a barefoot summer

Also by Jenny Hale

Christmas Wishes and Mistletoe Kisses
Coming Home for Christmas
A Christmas to Remember
A Barefoot Summer
Summer by the Sea
Summer at Oyster Bay
All I Want for Christmas
The Summer House
We'll Always Have Christmas

a barefoot summer

JENNY HALE

Bookouture

Published by Bookouture

An imprint of StoryFire Ltd.
23 Sussex Road, Ickenham, UB10 8PN
United Kingdom

www.bookouture.com

Previously titled *Love Me for Me*

ISBN: 978-1-909490-36-9
eBook ISBN: 978-1-909490-34-5

ACKNOWLEDGMENTS

I'd like to thank Patty Larson for sharing
her knowledge of small-town coastal living.

I'm forever grateful to my husband, Justin,
for his continued support and extra help
as I spent so many nights clicking keys.

As always, a big thank you to Oliver Rhodes
for his guidance and expertise.

I'd also like to thank Kate Ahl, my editor.
I cannot express how thankful I am to work with her.

For Patty,

with whom I share so many memories, including a few from a town a lot like this one.

Chapter One

Don't cry, Libby said to herself as she scraped mud off the Tory Burch wedge pumps she'd just bought in Manhattan last week. They'd cost nearly as much as her airfare. Her perfect shoes were probably ruined. Truthfully, though, it wasn't the soiled shoes that had upset her; she was on the verge of a nervous breakdown in general. In an attempt to alleviate the distress that was now consuming every inch of her body, she allowed her gaze to settle on the dogwood tree in the yard.

It looked just like the one she had climbed as a kid. Back then, her thin frame had allowed her to climb its narrow branches easily. Putting her foot at just the right spots where the branches forked out from the trunk of the tree, she'd grab a higher branch. She could feel the grit on the palms of her hands despite the tree's smooth bark. With every step, the branches wiggled under her feet, shaking the white flowers bunched at the ends.

When she reached the top, she'd lean against the trunk and pick the blooms, making a miniature bouquet. She could see all the way to the bay. She relished the quiet of her little spot at the top of the tree. With nothing but her thoughts, she'd sit, away from the demands of her mother, the pressures of growing up, and the drama surrounding her family.

But it was never long before her mother saw her through the kitchen window. Celia Potter would yell up to her, telling her that *ladies* didn't climb trees, and she had better get down before anyone could see her. She always obeyed. She didn't necessarily agree with her mother, she had just wanted to make her happy. The memory of it took her off guard.

Three familiar chirps came from her bag, and, still dragging her shoe along the cracked sidewalk, she retrieved her phone. She shifted her bag on her shoulder and looked around. Libby was in the middle of nowhere. She couldn't even see the next cottage over.

"Hello?"

She knew who it was, but at this point they barely spoke to each other. She used to answer his call with something witty and flirty, but now she could hardly muster a "hello" when she answered. The line was silent, and Libby checked the phone to be sure that she hadn't lost the call. With a grimace, she remembered about the bad cell phone reception, and inwardly cringed at the thought of the lack of service. Even her mobile hot spot wouldn't work consistently at that range.

"Hello, Libby. I just wanted to confirm that you're planning to send me the paperwork on the cottage," Wade's voice came through smooth and unbothered—whereas she wanted to sob into the phone. The pain of losing him was still right there in her chest, waiting to be unleashed. She took in a breath to center herself before answering.

"I just got here, but yes, I'll send it as soon as I finalize everything," her words came out carefully controlled in an attempt to keep herself together. She cleared her throat to try and remove the lump forming there.

Wade Foster was someone with whom she thought she could be happy. He had been the kind of boyfriend she could call any time, and he'd listen if she needed him. He'd brought her flowers on all the major holidays. He knew just when to be romantic as if he'd read a manual or something. Every time, he was right on the mark. So when he proposed and asked her to move in with him a year ago, she was over the moon about it. It was a step in the right direction, a step toward her perfect future.

A planner by nature, she'd mapped it all out in her head: She'd had a quiet, unfussy proposal—nothing drawing a lot of attention, which was exactly what she'd always wanted. Wade had simply gotten down on one knee over a candlelight dinner at a secluded table in the wine cellar of a restaurant. She'd hoped for a small summer wedding, the Vera Wang dress that she'd torn out of her latest bridal magazine, a separate reception held over the weekend at Wade's family home in the Hamptons, and a honeymoon in St. Croix.

Even more important than all that was the promise of a family. Growing up, it had only been Libby and her mother after her father left them, and she'd relied on close friends to be like family. Libby wanted nothing more than to have a *real* family with Wade—big, family holidays, the patter of little feet. And it had really looked like it was all going to happen. Until he'd knocked her to her knees by leaving her at her lowest moment.

After the merger at work, things seemed to be going along fine, until out of the blue, she was told they were restructuring her department and she would no longer be needed. Finding a new job was proving difficult, and Wade started working longer hours, spending weeks away on business. Feeling depressed and anxious about the future, she'd turned to Wade for support. That's when he'd left her.

And now here they were, having a businesslike phone conversation, like strangers.

"Okay, then," he said finally.

That's all you have to say? she wanted to scream into the phone. She clenched her phone, feeling the tightness in her knuckles. Leaving her hometown, becoming an adult and a successful professional, she'd felt in control of her life. This—her fiancé falling out of love with her—was out of her control, and it drove her crazy.

She fumbled with her keys and found the newest one on her key ring. "I'll be in touch," she said, a little more snippy than she'd meant to, and hoisted her carry-on suitcase onto the stoop.

She had to wiggle the key back and forth in the old lock to loosen it. With a pop, the knob finally turned. The line was dead on her phone, she realized, so with another deep breath, she ended the call and dropped the phone into her bag.

There had been absolutely no way Libby was going to stay with her mother while she was back here. But after actually coming home to the cottage, she wondered whether staying had been a good idea. Memories swam through her head faster than she could process them. She'd spent so many happy times there. Before she'd left for good.

She and Wade had bought the cottage together. It had belonged to Hugh and Anne Roberts, who happened to be the grandparents of someone she'd known very well, someone she'd cared for very much: Pete Bennett, her childhood best friend and high school boyfriend. When her parents were struggling with their marriage, Libby had escaped to the Roberts' cottage with Pete. The Roberts were like her own family. She even called them Pop and Nana just like Pete did. Standing there, she could almost hear the sounds from those happy days.

The new furniture that she'd purchased with Wade looked out of place and a little too modern, but she was able to look past it into her memories—memories of card games and laughter, lemonade on the porch, apple pie and lightning bugs at dusk. Seeing what was left of it made her feel as if she couldn't breathe. But she was a fighter; she'd come through a lot to get where she was, so she could handle it. At least that's what she kept telling herself. Her chest tightened, despite her efforts to think positively, as the new décor came back into focus.

Wade had wanted to sell the cottage as is, but she'd suggested that with some renovations they might actually make a profit. He'd agreed that she could go there and do the work, but now the weight of it was nearly crushing. The sun streamed through the tiny windows next to the front door, letting in the only light in the room. With her bag at her side, Libby watched the dust settling in the beam of sun, her mind racing.

The apartment she'd shared with Wade in New York had been small but open with an unusual amount of natural light, bright white walls, and modern furnishings. When she'd moved in with him, she'd wanted to add some femininity to the place. She'd torn out pages in magazines and she'd copied the very best in design until their apartment was perfect. It was a stark contrast to what was before her now. This cottage was dated and weathered, the walls screaming out memories of a different time.

The wall in front of her still had five nails jutting out. Five nails for five pictures, and if she closed her eyes, she could see them exactly the way Nana had arranged them. Now, just like Nana, the pictures were gone. Like ghosts, however, the memories were still hanging there right in front of her.

Libby was supposed to go to her mother's as soon as she'd gotten into town, but she didn't want to see anyone just yet. She worried about running into people who knew her, about seeing her mother. At eighteen, she'd sped out of the little town of White Stone as fast as her feet could take her. And with her life in the state it was now, she didn't want to face anyone, especially her mother. She'd come to the cottage she'd purchased with her ex-fiancé where she could be alone.

Originally, she'd never planned to even set foot in that house; the acquisition of it had all been her mother's doing. Libby had been a little apprehensive about purchasing the property since it had belonged to people she'd known so well, but her mother assured her that it would be no problem at all. And the one thing she had learned over the years was that when her mother was happy, she was a much nicer person. Libby had made it her life's goal, after her father left, to make her mother happy. And Libby's buying that cottage had delighted Celia Potter. It was a physical demonstration of Libby's success. It was her mother's way of showing off.

One of her mother's flaws was that when she was in good spirits, she got chatty. When she got chatty, it was cringeworthy. Libby guessed at the conversations that Celia probably had at the local market: *My daughter is living in Manhattan—she's got a top accounting job up there—Big Four firm!—and she had a little spare cash, so she bought the Roberts' place. I told her as soon as it went up for sale...* Her mother would lean in as if she were telling a secret, but hoping others would hear. *You know*, she'd say in her loudest whisper, *how Hugh Roberts can't take care of himself anymore after Anne's death. It's all so sad...*

The idea of it made Libby shiver. She was very protective of Hugh and she didn't want anyone speaking poorly of him in any way. He had been the most supportive, genuine person she'd known as a child, and the thought of what had happened to him was more than she could bear. She'd heard bits and pieces about him from her mother, but she hadn't seen him in years. As she walked down the hallway, she dragged her fingers along the wall where his hat rack had been.

She couldn't imagine Pop not being able to take care of himself. He'd always been the one who had taken care of everyone else. Once, when Libby was sixteen, she'd driven her mother's car to the movie theater, and something in the engine had rattled all the way there. Her mother didn't know a thing about cars, and she didn't want to upset her with news that something may be wrong, so she'd called Pop. Without even a hesitation, he set her mind at ease and told her to swing by after the movie. She could still see his reassuring eyes as he opened the door and went out into the afternoon sun to check her car. She'd stayed inside with Nana until he returned with oily hands and told her that it was all fixed. She wouldn't have to worry anymore. She never had to worry when Pop was around. He always made everything okay.

As she walked through the house, empty of Pop and Nana's things, she felt more depressed with every step. Being there, she was forced to face her memories, and they were coming back—all of them at once—like a giant tidal wave. In New York, she'd compartmentalized her memories, neatly tucking away the ones from childhood where they couldn't interfere with the new ones, but in the cottage that she'd spent so many days and nights, everywhere she looked she saw reminders of people she'd known—people she'd left—and it hurt. Terribly.

She carried on through the house. The hardwoods weren't in bad shape in most places, Libby noted, when she reached the back of the cottage. The kitchen was outdated, however, the sink dripping. The old linoleum floor was beginning to peel, and dated floral wallpaper stretched from the small dining area all the way to where she was standing.

She tugged on the faucet knob to stop the dripping, but was unsuccessful, so she just leaned on the edge of the sink, watching the drips—one at a time—hit the basin. *Tap, tap, tap.* The sound was relentless, like the pounding in her temples. A twinge of anxiety pecked at her as she wondered why Pop's sink was leaking. Surely he could've fixed it, unless his health was failing too much now. Pop had been her rock. He'd always been strong. The idea of weakness overtaking him was almost unbelievable. It all made her feel vulnerable, helpless.

The back door of the cottage was in a small breakfast nook area. It had a pane of glass in the center and let in a blast of blinding sun. The door was stuck so Libby had to pull with all her might. When she got it open, suddenly she remembered what an investment the house actually was.

She hopped off the concrete landing onto the lawn. Still dewy from the shade of the pines, the grass crunched beneath her shoes, so she kicked them off to save any further damage and set them on the edge of the sidewalk that extended the length of the property. With the wind picking up, blowing her hair in her face, she walked until the cool of the grass was replaced by the softness of sand. In front of her, as far as she could see, were the blue ripples of Virginia's Chesapeake Bay. The division between water and sky was so minimal that they almost looked like one entity. She wondered about Nana, where she was, if she could look down on her.

Anne Roberts had been like a grandmother to her. Libby remembered her powdery scent, the way her gray hair fell toward her eyes when she laughed, the soft touch of her hand as she patted Libby on the back when they hugged. Anne had a formality about her—her pressed cotton shirts buttoned down the front, tucked into her trousers perfectly, not a wrinkle in sight, her nails always manicured. But there was something so uncomplicated, so relaxed about her, that made everyone fall in love with her. She told stories that could pin Libby right to her seat as she hung on every word. And when Libby was in her presence, Anne had made her feel like she was the most important person in the world, so interested in her, so ready to listen.

Libby had been in New York when Anne passed. She remembered the day her mother called to tell her. That was the second time she'd cried about someone from back home. Just the way Anne would have planned it, she had gone to sleep and she never woke the next morning. Like everything about her, she'd spent her final moments peacefully.

The funeral had been on a Thursday and Libby could've taken time off to attend, but she didn't. There were reasons why—she wasn't heartless—and she still held onto the guilt of not seeing Anne that one last time to pay her respects. Being there in Nana's house, she was ashamed about her absence. The feeling of not being able to fix it consumed her—she couldn't go back in time and make it right. She took in a deep breath and let it out slowly, but it did nothing to lighten the guilt.

Libby's phone rang again.

She pulled her bag off her shoulder and dug out her phone. "Hello?" she said, taking in the magnificent view in front of her and trying to shake the memories as they flooded her mind. She walked closer to the water and let the foam slip between her toes, the sea breeze ballooning the bottom of her dress like a parachute around her legs.

"Are you here yet?" she heard the shrill but friendly voice of her mother.

"Yes."

"Where are you? I've been waiting about fifteen minutes, hoping you'd get here." Without so much as a pause, she continued, "How are you dressed?"

Libby looked down. Her golden hair—a two hundred dollar *investment*, her hairdresser had told her—dangled in her line of vision. "I have on a sundress." She thought of her shoes, pondering how she'd clean them up with no cleaning supplies in the house.

"Oh, good! I want you to meet me at Miller's."

"Miller's?" The only time they ever went to Miller's restaurant was for Sunday dinners. It sat right on the water and had the most spectacular array of seafood in the area.

"You're home! I'd like to celebrate!"

What Celia really meant, Libby was certain, was that she needed to keep her head held high, her chin up, and act as though her trip home were just a blip in her path to success. *Coming home is just a slight setback, nothing more*, she could almost hear Celia saying. Libby felt like crawling into a hole somewhere to hide in embarrassment. She couldn't keep her head held high feeling the way she did. She *wasn't* successful. Anymore. And the insecurity she felt because of it was nearly more than she could handle.

"Can I meet you in twenty minutes?" she said, trying not to fall apart right then and there. When she ended the call, she turned back toward the sea air to give her calm. She'd need it before facing the town she'd run away from so many years ago, never looking back.

Chapter Two

Libby tried not to notice the scenery outside as she drove the rental car down the familiar route to meet her mother. In twelve years, it hadn't changed at all. Every single place that she passed by had a story: the library, the place she'd spent so many silent hours, where she found solitude from her battling parents; the recreation center where she'd practiced day after day, trying to secure a swimming scholarship; the park, her escape when she needed time to think.

She pulled the car along the curb outside Miller's restaurant in front of a small strip of shops and got out. She pretended to fiddle with something in her handbag, but she was really stalling. The very last thing she wanted to do was to meet her mother there. Just thinking about it she felt anxious.

When she was young, she'd worried that she would disappoint her mother, but now, she knew that she probably had already done that, so the thought of facing her, listening to her try and spin the situation into something that she could boast about, was horrifying. From the time she was a little girl, her mother had paraded her in front of her friends: *Libby knows all her ABCs! Show them, Libby!* Or,

Libby just got first place in the swim meet! Now, there she was again, most likely going to make a show. *Libby!* She could hear her now…

"Libby?"

She stopped moving. She knew that voice—and it wasn't her mother's. With one word, he'd sent her heart thudding inside her chest. Her eyes still on the items in her bag, she was too mortified to look at the person in front of her, yet the excitement of hearing his voice made her lightheaded. Her hands began to tremble. Whenever she got nervous, it was very difficult for her to calm down, and she hoped she wouldn't rattle right off the sidewalk.

"You decided to grace us with your presence?" he said.

She shut her bag and looked up. There he was. It had been more than a decade since she'd seen him, but he looked just as he had back then. His sandy brown hair was a little longer but not much. His green eyes still light against his suntanned skin. She waited for the crooked grin that went all the way up to his eyes, his gentle expression as he looked down at her, the protective way he put his arm around her waist—but as she snapped into the present, she realized she wouldn't get any of that. Her heart was drumming so loudly that she was nearly sure he could hear it. She searched his face for any indication of how he felt about their meeting. Other than the shortness in his tone and the tiny crease between his eyes, his face was expressionless. That alone gave her enough of an answer.

"Pete," was all she could get out. Memories of all the insensitive things she'd said to him so many years ago were clouding her ability to form words. It made her flustered.

He swung his gaze up to the sky and then looked back at her, his head shaking so subtly that she had almost missed it. "Fancy seeing you here," he said, his eyes taunting her for a reaction. "I can't imagine why you'd come back." His arms were crossed, the muscles tight and flexed, as he glared at her. His hands looked more weathered, older, but she remembered them perfectly—the way they'd felt as he dragged his fingertips up and down her back while she rested on his shoulder, the coarseness of them as he held her face in his hands.

His words cut her right through to the bone. He hated her for the way she'd left, and she didn't blame him. Pete had wanted them to go to college together. He'd applied to Virginia Tech and the University of Richmond so he could stay close to his family. He wanted to be able to do things like go out on the boat with Pop when he felt like it and help his mom around the house if she needed him. He wanted Libby to be by his side like she had been since they were kids. Going to a state school would have allowed them to come home and be with their families more often while still giving them enough distance to be on their own together. But Libby's mother had always told her she could get into the Ivy Leagues if she just put her mind to it, and, in the end, her ambition won out. She applied to Columbia University in New York City and she got in. Breaking the news of her acceptance to Pete had exploded into the type of argument that changes everything. It wasn't just a disagreement; it was a complete attack on the kind of life he'd chosen to pursue.

The day she'd told him about Columbia was the first time she'd ever seen disappointment in his eyes. She'd sent off her applications for Virginia Tech and The University of Richmond along with the one for Columbia, but she knew she couldn't spend her days in White Stone—and with Pete, she knew she would.

"Give me one good reason you should go there, Libby," he had asked that day.

"Because I need something more. I need to get out. There's *nothing* for me here," she'd caught herself saying. She bit her tongue, knowing she'd made it sound as though Pete wasn't worth staying for. She hadn't meant it to come out that way, but it had. What she'd been trying to say was that for her whole life, she'd learned she had to achieve to be successful. In White Stone, she just didn't have enough opportunity to achieve to her potential. It wasn't about Pete. "I can't get anywhere in life if I stay in White Stone. It isn't the place for me." She'd called it an *insignificant town*.

"I refuse to believe this," he'd said. "That's not what you want. It's what your mother wants for you." His cheeks were flushed, his jaw clenched. She'd never seen Pete Bennett cry before, but his face in that moment was about as close as she'd ever gotten to seeing it.

Pete's implication that she couldn't make her own choices rubbed Libby the wrong way. She was old enough to decide for herself what she wanted from life and, while her mother had strongly urged her to apply to an Ivy League school, ultimately it was up to Libby. And she wanted to get out of White Stone. "Then you must not know me as well as you think you do," she'd said, irritation pelting her insides.

What she'd been too proud and angry to admit on that day was that, while she wanted out of that town, she was heartbroken about leaving Pete. He didn't see her cry into her pillow every night for weeks after she'd left him. He didn't know anything about the emptiness she'd felt day in and day out as she spent nights away from him, alone, in a new place where no one knew her. On more than one occasion, she'd almost picked up the phone to call him, to hear his voice, but she was too afraid he was angry with her. So she'd shut her eyes and imagined the crooked way his mouth turned up as if he were about to break into a laugh, the way his eyes squinted when he smiled. But that image always changed to the last expression of Pete's that she'd seen: the sadness, hurt and disappointment.

The guilt that she carried still sat deep within her, and it hurt like crazy to feel it again. But it had been for the best! She had too much drive, too much ambition to be stuck in that town without any opportunities for something bigger, for life on a grander scale. *What is life without achievement?* she thought. Working hard for things made her feel like she was doing something worthwhile. Hadn't he realized that by now?

"There you are!" her mother's voice plowed right through the heaviness hanging in the air. Libby pulled her attention from Pete to find her mother walking out of the door to Miller's, an apprehensive look lurking beneath an artificial smile. "Hello, Pete," she said, sending a fluttering look over to him and then away. Her eyes settled on Libby. "Our table's ready."

Libby turned back to Pete, but he was already walking away. She had so many things she wanted to say, so many feelings about the last twelve years, but she'd missed her chance. What kind of life had he made for himself? Was he married? Did he have children? The image of Pete swinging a child up onto his shoulders, a woman by his side, sent a wave of jealousy through her stomach and up to her cheeks. It was a shocking feeling to have, but it was clearly there, raging inside. She'd rolled her dice, put everything she had on her choice, and, in the end, the odds had been against her. Now she was right back where she'd started, and she didn't even have the comfort of the ones she loved to help her through it.

"Come in, Libby," her mother said, patting her arm and ushering her inside. As Libby walked up the wooden steps to the restaurant, she watched Pete out of the corner of her eye, and she could have sworn that he'd looked back, just once, in her direction.

The hostess showed them to their table. Libby sat down and wadded her linen napkin in her lap. *Why is this happening to me?* she wanted to yell out. *I planned perfectly! I did everything right! It wasn't my fault they cut staff at work. It wasn't my fault Wade left me… Right?* The more she pondered her problems, the more unsure she became. She started to question her presumptions, and more questions filled her mind. *Did I do something at work to be the one they let go? Am I not as sharp as my colleagues? Did I become a burden to Wade?*

"Can I get you anything to drink?" a waitress asked as Libby scooted her chair farther under the table as a nervous impulse. She couldn't tell if it was just her own paranoia, but it seemed like the waitress was looking at her as if she knew her. But then she wondered if, perhaps, the woman thought she looked out of place there.

The culture in White Stone was different than in New York. Libby hadn't really noticed it until she'd been away. They dressed differently, more casual. Businessmen wore polo shirts and trousers on dressy days and jeans on Fridays. The women wore informal clothes to work mostly, and everyone, no matter who they were, wore T-shirts and shorts in their off time. The only time people felt the need to dress up was for church and special occasions. Libby looked down at the Diane Von Furstenberg sundress she'd gotten at Barneys last week. It made her feel like an outsider.

"I'll have a water," she said before looking down into her menu and trying to hide there.

"Nonsense!" her mother piped up. "Let's have wine. Don't you want a glass of wine, Libby?"

She peered over the menu at her mother. Celia Potter was the only person she knew who didn't follow the area's dress code. Her mother had on a brand-new-looking red and white dress, the fabric some sort of textured cotton. Her lips were as red as the flowers splashed across the garment. Her make-up, her hair, it was all done to perfection, so much so that it looked odd. Libby wished, for once, that she could reach over and tousle the over-sprayed salt-and-pepper waves that framed her mother's face.

She didn't want to hurt her mother's feelings, but the thought of alcohol made her insides turn over. In the state she was in, it would give her a pounding headache. "No thanks, Mom. I don't want wine."

"Well, I'm not going to make a scene by arguing," she smiled a tight smile, her eyes darting around, probably to see if anyone had noticed the exchange. "I'm just glad to have you home, that's all."

The waitress waited politely by their table, her eyebrows raised in expectation of Celia's order. Libby wondered why that girl had ended up in White Stone. For Libby's entire life, her mother had told her she could do better than her home town, go away to college and do something grander with her life. She was taught to produce only perfection in the hopes that she could get out of there. And yet, Celia Potter had stayed.

She probably likes being the big fish in a small pond, Libby thought. If she did, that was the only thing she liked. She had been a stay-at-home mom for Libby until her father left them. Celia Potter had grown up in Las Vegas, and she had been a PR representative for one of the casinos, where she'd met Libby's father. She followed him to Virginia but after he left them, there wasn't a whole lot of corporate PR work to be had in the area. And by that time Celia had been out of the game so long she didn't have much to show for herself in terms of experience, so she'd settled on a job as a receptionist at the local dental office.

The waitress was still waiting on Libby's order.

"I'll just have an iced tea… and another iced tea for her. We'll both have a salad," Celia ordered without consulting Libby.

After the waitress left them alone, Celia leaned across the table. "You don't have to be so gloomy, honey. Be *glad* to be home."

There was no reason to be glad. She was the exact opposite of glad. Libby had been completely happy in New York. She didn't belong in White Stone. She didn't look like the people in town, she didn't act like them, and certainly she didn't live like them. But now, who was she? She'd lost her job in Manhattan, she had nowhere to live, and Wade had left her.

The conversation the night Wade broke up with her had been surreal. He was away on business, and she wanted to feel closer to him. Libby was reasonable enough to know that if she hadn't called him that night, she'd have eventually faced the same outcome, but she still wished it could have happened differently.

I don't think we're compatible anymore.

After two years of being together, that was how he'd ended it. With that one statement, Wade showed a side of him that Libby had never known existed. She knew why they weren't compatible and, until that moment, she hadn't wanted to admit it. They weren't compatible because she wasn't successful anymore. When she'd had a lucrative career, he'd been very attentive, romantic, interested. But the longer she sat in their apartment looking for jobs, not going anywhere, not getting out of her pajamas until late in the morning, the more he'd distanced himself. He'd been so busy on his trip that he was unable to take her calls for most of that week. That's the way she'd rationalized his silence before their break-up. In the end, he'd left her with barely an explanation. He'd come home long enough to suggest that she find somewhere to go as soon as possible, and then he'd left again—where to, she had no idea.

All the plans she'd made for their wedding—the reservations, the deposits, the appointments—had to be canceled. With every phone call, she sank further into her depression, constantly reexamining herself and wondering if she'd achieved what she had based on her merit or if it had all been some terrible fluke. She'd hit her very lowest at that point, and she wondered if she'd ever get back up to the top. It seemed like a daunting climb.

"Hello-o!" Celia waved a hand in front of her face.

"Sorry."

"Honey, I… I'm just going to say it. You look depressed."

Ya think? "Really?"

"Would it help to see someone about it?"

"Who? Taylor's mom? She's the only shrink in town, and, since I spent most of my childhood at her home playing with Taylor, I don't think she could be very objective." Libby noticed her tone and shrank back into quiet. It wasn't her mother's fault she'd lost everything. The last thing she wanted to do was upset her mother. *I'll bet you're doing damage control in your head right now*, she thought as she looked at her. Libby had already ruined her reputation as an overachiever for her mother. She'd better not make it any worse.

Celia waved her hands in the air. "Let's not talk about it. I'd much rather discuss what you thought of the Roberts' place. Is it livable?"

"Well, there's no way I can sell it and make a profit the way it is currently, but that's okay because I'll be here to oversee the remodel."

The realization of what was ahead of her was slowly sinking in. She was about to start living and working in the town she'd worked so hard to leave. Was she destined to live out her years like her mother had? In New York, she felt there was nowhere to go but up, but in White Stone, there was just nowhere to go.

Her mother had gotten her a job at a small firm in town owned by an acquaintance of Celia's named Marty Bruin. Libby was over-qualified for it, but it had been the only offer of employment she'd received. It wasn't even a full-time job; it was a temporary, part-time position that she'd only gotten because she was Celia's daughter. It was just something to keep her afloat until she could get back to New York.

Compounding things, she hadn't told Wade that she'd planned to prolong putting the cottage on the market until she could get back on her feet. She didn't really know what to tell Wade, and she didn't re-ally know what she wanted to do with the cottage. In a perfect world, she'd sell it, get a job back in New York, and return to her happy life, but that wasn't an available option at the moment. At least she could use the house to hide away until she figured out what to do. She couldn't hide, however, from the inadequacy she felt coming back.

"I know the house isn't much." Celia pulled her from her thoughts, "Your investment is the property."

Libby nodded as the waitress brought their drinks and set them on the linen-covered table. As she looked around at the tiny, southern restaurant's interior, over half of the faces recognizable, she thought to herself how much she wanted this to be temporary. Even if the only things she had were her laptop and a change of clothes, the first thing she'd do after lunch was get online and start sending in job ap-plications. She was getting out of there as soon as she possibly could.

Chapter Three

L ibby could feel the sting of salt in the air as the breeze hit her sun-warmed skin. The sun's rays were finally behind the trees, but they'd been on her face all day. Cocooned in the latticework of rope that comprised the hammock, bolted to two towering pine trees near the shore, she closed her eyes and let the lapping of the waves lull her. There was something so peaceful about it. It was like being on vacation but with no one to share it.

She'd sent off a dozen applications all over New York this afternoon, each one taking double the time to send as the wireless went in and out because she was so far away from town. She resolved to do the rest at the coffee shop since they had advertised free wireless. She was hopeful that they had a better connection. For now, though, she kept her eyes closed and tried to block out the last month of her life.

The moment of tranquility didn't last. Her cell phone was chirping on the towel in the sand. She rolled out of the hammock, catching herself as it twisted in a circle and spun her outward. "Hello?" she answered. "Trish, how are you?"

Instantly, all the tension that her rest had eliminated came flooding back. The call from her friend, Trish—newly engaged and full of excitement about her wedding—brought her back to reality and filled her with the uneasiness that came when she thought about how she'd lost everything.

"I'm well! How are you?" Trish sounded extra chipper.

Libby pushed her toes into the sand. "Okay." Even though she wasn't.

"I called to say happy early birthday!"

"Oh, thanks."

"Kevin and I are going to be up to our eyeballs in wedding planning tomorrow picking china patterns, so I knew I wouldn't have a chance to call…" Libby could hear traffic in the background, the sound of it making her homesick.

As much as she loved Trish, she disliked how she brought out the competitive side of her. Trish always did that: she always said something to put herself above Libby, like how she'd be too busy to call on her actual birthday, and then, right away, something exciting about herself. Not that Libby wanted to drone on and on about the situation, but the way Trish did that, it was almost like a challenge—one negative, one positive. One-to-one: *Happy Birthday—so sorry! I'll be too busy planning my wonderful wedding with my fiancé—who didn't leave me like yours did—to call.* As if to say, *Your turn. What can you offer?* When she'd had something to offer, it hadn't been a problem at all. It was as easy as lighthearted sibling rivalry. But now, with her confidence shattered, it was a blow to her ego.

"Would you be my Maid of Honor?" Trish asked.

"Of course!" she said. She was honored to be asked to be in Trish's wedding. She just wished she could be happier about it. She felt so low, it was hard to be anything but miserable.

The sun had completely slipped beyond the horizon, sending out a bright orange and pink glow in the sky. The spring air was still cool in the evenings, and Libby felt a slight chill against the heat of her skin. She sat down on the hammock and hung her head, the ropes creaking beneath her.

"I'm so glad! I was nervous to ask, given what's happened in your life recently. I didn't want to upset you or anything."

My wedding! Your disaster of a life. There it was again. One-to-one.

"It's fine, Trish. I'm happy for you! So, what are my duties?" she asked, trying to sound as chipper as one should sound when her best friend had asked her to be her Maid of Honor. Shame was swelling in her gut in the form of acid as she thought about how bad a friend she was for not being happier. It was just too hard. How in the world would she be able to help Trish plan her wedding festivities when she'd just had to cancel all her own? It made her feel hollow and exhausted, and she hadn't even started yet.

"I'll send you a list of addresses—most of the people you know—and you can send out invitations to the shower. Would you mind planning that?"

"Of course not. Do you have anything particular in mind for the shower, or do you want me to surprise you?"

"Why don't we have that shower game that Becca had at hers? Do you remember it?"

Libby remembered it. It was the shower game she'd wanted to play at her own bridal shower. The shower she'd booked at the 21 Club on West 52nd. The shower she'd squealed with delight about because she'd been able to squeeze in her reservation after another group had canceled. The shower that she'd had to call about and tell the event planner that, after all his hard work getting her an open banquet room for thirty-five people, she wasn't going to make it after all.

"Sure. We can have that game," she said. "Any other requests? I want it to be perfect."

"I trust you. You'll make it better than I can think up. You're so good at planning these sorts of things. Just keep it classy—nothing too frilly—and I'll be happy. You sure you're okay to do all this?"

She wasn't okay. The thought of making wedding plans after she'd just seen hers vanish into thin air made her chest hurt. It was another one-to-one. Then, as if something in her snapped, she didn't want one-to-one anymore. She wanted her own happiness. Why should Trish get all the good luck? "Of course," she replied. "I'd forgotten how beautiful it is here," she heard herself saying. "It's like being on vacation all the time! Renovating won't be hard work at all with this gorgeous view."

"Wow, that's really nice," Trish returned, causing the competition to take a turn. Trish hadn't said anything about herself yet. Time to throw in an oh-for-two!

"I'm really enjoying it." Inwardly squirming, Libby thought how she seemed, at that moment, an awful lot like her mother. It was official: she was falling apart.

"Libby, I'm so glad to hear that things are looking up!"

"I hope so." *What am I doing?* she thought. *Things aren't looking up. If anything, they're looking down, further into the abyss that is my life!* She grabbed her towel to shake it out, the phone wedged between her ear and shoulder. The wind blew as if to spite her, sending a storm of sand from the towel into her face. "Hey, Trish. I need to go. I have something I need to do." *Wash the sand out of my eyes.* "Can I call you later?"

"Absolutely."

She ended the call, dropped her phone into her handbag, and then sat down on the shore. With sand still in her eyes that were now watering uncontrollably and causing her to blink in an effort to relieve the scratching feeling, she threw her head back and laughed at the absurdity that was her life. There she was, sitting on the beach with a ridiculously small bath towel (that had been in the one box of things that she had) and her Michael Kors tote. The designer handbag sat half buried in the sand. Just like her, that tote was made for city life; it was in the wrong place.

Libby missed New York horribly. All her life, her mother had groomed her to be successful. She'd been in the top five in her high school class, she was an accomplished swimmer, her memberships in school clubs and organizations were a mile long. Those things made her different in her small town, but once she got to Columbia, she met so many other kids like her. There, she felt normal. She wasn't an overachiever anymore because the others had worked just as hard as she had to get there. Then, as she took her first job in the city, she fell right into place. Working in New York, she was able to mingle with people who had the same ideals, the same goals. She had friends there, friends just like her. There, she could be successful and driven—and not under the judging and boastful eye of her mother. She could just be herself. She felt a freedom that she could never feel back home.

The minute she'd returned to White Stone, that freedom had all but dissolved. She'd sunk a ton of savings into the cottage, she was still paying the loans for her Columbia education, she had nowhere else to live, and she was stuck where she'd never hoped to return. *I'm turning thirty tomorrow*, she thought, *and what do I have to show for it?* Her failures made her feel as if she were being held down and unable to move. Having felt the joy of success, coming back was unbelievably demoralizing, as if being so low, she'd never be able to get as high again. *I will get through*, she told herself, but deep down, it was difficult to believe, given how much had happened to her.

A pinch on the arm sent her hand slapping in that direction, and she remembered that as the sun went down, the mosquitoes came out. Unable to tell at that point if the tears were from the sand or the misery that she felt, she got up and started toward the house.

❊ ❊ ❊

"Good morning!" her mother's voice chirped through the phone.

"Morning."

"It's someone's special day today!"

She'd nearly forgotten, and probably would have if Trish hadn't called last night. Originally, she and Wade were going to take a trip to the Cayman Islands to celebrate, but he wouldn't ever finalize their plans.

"I know you probably don't want to, but it would be good for you… I've got a late brunch scheduled with Jeanie and Sophia in town. Won't you come?"

Mom, you're asking me to meet you and two other women your age for brunch on my birthday? It's not exactly what I'd have planned. Libby shook her head. *She's trying*, she thought. *I should at least go for that reason.* The guilt that rose up due to her lack of enthusiasm for going to brunch made her feel even worse. She should feel lucky to have anyone want to celebrate with her, but she didn't feel lucky. She felt awful.

"Sure," she said.

"Perfect! We're meeting at Jeanie's house. Do you remember where she lives?"

Libby pursed her lips and nodded even though her mother couldn't see her. Finally, she verbalized her thoughts. "Yep."

Of course she remembered where Jeanie lived! Jeanie, unbeknownst to her mother, had been her confidante. She'd always been able to tell Jeanie when her mother's demands had become unbearable, and she had listened. Jeanie never had children of her own, but she was amazing with them, and Libby wondered if maybe she hadn't been able to have any. Since that's something one could never ask, and Jeanie hadn't shared anything regarding the issue over the years, she was left to wonder.

"It's at eleven. I'll meet you there."

"Okay."

"Libby?"

"Yeah?"

"Happy birthday, honey."

She took in a deep breath. "Thanks. I'll see you at eleven."

All Libby had was the spare outfit she'd packed. She was supposed to pick up her boxes of things from New York at the local post office, but they'd said—twice—that the boxes had not arrived. She decided to have a look at her change of clothes, wondering how many wrinkles she would find.

She pulled her trousers from her bag and shook them out. They weren't too bad, but they didn't go with the pair of shoes she had. She draped them on the bed and paired them with the shirt she'd packed. The shoes would do, she decided after a debate with herself, since they matched her handbag.

Mentally reexamining her packing choices, she got up and got ready with what she had. The only silver lining to it all was that she didn't have groceries yet, so she could justify a visit to The River

Market where they had delicious coffee and an enormous array of freshly baked muffins.

The spring air, striving to be as hot as summer, but maintaining its chill every morning, had put a layer of dew on the grass that lined the front sidewalk of the cottage. With the late-morning temperatures only slightly cooler than room temperature, Libby decided to park the car and walk through town.

She worried about what she'd say to Celia's friends. Her perfect life wasn't perfect anymore, and she didn't know how to do anything less than perfectly. For as long as she could remember, her mother had always expected perfection. Libby had thrown fits about the clothes her mother had made her wear as a child, the curls in her hair. In school, if her homework wasn't in her neatest handwriting, she'd have to erase it, rubbing holes in her paper until it was her very best effort. Ultimately, it was her mother's way or no way.

It occurred to her that her father should have stuck up for her, but after her parents divorced when she was ten, he had always let her mother make the decisions when it came to Libby, the Potters' only child. He'd only been around to voice his opinions every other weekend anyway. By the time she was about fourteen, he'd moved to another state. So her mother went on with her rigid childrearing.

As an adult, Libby could rationalize this behavior, try to explain it. Her mother, resentful and bitter about having to live in a town she'd never have chosen for herself, had put all her hopes and dreams of success into Libby, and if Libby didn't succeed, neither did her mother as a parent. All this made perfect sense to her as an adult, but it didn't do anything to change the way it had affected her personality.

She worried that she wasn't as good as her mother had made her out to be, and she worried that she had let her down. There she was, back home, having taken a job for which she was far overqualified, with no hope of a wedding or family in her future. Certainly her mother was disappointed. *Could I have changed anything about the cuts at the office?* she wondered again. *Could I have been a better fiancée in some way?* She went over and over it all in her head. She was an intelligent woman; she knew how to solve her own problems. But she couldn't solve those.

Standing at the corner of Windmill Point Road and Rappahannock Drive, she had arrived at the only stoplight in town. As a kid, it had been a cautionary, blinking, yellow light, but having moved along with the times, all three colors were now represented, and the light was red. Libby didn't notice the red light, but she noticed the truck that was stopped there. It was a vintage yellow 1969 Bronco.

She only knew that because she'd been with Pete when he'd bought it. She remembered sliding across the tattered seat toward Pete who was sitting, poised in the driving position, his hands on the wheel, considering the purchase. "How do we look in it?" she'd asked playfully. His expression was frozen in her memory as if she'd seen it just yesterday. Pete turned to her with fondness in his eyes, a grin on his face, and said, "Well, I must say it looks a whole lot better now that you're in it." He and his brother had spent the rest of their high school years saving money to restore it.

As she surfaced from her memory, the window slid down and Pete called out, "Still here?"

Libby turned to face him, her eyes narrowing. With an empty lane between them, she glared in his direction. *Of course I'm still here!* she wanted to yell. *I can't go anywhere else! I'm stuck here against my will, which should make you happy, so leave me alone and let me stew in it!* Instead, she said nothing.

The light turned green and, to her dismay, she saw him put on his turn signal and move closer to her. He kept going and rounded the curve, pulling the truck to a stop on Rappahannock Drive. A few cars passed, and she watched them go, not wanting to look in Pete's direction.

"I thought you'd be gone by now," he said, closing the door and stepping up onto the curb. She recognized two women from her childhood church gawking at them from the window of the market.

He took a step closer to her and slid his hands into the pockets of his jeans, bunching the shirttails of his oxford button up. Even when he wasn't spruced up, he looked perfect. She had so many things she wanted to say to Pete Bennett that all the thoughts bumped into one another, and she couldn't sift out a single one. She stood there in silence, the irritation of her lack of coherent thought nibbling away at her from the inside.

"What are you doing back here, Libby?" He said the words in anger, but she'd known him over half her life, well enough to see the softness behind his expression, and she could also see the hurt she'd caused.

She wasn't about to tell him what had transpired during the last month of her twenties. She wouldn't give him the satisfaction. He didn't need to know any more than she was willing to tell him. "I'm here to sell the cottage," she said matter-of-factly.

The anger that had been evident on his face deepened, and the softness was now gone completely. "You're getting rid of it?" he asked, his green eyes shooting daggers at her. His face was flushed, his jaw set in a rigid line.

The cottage *had* belonged to Pete's grandparents. But now that Anne was gone, and Hugh was living with Pete, she didn't know why he cared one way or the other about that cottage. Especially since she'd heard from her mother that he had an amazing house he'd restored himself, right on the water and not far from her own childhood home.

"Yep."

"Why? Isn't it good enough?"

This wasn't about the cottage. "Pete," she took in a breath, trying to decide how to start. Her arms were crossed around her body, and anyone looking would think she was cold, but it was really an effort to keep herself from trembling. She felt as if she'd fall apart if she let go.

"You waltz back into town like you own the place, with your," he swung his finger up and down in the air at her, "high and mighty, too-good-for-this attitude. You show up just to sell off the cottage, fluff out your feathers. Well, I don't care about your wealth or all the airs you're putting on. *None* of us care."

Libby opened her mouth to retort, but the words weren't there. She could feel the sting of tears, but she wasn't about to let them show. Irritation burned in her stomach. She pressed her lips together to keep from screaming. What did he know?

The two ladies in the shop window were talking to each other, their knobby fingers pointing in the direction of Pete, and Libby felt like she wanted the ground to open up and swallow her. She'd lost everything, and now Pete was making a show of her poor choices for everyone to see. Her cheeks were on fire, her hands trembling. "You don't know what you're talking about," she said through clenched teeth.

"Oh, yeah. I forgot. We're not smart enough in this *insignificant* town to understand anything." He took a step back, his eyes still on her. Then, without another word, he walked around the front of his car, got in, and sped away.

Libby stood still for a moment, shock and confusion swimming around inside her.

The light turned green and a few more cars passed, bringing her back to reality. She went into the market and tried to avoid the curious glances of the women in the window, who were now following her every move, their gazes burning into the back of her.

"That's Celia's daughter," she heard one of them whisper before saying something else that she couldn't hear. Libby's mother had made her thoughts about the town quite clear, while Libby was growing up, and she'd been sure to let everyone know Libby's plans for the future. All those carefully executed plans had come crashing down, and Libby felt like it was her failures that everyone saw when they looked at her. She continued walking past the counter and into the bathroom where she finally allowed herself to cry.

Chapter Four

Once she'd gotten herself together, Libby walked the few shady blocks from the market toward Jeanie's house, shaking her head at how small a block in this little town was compared to the city blocks she used to walk in New York. She'd heard once that about twenty New York blocks equaled a mile. The entire width of White Stone seemed to equal a mile. The Maple trees that lined the sidewalks had grown in her absence, casting dark, thin shadows toward her destination.

With a rolled white paper River Market bag in her hand, containing muffins bigger than a grown man's fist, she took in the fresh, salty air. She knew that the other women would show up with dishes of breakfast casserole wrapped in warming blankets that they'd prepared early that morning, but, given the circumstances, they'd have to be happy with her offering of muffins. They *were* made by hand, just not by her.

Jeanie lived in a white bungalow with rectangular boxes of red geraniums hanging from every window. The porch took up the entire front of the house. Sophia and Celia were there, swinging on the bench-style front porch swing. Libby wondered if they had done anything else in the twelve years she'd been away. When she'd left at eighteen, they were having brunch together, playing card games, and sitting on Jeanie's front porch, and there they were, right in the same place twelve years later.

"Hey there, honey!" Celia waved to Libby as she made her way up the walkway, a nearby gardenia bush filling the air with its sweet smell. The front door had been left wide open with only the glass storm door between her and Jeanie, who held her Yorkshire terrier nestled between her voluptuous bosom and the crook of her arm while waving madly at her with her free hand. Libby smiled despite herself.

She had missed Jeanie.

"Welcome home!" Jeanie said, now holding the glass door open with one hand and allowing her dog, Rascal, to roam free on the porch. "How's my birthday girl?" Jeanie smiled a smile that enveloped her entire face, her prematurely silver hair flipping out around it.

"I'm well," she lied. "I brought these." Libby held up the bag of muffins.

"Bless your heart!" Jeanie took the crumpled sack from her and peeked inside, her eyebrows bouncing up and down with excitement. She reached in and pulled out a blueberry muffin with sugared crumble on top. "I'm just cookin' inside. I'll go and get you a chair." She offered the muffin to Libby.

"Don't go to any trouble, Jeanie. I can sit on the steps." She noticed a slight look of disapproval on Celia's face as she said it. Her mother had already scooted to the far side of the swing, creating an open space in the middle between herself and Sophia. Libby broke a piece of crumble off the top of her muffin. "I'm fine," she said to the ladies, taking a seat on the porch step. The two women wriggled back into a more comfortable position. Libby watched her mother's reaction, worried that she'd upset her by sitting on the steps and not in an actual chair, but it hadn't seemed to bother her too much.

She could tell that Sophia wanted to make conversation, but all she did was grin. A good friend of Celia's, she probably knew why Libby had returned, and that made it awkward. What could she say? *I'm glad you're back?* That would be rude if she knew the truth. Or even, *How was New York?* Clearly a poor choice of question.

"You're gonna get your fancy clothes dirty on those steps," Sophia finally said. Leave it to her to figure out something to fill the silence.

"It's fine, really."

Rascal meandered up to the porch from the front yard and sniffed Libby's new shoes, causing her to focus on how very out of place they were there. She needed to be back in New York with other people like her, not lounging around on a front porch in the middle of nowhere.

Libby hadn't been back in town since she was eighteen. Her mother had always come to New York to visit, saying she'd rather spend the holidays at Libby's where she could enjoy the city, and it got her out of White Stone. So basically, one could say that Libby had grown up in New York. She didn't know how to socialize on a front porch and nibble on a muffin as it balanced on her lap. She knew how to network and drink martinis and hail a taxi when she needed to get somewhere. She knew White Stone inside and out, and, to her knowledge, there wasn't a single place there that she could even order a martini, let alone find a friend who would drink one with her.

Time was valuable in New York. People had things to do. In the city, she felt like hard work would move her up the corporate ladder and generate a good income. A good income produced a successful life and more opportunities. Not spending every day sitting on a porch swing, in a town where the nearest city was an hour away and there was nothing but home and beach. Until she left, she'd known nothing of the world around her except what she'd seen on television. She didn't want that for herself or, God forbid, her children.

There was a tiny scratching sound, and Rascal stood, wagging his tail, awaiting Libby's assistance with the door. She was glad for the slight diversion. Before she could get up to let the dog in, Jeanie opened the door and scooped the puppy into her arms. "Y'all come on in and eat. Food's ready."

Libby held the door open for Sophia and her mother. "Libby, honey, you *need* to eat. You look so thin," her mother said as Libby followed behind them into the house. There was entirely too much food for four people, but that was how things were done there, she did remember that. The table was set with the Willow plates Jeanie had collected over the years at antique stores. Each plate was piled high with different variations of eggs, potatoes, and sausages.

"So, I hear you're sellin' Hugh's place." Jeanie said as Libby took a seat in front of one of the plates.

The other ladies were looking back and forth at each other, clearly uncomfortable. *Is my life the elephant in the room?* she wondered. *Probably.* Celia, who always praised her publicly, may just as easily seek the pity of her friends by telling Libby's sob story about her depressing life.

"Yep," she said, setting her muffin on a napkin and scooping a bite of casserole onto her fork.

Jeanie, now seated beside her, nodded and draped a cloth napkin in her lap. "That place is so nice, and nobody seems to want it," she pointed out.

though, once they realized that most of the people there weren't selling, and vacation cottages usually stayed in the family for generations. She wondered how this one had gotten wind of her intent to sell. Had Wade sent her?

When Libby didn't respond, the agent added, "Pete Bennett said you wanted to put the house on the market."

Pete? What does he care? "I hadn't planned on selling just yet…"

"Oh!" the agent seemed surprised. "Pete called on your behalf. He had thought you were going to stay, but when he found out you intended to sell, he wanted to do anything he could to facilitate that process to get you back home as quickly as possible."

"Did he now…?" Her mind was racing with the things she wanted to say to Pete Bennett. It was bad enough that she didn't want to be there, but the fact that Pete didn't want her there either made her almost want to sell the cottage immediately—for whatever profit—take the money, and run away never to return.

"He was mistaken. I'm not quite ready to put the house on the market yet. I'm so sorry that he sent you all the way out here." She said the words, trying to maintain composure, but she wanted to explode. Being back was exhausting. What if it took months, not weeks, to get another job? What if she was stuck there and months turned to years? Suddenly, she could feel what her mother must have felt.

After making small talk for a brief moment, Veronica Redgrave got back into her car and drove away leaving Libby alone once more in the cool breeze. She walked around the house to the backyard and put her hands on her hips as the sea rippled in the sunlight. This beautiful bay was the only thing that made her nostalgic.

She remembered the old tire swing in her neighbor's backyard that dangled from a pine branch the size of her torso. Her mother wouldn't let her on it because she'd said that it was too dangerous, but her friends had convinced her to do it on the days her mother was at work. It was positioned right at the bank, and when she pushed herself off the tree, the long rope swung her out over the water, the movement of the waves beneath her causing blinding white sparkles in her vision. Like a life-sized pendulum, the wind picking up with every swing, she held onto the rope, her hands sweaty from the rush of adrenaline as it suspended her over water only briefly before pulling her back to the shore. The wobbly rubber tube beneath her as her only security, she had trembled her way to a standing position, her fingers crawling up the rope until she was ready. Then, with a shot of panic to her chest, she leaped, splashing into the water below. There was that one moment just before the splash, when she was suspended in air, falling, knowing her fate. She loved that feeling, no matter how much it terrified her.

That's what it was like when she'd left home to live in New York. She was leaving the security of what she'd known, but she was soaring, floating, on her way to that final splash where everything felt right. She wanted that feeling again of knowing her fate. She wanted it more than anything in the world. *This—this small town with its quirks and gossip and ghosts of people I left behind—this is not my fate*, she thought.

Her mind went back to Pete. She did wish she could explain things, say something to make him understand. Then, shaking the thought free, she turned around and walked toward the rental car, her gift card in hand. Maybe she'd run into him in town and she could give him a piece of her mind for sending out that real estate agent.

Chapter Five

Wentworth's Hardware looked exactly the same as it had when her father had made her go with him as a kid. She still disliked the musty smell of it and the sandpaper feel of the concrete floor beneath her shoes as she walked. In the last decade, she'd seen the invention of file-sharing, learned various new forms of social networking, and marveled at all she could do on a smart phone, yet at Wentworth's it seemed that absolutely nothing had changed right down to the push-button cash register.

Choices were limited. There were no interior designers in town that she knew of, so she'd have to rely on her own tastes and what was available to make the changes necessary to put the Roberts' cottage on the market—or at the very least make it inhabitable for advertisement to out-of-town renters.

All the gadgets, screws, nuts and bolts before her reminded her of the odds and ends in her memory box. On separate occasions, her mother had tried to empty out her memory box, telling her that she needed to rid it of all of the *junk* that was inside—rocks, old pieces of cement, ribbons—but she'd refused.

The last time she'd put something in it was right before she'd
left New York. She'd picked up a runaway flier, a pink half sheet of
heavy paper advertising a stage show off Broadway. It had floated
past her on her way home to her apartment for the last time. She'd
picked it up, folded it twice, and placed it inside her memory box
before packing it up to ship to the cottage. It was at that moment
that the flier had crossed her path that she'd stopped to watch all the
people crossing the crosswalk in front of her. All those faces of New
Yorkers—driven, busy, walking at a clip, oblivious to her stares. The
flier would be a tangible reminder of those faces.

There were other memories in the box too. The pebble she'd taken
from the driveway outside her house the day her father had packed
the last of his things in his car and moved out for good. She'd held it
in her hand as the other pebbles had crunched beneath his tires, his
car pulling out in front of her, his eyes visible in the rearview mirror.
She had also held on to a twig that she'd taken from the butterfly
bush next to Pete's window the day she'd snuck over to his house to
take one last look at him before leaving him and never coming back.

Libby had known that the only way to get Pete to understand
and not try and convince her to stay was to tell him straight out
what she thought about leaving. That day was burned into her
memory—every bit of it as clear as if it had happened yesterday.

"How can anyone be successful here?" she'd said. "I want to be
around people who have ambition."

"So going to a school closer to home doesn't show ambition?"
Pete had said, his face indignant. "I can't believe you just said that."
He looked down at the floor, his jaw clenched. When he looked up
at her, it was as if he were just seeing her for the first time, his eyes
scanning her up and down. "Is that all that matters to you? What

about your family? What about Pop and Nana? Don't you want to be close to them? What if, God forbid, something happened to one of them? Wouldn't you want to be able to come home and see them? Is your ambition worth that much?"

She did care about Pop and Nana. She did care about being able to see them, but she couldn't do anything about it. She needed to attend an elite university to be surrounded by other people with goals like hers, people who could challenge her, push her to be the very best version of herself that she could be.

"I need a competitive university to get me where I want to be in life. If I go to college around here, I know I'll end up staying in White Stone." His expression looked annoyed, irritating her. "The best I can hope for here is an unimportant job at one of the little office buildings in town!" she could hear her voice rising. "This is an insignificant little town with no opportunities."

"Wow," he'd said, shaking his head, incredulity in his eyes. He was quiet for a moment, just staring at her as if he could not believe what he'd just heard. Then, quietly, he said, his face turning red from the anger that he was clearly attempting to control, "Then go, Libby." That was all he'd said before he walked out of the room and left.

Libby remembered feeling helpless in that moment because there was nothing she could do to change the situation or what Pete wanted for his future. She had hurt him, but being honest with him was the only way she'd be able to leave. When the day came, she was more than ready to get out of town, but she couldn't leave without seeing him.

Growing up, she'd always come to his first-floor window by the butterfly bush and knocked. He'd see her and sneak her inside. She hadn't told anyone about going to see Pete the day she'd left. No one would've understood. She had snuck over and peeked in on him in his room, but she didn't knock. It was only for a second, just to say goodbye. He was lying on his bed, reading a book. His face was calm, his expression neutral—a change from the last time she'd seen him. He had the palm of his hand on his temple, leaning on his elbow, and it struck her how she'd never get to hold that hand again. She took in his fingertips, the strength in his forearm, his eyes as they studied the page in front of him, the way his back rose with every breath. It may be the last time she'd see him. After their argument and the hurtful things she'd said, he certainly wasn't going to show up for a visit.

The finality of it sent a wave of sadness over her, sadness like she'd never felt. Through that window, she saw the first person she'd ever kissed, the one who'd been by her side whenever things were tough, the only person she'd ever loved. She let the tears cloud her eyes on purpose so that she didn't have to see it anymore. A stab of fear shot through her like a bullet as she thought about what she was giving up. She was leaving everything she knew for an unknown future. She tried to rationalize it in her head: They were only eighteen. Surely she'd move on, make a life in New York, and forget the hurt that was sitting on her chest like a cinder block at that moment.

Her fingers were wrapped around the twig, not wanting to let go, gripping it so tightly that it snapped right off in her hand. It was that snap that had brought her back to reality and, with it still in her hand, she'd run as fast as she could in the other direction.

"May I help you?" an elderly man's voice came from behind her, yanking her out of her memory.

She pulled in a large breath of the musty air to send her back to the present. "I'm just looking, thanks," she said, willing herself to smile in his direction. The man grinned at her warmly, his lips hidden beneath a white mustache. She recognized him. He was the same person who had worked there when she was a child.

"Let me know if you need me. I'll be up front," he said, walking away from her toward the door.

After she'd been left alone again to immerse herself in her memories, she took a moment to look around her. The hardware store hadn't left any sort of impression on her before, but it was so clearly representative of the town, so different than anywhere she'd been in New York, that it pulled her back to another time. Everything in White Stone was like that. All her memories were right there, lurking around corners, each one startling her as it revealed itself, bringing her emotions to the surface.

The fear that she'd felt that day, seeing Pete in his room, came rushing back in full force—the fear about what she'd given up, about leaving him. Now that it all had come crashing down, she wondered if her choices had been the right ones. She couldn't focus on the items in front of her. She felt stifled, as if she couldn't get to the door fast enough, the air around her turning to liquid, like being underwater. Her chest was tight, her heart beating fast; she needed to get out of there. Memories of her childhood, leaving Pete—they were too much. She paced past the man, ignoring his inquiring stare in her direction, and she pushed through the door, sucking in a breath of fresh sea air. The sun was shining, the heat of it calming her. She moved over to the bench that sat between the hardware store and a gift shop next door and took a seat.

At eighteen, she'd thought mostly about herself, how much she missed Pete, and how hard it had been to get over him. He'd always been the one who could calm her, take away the anxiety she'd had about her family or school. When she was with him it was as if nothing else mattered. Being without him, alone in her dorm room every night, knowing that she couldn't call, couldn't hear his voice, made her feel as if her heart were actually breaking. She cried into her pillow until she couldn't breathe some nights, the ache in her chest nearly too much to bear. Mostly, she'd been consumed with how she'd felt, but now, at thirty, her perspective had changed. Now she wondered what *he'd* thought when she'd left that day, what he'd felt.

A car pulled over to the curb, and she looked up to see if it was him, but it wasn't. A woman got out and went into the gift shop. Relief flooded her; she wasn't sure she was really ready to see him yet, she'd decided. She hadn't worked out what she wanted to say because, unexpectedly, she wanted him to know her side of things. How could she possibly explain it to him—and would it even make things any better? The truth was that the only place where she could have the success she'd had was in New York. And Pete was happy in the life he'd made for himself. Perhaps she should just let it go, let him stay irritated with her…

"Libby Potter?"

She looked up to find a petite brunette with dimples and straight, white teeth grinning at her, her hand on her chest, shopping bags hanging from the crooks of her arms. "I can't believe it!"

"Catherine?" Catherine had been one of her best friends in school and her neighbor growing up. She hadn't spoken to her in years apart from the annual Christmas card, but she was one of those people who could be absent from her life for ages and yet when they came back together, it was as if they hadn't been apart a day.

She embraced Libby, nearly knocking her over, her carrier bags thumping into her as they slid down Catherine's arms. "It's been so long! *Where* have you been?" She pulled back, shaking her head.

"New York."

"Well, I know that. *Everyone* knows that. But I meant, why have you just come home now? We've all missed you so much!"

"I've missed you, too," Libby said, and for the first time since she'd gotten there, she meant that. She was truly sorry not to have kept in touch better. It was all just hitting her, and it was a little overwhelming.

"Does Pete know you're home?"

Worry and hurt and shame churned in her stomach. For Catherine, it was just a simple question about two people who had once been very close, but for Libby it was an inquisition, a judgment. She felt as if Catherine were really saying, *I know what you said to Pete when you left, and I live here too, you know. Am I insignificant?*

"I've run into him, yes."

"Here," she held out her hand, "give me your phone. I'll put my number in, and we can catch up." Libby handed her cell to Catherine. "I'd really love to get together. How long are you staying?" she asked, her fingers moving at warp speed across the keypad.

"It would be nice to get together," she smiled. It was good to see Catherine, good to have a friendly face. "I'm getting the Roberts' cottage ready to sell, so I'll stay as long as that takes. Maybe you could offer some ideas. Remember when we painted your bedroom?" Libby laughed.

"Oh, yeah! We thought the paint was a light yellow, and it was chartreuse! All my furniture was brown—do you remember?—and so we tried to paint it all white to tone it down. I thought my parents would kill us!"

They both giggled together and Libby was glad for the moment of relief.

"Well, you'd better call!" She stood up and handed Libby her phone.

"Of course I will."

"See you soon!"

"Bye." Libby thought about how much harder facing everyone was compared to leaving them. She decided to hurry back to the cottage. She didn't want to run into Pete. She needed to get herself together before seeing him again.

Chapter Six

The rental car still running, she looked at the gas gauge. *How long can I sit here?* she wondered. She eyed the door to see if Pete had come out. In her rearview mirror, she had a glimpse of one side of his Bronco parked in front of the post office. *What is taking him so long? Why won't he come out, get in his car, and leave?* She wasn't ready to see him yet. She hadn't worked out what she wanted to say or even how to emote.

There was a knock on her car window, sending her jumping with fright.

"Don't you have anything better to do than stalk me at the post office?" Pete said as she put her window down.

He was wearing a blue T-shirt and tan shorts that came just to his knees, his hair messy from the wind outside. He leaned on the door with one hand, his fit arm showing through his sleeve. He'd always been thin, despite his attempts to bulk up, but she liked that about him. She frantically searched his eyes for any hint of affection, any lapse in total hatred for her, but there was nothing there. His all-too-familiar grin was absent, his strong jaw clenched, his face vacant.

"I waited for you to come in, but you kept sitting in your car," he said.

"You were waiting for me?" She turned off the engine.

"Yeah. I'd like to know when you're leaving."

"I don't know," she said quietly. She looked down at her lap, her eyes stinging from the tears that wanted to come. Seeing him brought back all the feelings she'd had for him, as if she hadn't been gone a day. She wanted to see him smile, feel him fiddle with her fingers when they held hands like he had so many years ago. He was right there but so far away at the same time. She wanted to make him happy, make him understand how terrible she felt for hurting him. But if she tried to tell him all those things, it wouldn't do anything but make it worse. Eventually, she had to leave. She needed opportunities that were not available to her in White Stone. The conversation would inevitably return to that fact. "I'm leaving as soon as I can," she said.

"Right." He blew air through is lips and looked out over the top of her car as if searching for something.

"Look, I get it that you don't want me here. The real estate agent was message enough."

Pete didn't say anything, but she thought she saw contemplation in his eyes.

"Can you let me out please?" She swallowed to alleviate her drying mouth. "I need to pick up some boxes…"

Pete took a step back to allow her to open the door. She got out, pushed the door shut, and stood across from him, still wanting to tell him everything she'd been thinking. Not knowing how to begin or what to say, she settled on simply an apology. "I'm sorry I said what I did before I left," she said.

She looked up at him, the sun in her eyes, which was a good thing because she could blink away more tears and pretend it was due to the bright light. She looked again for friendliness in his face, but if he felt anything, he wasn't allowing it to show.

"Pete," she took a step closer to him. "I left this place more than I left you. I didn't want to miss out on an opportunity for something bigger, something better. Our relationship was a casualty of that choice. I didn't like leaving *us* any more than you did."

Pete ran his fingers through his hair. "You still don't get it."

Libby caught herself looking around to be sure no one was staring at them. Luckily, they were alone. What didn't she get? She waited for further explanation.

"You look down on where I live." Her skin burned with unease at the sight of the irritation on his face. "You act like we're all a bunch of idiots around here; no one's as good, as smart, as you."

She could feel the tears coming and the heat on her face from embarrassment and anxiety. She was so confused, so lost all of a sudden. She tried to formulate a solution, but her mind was empty. "You're twisting my words." Her voice broke.

"No I'm not." He paused. "Growing up, you hated the way your mother was. It drove you crazy—but guess what, Libby? You're just like her."

How could she ever fix this? He was right. She wanted success and achievement—it made her feel like she'd done something in life—and he had a different perspective on both of those things. By putting down where he lived, she was putting him down as well. She'd never meant to make him feel that way.

What she'd wanted was to be with him. She'd asked him to apply to Columbia with her and he'd refused, saying he didn't want to be that far from the people he loved. So, *she* was a casualty of his choices as well. How was he much different than her?

Against her will, a tear escaped and slid down her cheek, and his face softened considerably. He never did like to see her cry.

Libby wiped another tear away with the back of her hand. "Can you let me by? I just need to get my boxes." The words came out all sputtery as the tears finally started to fall. She pushed past him and jogged across the parking lot, tears streaking her face. She caught a glimpse of him as she entered the post office, and he was already talking to a man she recognized from her childhood. She was a wreck after their confrontation. Had it not fazed him at all? She pushed the thoughts away as a sob swelled in her throat.

After a few minutes' wait inside, she was able to hold in her tears once more, and a couple of the postal workers, clearly noticing her state, started carrying boxes out one by one until all Libby's things were stacked like Legos in the hallway. She signed for them and opened the door with her foot. She leaned toward one of the stacks of boxes, scooting it along the floor toward her while she held the door open. She could feel the dust settling on the palms of her hands and between her fingers.

The door kept shutting on her as she struggled to move the heavy boxes. She could see the postal workers' glances from around the corner as if they wanted to lend a hand, but the line was quite long and they were busy helping others with their packages. Leaving one box wedged in the door to keep it open, she hoisted another into her arms, the weight of it nearly causing her to drop it.

"Are you carrying boxes in *that* outfit?" Pete said from across the parking lot. "There's no way you'll get all those in your car." He was leaning against the Bronco, his arms folded. He squinted toward the rental, and she noted how his vision seemed to have gotten worse since she'd seen him last. His chest rose with his breath and he blew it out—it was a giant, frustrated huff. He walked over to her. "I'll put the big ones in my truck and we can squeeze what's left into your car. Just stand over there," he pointed, "and I'll get the boxes."

Libby moved over to her car, stopping at the back of it to open the trunk. Her phone buzzed in her handbag and she pulled it out. She didn't want to take the call. If she had to speak at that moment, she was liable to have a full-on tear fest. But it was Wade. Since she'd already told Wade about the paperwork, her curiosity about the call got the better of her. The call could be about the cottage or something of hers she may have left behind, both of which were worthy of answering. At the very least, she could tell him she was busy and call him back.

"Hello?" she said, watching Pete out of the corner of her eye. Answering Wade's call was causing an angry punching sensation behind her temples.

Without even a "hello," he started in, "I was wondering how much longer you'll be before the house goes on the market."

She rubbed a knot that had formed in her shoulder. "Wade, I need to keep the cottage for just a little while. I'd like to live there until I can get back to New York."

"What? I don't think that would be a good idea."

She looked over at Pete who had parked the Bronco next to her car and was on the other side of his truck, loading boxes into the backseat. She whispered into the phone, "Wade, be reasonable. I'll pay the entire mortgage while I live there. I *need* a place to live." She knew he didn't feel anything for her anymore, but he wasn't completely merciless.

"This is *temporary*, Libby. You still need to get the place in order, and get it ready to either sell or rent. I'd like to actually make some money on this investment."

"Don't worry. I don't want anything other than temporary," she assured him, then jumped as she turned to pick up a box and bumped into Pete. He looked down at her, his lips pressed together in an unreadable expression.

"Look, I'll talk to you later." She ended the call.

Pete clapped the dust from his hands. "I need to hurry up if I'm going to help you. I have to check on Pop."

* * *

Pete and Libby had called his grandfather "Pop" the entire time Libby had known him, which was over half her life. Pete's dad hadn't been around while he was growing up, and neither had Libby's. At the young age of eleven, when Libby had first started getting to know Pete, their mutual lack of a paternal figure had drawn them together. His mother, Helen, had done well for herself. She'd raised Pete and his elder brother, Ryan, on her own, but Pop and Nana had always been right there, just down the street, ready to offer a helping hand for their only daughter and her children.

Pop had always been special to Libby. He seemed to understand her, to accept her without any reservations. When she'd left, she'd missed Pop so much, and she'd wanted to contact him and keep in touch, but she hadn't. Thinking of him, she had a heavy heart. His health was failing him—she knew that much—and she'd missed twelve good, healthy years with him.

She pulled up behind the Bronco, turned off the engine, and got out of the car. Libby jogged up ahead of Pete, who was carrying the biggest of the boxes, his biceps straining under the weight of it. Libby unlocked the door and pushed it open. He carefully set the box down in the front foyer and scooted it to the side with his foot.

"I like what you've done with the place," he said, looking around.

Considering that the room only had a sofa and one table with an extremely small television, she figured his comment was meant sarcastically. Sarcasm was good; she'd take it. It was much better than the disgust she'd seen before. She wondered, though, if it hurt as much for him to stand there, the two of them together, as it did for her. Seeing him was her real *coming home* moment, because it was he who had been everything for her, growing up. When her mother had pushed her too hard and she didn't think she could take any more, Pete had had a way of lightening the mood, showing her how to be happy despite all the drama.

But most of all, he'd loved her. He told her all the time, and it made her feel untouchable. Like many high school romances, they had gone on in different directions in life, and now they were caught in the empty space between reality and the past. The feeling of it overwhelmed her. Her eyes filled with tears. She blinked, but that only sent them spilling over. She dragged her fingers under her eyes and sniffled.

"I was just kidding," he said, his eyes a little gentler than they'd been before. "I'll go get the next box if you'll just keep the door from shutting."

She nodded, her mind still stuck in the empty space. She wasn't the person who had loved him anymore. She was someone else. It was as if she were two entirely different people: One side of her wanted to hold on to him and never let go, tell him again how sorry she was. The other side yearned to get back to the city—her real life.

Pulling her out of her contemplation was the sound of children's laughter. She stood in the open doorway and saw two boys, one tall and lanky, his feet like those of a Labrador puppy—too big for him—and the other, a dark-haired boy, shorter, and running with a football under his arm while Pete playfully chased him.

"You can't catch me!" the smaller boy shouted.

"Oh no?" Pete picked up speed and scooped the boy into the air, the football dropping down onto the grass. The little boy shrieked with delight.

"That's a tackle," Pete said, setting the boy down and tossing him his ball.

Libby wondered who they were, and a wave of anxiety rushed through her veins. Were they *his* children? Did he have a loving wife at home, and his own family? Pete looked so comfortable with them, so happy. She'd seen that playful side to him as kids, but to see him as a grown man, the kind way he handled them, hit her hard and made her feel like she was missing so much more than what she'd already lost.

"When're you gonna set up that swing for us?" the lanky one asked.

Pete stopped, as if pondering the question, but noticed Libby and, for the first time in twelve years, she saw that smile. He hadn't been smiling at her; he'd smiled for the benefit of the boys, but she didn't care. The sight of it caused a flutter that started in the pit of her stomach and rose all the way up through her chest. The two boys looked her way; they seemed to just now notice that she was there.

"Who's that?" the small one asked.

"That's Miss Libby. Miss Libby, this…" he tousled the boy's hair, "is Thomas, and this…" he gestured toward the tall, lanky one, "is

Matthew." Then he looked back at the boys. "This is Miss Libby's house now. Pop doesn't live here anymore."

"Are you going to come over still?" the taller one asked.

Pete glanced over at Libby. "Maybe," he said, his face turning serious before looking back to the boys.

Libby knew what Pete meant by "maybe." They used to joke about it when they were young. Whenever he wanted anything from his mother that she wouldn't let him have, to quiet him, she answered, "Maybe." He used to say, "My mother has three answers: yes, no, and no, but she calls the second 'no' *maybe*." Because of this, Pete and Libby always used to say "maybe" instead of "no."

Another memory came back like a flash of lighting. It had been years since she'd thought about it. Pete would pin her down, kissing her relentlessly, tickling her, and she'd scream, "Let me go!"

He'd tighten his grip on her, that smile across his face, and, just before kissing her again, he'd say, "Maybe." She'd squeal and wriggle underneath him until he finally loosened his grip and let go of her wrists so she could wrap her arms around his neck, still giggling. She wondered why that particular memory had surfaced. There were tons of times they'd used "maybe," but it was that time that she'd remembered.

Even though Libby knew that it was probably better that way, she still felt a little sad when she heard his answer to the boys. She shouldn't have him around though, because it would just make leaving too hard if they became friends again before she left for New York.

"I have to help Miss Libby now. Can I catch you two later?"

The boys ran off, the lanky one waving at Pete and the little one tossing the football into the air. They ran down the gravel road adjacent to the cottage.

"Who were those boys?"

"They live down the beach. The next house up. I promised them a tire swing about a week before Nana died—like the one we used at Catherine's house."

She remembered him pushing her so far out over the water that the tickle in her stomach had almost made her lose her grip. It seemed like so long ago.

"But with Nana gone and Pop…" He looked down at the ground and scuffed his shoe along the loose dirt. Libby could tell by his demeanor that he was dealing with something. Seeing his face like that made her want to protect him, help him through whatever it was.

"Leave the boxes. Come in. Tell me about Pop. I miss him so much." Why had she just asked him to do that? It went against everything she should do… By getting closer with him, she was making things more difficult than they had to be, and she was afraid it might hurt again when she left.

"I can't. I really have to go," he said, and she could tell that her concern for Pop had softened him a little. He knew as well as she did what Pop meant to her. "Let me get these boxes out of the car for you, and then I'm off. I have to check on Pop. He's been alone all morning and sometimes he thinks he can take a walk when he's been by himself for too long. He forgets…"

"He can't take a walk?"

"Not when he doesn't remember how to get home. He has dementia."

Hugh Roberts, who had been so strong and so intelligent—she couldn't fathom anything like that happening to him. He was a salesman—medical supplies. People said that he could sell *anything* because he was that sharp, that much on his game. So the thought that someone so bright could have a disease of the brain was tough to take. It seemed like such a loss. As if Anne's death hadn't been enough, now Pete was dealing with that.

"Does he… know who you are?"

"Yes. He remembers his family. He remembers Nana… It hasn't progressed that much yet. He's just a little forgetful right now."

A cool breeze rustled the leaves in the trees, causing Libby to look up. The sky was a piercing blue with cumulus clouds that looked like bowls of whipped cream. She wondered if Anne could see the two of them standing there. What would she think about all this: Libby living in her house, talking to her grandson after so many years, Hugh being cared for by Pete? She could almost feel her presence.

"Can you help me? Let's see if we can get the rest of those boxes inside," Pete said.

Libby followed him to the truck and, together, they finished unloading the boxes, piling them in the center of the living room, filling nearly the entire floor.

"Thank you," she said, wiping her hands on her trousers.

"You're welcome." He took a step toward her, and for that one second, she felt like time had stood still for those twelve years. It was as if she were the same eighteen-year-old girl she'd been back then when she looked at him.

"I'm sorry," she blurted. She didn't know what else to say. She was sorry she'd hurt him, sorry she didn't get to see Nana, sorry she hadn't spent time with Pop. She could keep listing the reasons for being sorry, and she felt like that one little word wasn't good enough, but it was all she had. "I'm sorry," she said more quietly, her eyes on the wooden floorboards by her feet.

"Okay," he said quietly.

What did he mean by "okay?" Okay, he knew she was sorry? Okay, he wasn't upset with her anymore? Okay, he didn't care one way or the other? She looked for an answer on his face but his expression was neutral, his smile gone. She wanted him to smile. She needed his smile. It always made things so much better.

"Hey," he said. "Happy birthday." The corners of his mouth turned up just a bit, winding her stomach tighter than a nautilus shell. That slight glimmer, that infinitesimal look of happiness, took her breath away. "Get anything nice?" he asked, clearly chewing on some thought. Had she finally convinced him that she was truly sorry for what she'd said to him? He had to know that, regardless of her opinions of where he lived, she didn't have the same opinion of him.

She had a strange urge to grab him by the pockets of his shorts and pull him toward her like she'd always done, but she knew better. "Yeah," she nodded, thinking how good it felt to be near him. That was gift enough. "I did."

Chapter Seven

Libby folded some of the empty boxes and leaned them against the wall upstairs. She'd contemplated not even breaking them down since she hoped that she'd be filling them back up sooner rather than later. She opened the door of the last bedroom upstairs. Tucked away inside the room, on the ceiling, was the attic, accessible by a pull-down lever door, where she planned to store the boxes until she needed them again. Libby tugged on the rope and the door fell open on its hinges, revealing a folded wooden ladder. She unfolded it and stood on the bottom step, testing her weight. It seemed sturdy, so she grabbed a couple of boxes and climbed up.

The warm spring air filtered in through two vents on either end of the house, causing a plume of heat to envelop her the minute she got to the top. The old wood interior smelled of dust and rain. She pulled on the chain of an uncovered light bulb to illuminate the small space. The light clicked on, exposing a roll of old flooring and a few spare tiles from one of the bathrooms.

Libby pushed her hair out of her face and tucked it behind her ears. With a nudge, she thrust the flattened boxes over the flooring. They sent up a cloud of dust as they came to a rest on the other side. She turned around to go back down the ladder but stopped, noticing a yellowed envelope peeking out from under the linoleum flooring. Curious, she pulled it from its spot, wondering if it had old family photos or something the Roberts had left behind. The end had been torn neatly to expose its contents. She flipped it over in her hand, and saw the name "Anne" written in heavy script on the outside. Inside there was only a single sheet of yellowed paper.

The humidity had blanketed her with a sticky, wet heat, so she decided to take the envelope with her downstairs where she could investigate it further in the cool breeze of the bay. With it still in her grip, she left the attic and went outside onto the stoop where the sea air nearly chilled her sweaty skin. Inside the envelope was a letter addressed to Anne. As an impulse, she looked around to make sure no one was watching, even though she was isolated at the Roberts' cottage. She was being nosy, and she knew it.

She chewed on her lip as she began to read the letter, and she wondered if she should read any further, since the letter had been written for Pete's grandmother. Libby looked around one more time to ensure that she was alone. Just to be on the safe side, she took the envelope and its contents down to the beach where she could sit in the hammock and read with no interruptions.

She sat down and got comfortable, the old rope creaking beneath her in time with the rising and falling of the waves. The wind caused the letter to flap in her hands so she smoothed it out on her lap, pinning the envelope underneath it, and read:

My Dearest Anne,

I hope this letter finds you well. Thank you for coming to dinner with the others to welcome me back home. I really enjoyed it. I wanted to pull you away and tell you all of this then, but I know that you are an honorable woman, and I would not put you in such a precarious position as to require an immediate response. So now on to the reason for this letter.

Anne, I am shamefully in love with you. My affections for you transcend duty and honor, and I am willing to take a knock to my reputation if it means spending the rest of my life by your side. While I know in my heart that you will not leave your husband, I wanted to put forth this gesture just in case you ever reconsider. Come to Chicago with me. We can live in the city, travel, do anything you'd like. I will buy you a ticket immediately should you want to come with me. You can just leave; I'll ensure you have everything you need. You know where to find me. I will be waiting, whether you come or not.

Forever yours,

Mitchell

This was not what she had expected to find. Nestling the letter inside its envelope, Libby folded down the jagged flap of paper at the end and pressed it down in her hands. She wondered what Anne had thought of this proposition. Had she considered it? What would her life have been like if she'd accepted Mitchell's offer and left Hugh to move to Chicago? Indignation swam inside her as she processed Mitchell's words in the letter. How could he think he could step in and try to ruin what Pop and Nana had together, she wondered? They'd always been the perfect couple, full of love for each other, completely happy. How could someone have tried to interfere with their relationship? She lay back on the hammock and closed her eyes.

She pictured Nana, and a memory of her and Pop one summer's day came to mind. Pop had a pontoon boat—a big, flat, slow thing that inched its way along the bay. It had a row of seating down each side and a canopy above the helm. Nana always insisted on having a cooler for mixed drinks, her bottle of wine and a picnic basket full of fresh vegetables, crackers, and fruit. Pop dutifully hoisted it all onto the boat before every voyage. Pete had taken Libby along with Pop and Nana on a ride out into the middle of the bay so they could go swimming.

Libby sat on the boat, hugging her knees to keep the chill off her, her tank top coverall flapping in the sea breeze as the boat made its way out into the bay. Pete sat beside her with his arm around her bare shoulders. Occasionally, he toyed with the tie to her swimsuit at the back of her neck. His soft touch, the sun's heat, and the lull of the waves against the boat were making her drowsy.

Pop came to a stop and lowered the anchor, the boat swaying on the water. Libby was too relaxed to swim, so she'd opted to stay on the boat and read a book. Pete stayed with her. Pop turned on the radio, beach music filling the air. Nana began unpacking snacks and drinks and setting them on the small table on the side of the boat. She had on a halter dress that fell past her knees, and sandals.

There was an ease to the way Pop and Nana communicated. Watching them move about the boat together was lovely. Libby had tried to read, but they were more entertaining. They'd done it so many times that they knew exactly what the other needed. One moved, while the other leaned, back and forth, as they laughed together, helped each other, and set up for the day. When they were finally settled, and Nana was sipping her Chardonnay, Pop gently took it from her hands and set it down next to the picnic basket. He pulled her close to him, placing a hand on her back and holding her other hand out to the side, and he started to dance with her. He spun her around, making her laugh, and then swayed back and forth in time with the waves. Nana lay her head on his shoulder and closed her eyes, a smile on her lips. The sight had made Libby lean toward Pete, and he wrapped his arms around her, intertwining his fingers at her shoulder. She thought how she'd like to be that happy one day.

The breeze in the pines above the hammock brought Libby back to the present and she opened her eyes, the feel of the envelope registering under her hand on her stomach. She wanted to find this Mitchell person, tell him how wonderful Pop and Nana were together and how nothing should have ever come between them. Had Nana considered his offer? The mere question made her shudder.

Libby swung her legs over the edge of the hammock, the sea grass tickling her, and tried to clear her mind of the shock of the letter. She was feeling uneasy because of it, and she already had enough making her uneasy. She needed to get up, get on with things, and try to put one more day in that town behind her. She walked back to the house to put the letter in her handbag when she heard her phone ringing through the screen door.

Chapter Eight

"We miss having you out with us," Trish said on the other end of the line as Libby finished hanging up the last of her clothes. They looked out of place in the cottage closet. "I had my first pineapple cocktail the other night. It was fantastic!"

Going out after work in New York was a regular occurrence. Libby wondered if this trend of having dinner and drinks any night of the week had started as a result of the stressful occupations many New Yorkers had. Most of her friends worked for big-name businesses, and with a big name came big demands. Libby's job had been the same. She usually started work before eight o'clock in the morning, worked through her lunch, and finally finished up after seven thirty. By the time she was done, she was ready for a drink.

"Who went out last Friday?" she asked, although she really didn't want to know; it was too depressing. The fact that her friends could still have drinks because they were all working and perfectly successful in their own lives only sharpened the edge of her failures, making her feel miserable. She opened up a small box containing jewelry and other accessories and fished through it, untangling her necklaces.

"Sonya and Babs. It was a small crowd."

She took each necklace and stretched it out along the oak dresser of her new bedroom. There wasn't a whole lot of storage in the cottage, so she'd have to get creative as to where to put things. For now, she was just focused on unpacking so as not to use up the entire evening. She wanted to try and send out a few more applications.

"Anything interesting happen?" she asked.

Trish sighed. "No, same old thing."

"Apart from the new cocktail."

"Yes! Apart from that. What have you been up to? Lots of sunbathing, I hope."

She rested the phone between her shoulder and ear as she tugged at two more necklaces. "A little." On vacation, one can lie around in the sun and enjoy it, but in her current situation, she saw it as a sentence for her shortfalls, a prison to keep her away from the successes she knew would make her happy.

"Well, I didn't want to bombard you after the last phone call, so I waited until you were a little more settled… I was wondering if I could offer some possible dates for the shower and the brunch? It looks like we have a few parties on Kevin's side to attend."

Everything sounded so festive—so many celebrations. She wanted to be happy for Trish. She was trying very hard despite the sinking feeling that she'd ruined her own chance. But, if Libby was an expert at anything, it was planning. All her life, she'd been a planner. As a girl, she'd always been *that* person who did all the inviting and organizing whenever she went out with her friends. She had meticulously structured her courses in high school to ensure the most attractive transcript for colleges. Her entire life she'd spent fine-tuning her years down to the last detail to ensure her success.

Sometimes, however, even the best plans went south. Look at where all of that planning had gotten her. But this would give her a project of sorts, which she welcomed. "Of course! What are the dates?" she asked, dragging another moving box toward her with her free hand.

While Trish told her the days to work around, she pulled a wooden container from the moving box. It had been sanded down until the surface was as smooth as glass, the grains evident under the clear varnish. On one side of the lid were two brass hinges with curling details, and on the other side, a brass latch. Her memory box. She set it down next to her necklaces and opened the lid. "Other than the dates you can't," she scooted the moving box to the side with her foot, "do you have any particular days you'd like better, or do you want me to pick?" she asked.

"Could you fit them in during the next month or two? I know that's probably a lot on you, given that you've just moved and you're trying to do renovations."

"It's fine."

"Okay! Then you pick the dates and I'll be there!"

"Will do."

After jotting down a list of possible times and dates for the shower and the odd detail about the brunch, they said their goodbyes and Libby stopped unpacking. It was time for a break. The sun was setting, painting the sky a vibrant pink. On the side of the cottage, off the kitchen, there was a small screened-in porch. It had a paddle fan and a comfortable porch swing. When Wade had mentioned buying furniture, the only piece that she argued over was that swing because from it, one could look across two acres of lawn, straight out to the sunrise over the bay in the morning, and the moon casting its glistening light in the late evenings.

She'd been on that porch with Pete enough to understand the necessity of a solid piece of furniture for that location, but her memory hadn't done it justice. The photos didn't let in the light breeze coming off the bay or the shushing sound of the waves as they kissed the sand during high tide, the rustling of the pines, and the almost electric sounds of the insects in the woods. All those sounds, together with the *clap, clap, clap* of the paddle fan, were more like silence than anything she'd had in a long time.

She just sat, gently rocking, her long strands of blond hair moving ever so slightly with the wind. The silence, while calming, made her more homesick. She wanted the velocity of the city, to be back in her reality where she could make progress toward her goals. But she was stuck in a place where nothing moved forward. If anything, it yanked her backward in time, like quicksand. Tears swelled in her eyes as she thought of it all. She tried to steady her breathing by matching her inhales and exhales with the tide.

A knock at the screen door behind her sent her leaping to her feet. She hadn't even heard anyone walk up.

"Sorry, hon. Did I startle ya?" Jeanie stood with a covered dish in mitted hands.

"It's okay."

She held out her dish, the steam escaping from under the foil. "I brought you some supper." Libby held the screen door open, allowing her to enter. "It ought to last you a few nights… You been cryin'?"

"No, I think it's just the salty air."

"You've been away too long if your eyes are tearin' up from fresh air!" she said, shuffling up the three wooden steps. She knocked her feet against the boards on the porch, Libby guessed to get the stray sand off her shoes. "You need some good chicken casserole to reac-quaint ya with this part of the world, Miss Libby!" She left Libby on the porch and headed inside toward the kitchen.

Libby had known Jeanie all her life, and she was more mothering than her mother had ever been. With her big bear hugs, concerned eyes and loving smile, she was one of Libby's favorite people. Once, when her mother had been telling a group of shoppers at the local supermarket all of the top universities she'd planned to visit with Libby, Jeanie caught Libby's eye, pursed her lips, and rolled her eyes. That had been the first time it had occurred to Libby that perhaps her mother's way wasn't always the right way.

She could talk to Jeanie.

"It's still hot so come and dish yourself some," Jeanie said as Libby pulled a chair out at the wicker dinette she'd put in the small nook in the kitchen. "Mind if I have some too? I've got some apple pie out in the car, but I couldn't get it in one trip."

"Not at all." She pulled out a second chair and then went to the cabinets to get dishes. She set them down on the counter and grinned at Jeanie who had already found a serving spoon in the drawer and was dishing out their servings. "Thank you, Jeanie, for thinking of me. You didn't have to do all this." She was so grateful to have Jeanie and so thankful that she had brought her dinner. No one had ever brought her a fresh-baked pie in New York. More than the food, she could tell that Jeanie cared, and it felt good to be cared for.

Jeanie waved a dismissive hand as if it were nothing, but Libby knew she'd taken a lot of time to prepare it, even if she didn't want to admit it. "You don't have an apron hangin' around here," she noted.

Libby shook her head. "Nope. Don't cook much."

"Hmm. Well, I'll help you out for now, but you'd better get to practicin' because no cookin' 'round these parts means no eatin'!"

Libby allowed a little huff of laughter to escape at that remark. Jeanie was right. If Miller's even did takeout, it would probably start to get really old by the end of the month, considering the limited menu, and the other few places around also served mostly seafood which would wear out its welcome after a while.

Jeanie set two glasses of tap water onto the table, pulled the chair across from Libby out a little farther, and lowered herself down. Draping a paper towel in her lap, she asked, "How are you *really* doin'?"

"Not great," she said, looking at her steaming chicken and pasta.

"Thought so. That's why I stopped by tonight. I could tell when I saw you last." They ate in silence for a moment. Libby knew that she was waiting for her to say something, but she just didn't know what to say. She didn't even know where to begin. Jeanie took a bite of chicken and followed it with a swig of water. "Wanna talk about it?"

She wanted to say "no," but with Jeanie, she knew that her secrets were safe. She took a deep breath and let it out like a burst pipe, the tension in her shoulders pinching her neck—and tried to figure out how to verbalize her thoughts. "It's hard coming back... hard to see everyone."

Jeanie nodded and took another bite. Through the glass in the door, a swarm of tiny bugs circled the porch light outside the kitchen window. "By '*everyone*,' you mean Pete?"

There it was. Jeanie just laid it all out there. But she was right. Libby couldn't lie to Jeanie. "That's a big part of it, yeah."

"Have you two had a chance to talk?"

"Some. I don't think he hates me anymore. Now he just doesn't like me," Libby smiled.

"I've heard of married couples worse off than that. Maybe you two can work things out then."

"Maybe," she smiled, knowing that she meant Pete's "maybe" and not the real one.

"If you did work things out, would you stay?"

"No." Her shoulders were tightening with the complete misery of her predicament. She could feel the stress welling up. Why did she even have to have dated Pete Bennett? They'd been friends for so long. Why had they taken that next step? It made everything so complicated. He was a fantastic person, just not the right one for her, and now it left them in a very odd place.

"You might surprise yourself. Not everyone wants to leave this town. There's a lot of good here, you know. Some people like it enough to spend their whole lives here."

Jeanie's comment brought to mind Anne's letter and the choices that she'd had before her. Regardless of what may have happened, *she'd* stayed. Libby wanted to tell Jeanie about it, but she knew it wasn't her secret to tell. She wondered if Jeanie knew anything about the man named Mitchell or if she had heard any stories about trouble between Pop and Nana. They had been so perfect together; it seemed unthinkable that anything could have put a wedge between them, yet the point crept into her mind that Nana had been given the chance to escape that town for something bigger.

"What're you thinkin' about?" Jeanie asked.

Libby set down her fork and put her hands in her lap. She took a moment to look around the kitchen, the old wallpaper still there where Nana had hung it. "I think about Nana and Pop a lot since coming home," she said. "Being here brings back so many memories."

Jeanie took a sip of her water and nodded, following Libby's gaze as she looked around the room once more. Jeanie had known Hugh and Anne Roberts quite well. During so many of the times she sought a retreat from the demands of her mother, and she'd come to the Roberts' place with Pete, Jeanie had been there. Libby had never said a bad word to anyone about her mother, but whenever she'd shown up, it was as if Jeanie already knew.

"Do you remember what they were like when you were young?" she asked, trying to ascertain how Mitchell could have even gotten into the picture. "They were always so happy. As a kid, it never occurred to me, but now, I wonder about their life together." She scooped a bite of casserole onto her fork. "Didn't you say that you'd attended their wedding? I'll bet it was wonderful."

"I did go to their weddin'," Jeanie smiled. "I was seven." The paddle fan clacked outside as it spun the warm air around on the porch. "I remember her dress so well because I was at that age where I still thought it might be possible to be a princess one day. And that's exactly what Anne looked like."

Libby leaned on her fist, her elbow propped on the table. "Tell me what she looked like."

"She had a long, ivory dress. The top was a mixture of lace and satin. It went right up to her neck and down her arms. She had a large sash of satin at her waist, and a train—I swear—the length of a football field. At least that's how I remember it." Jeanie stood up. "Come on out with me. Let's get the pie from the car."

The crickets hummed outside as they walked into the late evening air. The sun was still resting on the edge of the horizon, casting enough light into the night sky to make the trees look like silhouettes against the sapphire-blue background.

"I'll bet Nana was a pretty young woman," Libby said, opening Jeanie's car door and allowing her to take the pie off the passenger seat. With the open car windows, the smell of cinnamon and apples wafted up toward her as if it were just out of the oven.

"She was. I've heard she was the catch of the town when she was a girl." Jeanie stepped to the side, holding the tin while Libby shut the car door. "In her—I suppose—thirties, she always had red lips and her dark hair rolled up on the sides in pin curls. So pretty."

"How long had she known Pop before they got married?"

"I'm not sure. That was before my time. But I've never known a happier couple," she said as they went inside.

Libby opened a drawer and pulled out a knife. It was all she had for serving apple pie. As she dished the dessert, she was left to ponder the man named Mitchell and how he'd offered to take Nana away from Pop.

Chapter Nine

Libby felt strange to be dressed down. Even her casual clothes were out of place there—as Jeanie had pointed out last night after dinner—so she'd gone to the local clothing store and purchased a simple pair of shorts, a T-shirt, and a pair of flip flops. She had needed some clothes to wear when she worked on the cottage. The new outfit was also fitting for trips to the hardware store.

With her gift card in hand, she'd decided to try again and see if she could find something to get that kitchen wallpaper off. It didn't hurt matters that Jeanie had told her Pete was always in the hardware store and that he liked to take Pop there around noon before lunch. Since his dementia had worsened, Pop liked to build things, and he made Pete take him to Wentworth's almost daily.

There were so many things she wanted to say to Pete, to explain herself more, to make the situation between them better. She hadn't worked out exactly how she wanted to say it all, and she didn't know if she'd have the emotional stability to do it, but she still wanted to see him. She stood, staring at the various brands of paper stripper, scrutinizing the benefits of each, when she heard a familiar voice that sent flutters shooting through her stomach.

"Wow. That's an improvement."

She spun around to find Pete, right on time. The sight stunned her. It hadn't been Pete who'd captured her attention. It was Pop, who was standing next to him. Pop looked considerably older than the last time she'd seen him. His hair, now completely white, didn't stay down quite as easily anymore, and he seemed smaller, thinner. It took her by surprise so much that she didn't even speak for fear her mouth would gape open. Her strong and protective Pop had withered to this feeble old man. But his big, bushy eyebrows rose when he caught sight of her and his face lit up.

"Libby!" he nearly shrieked before wrapping her in a tight bear hug. He pulled back, his hands trembling with old age and covered in sun spots. With everything else in town, time had stood still, but not for Hugh Roberts. He had definitely moved along with the years. But upon closer inspection, his smile was the same and his eyes were still friendly. "I've missed you so much."

"I've missed you too," she said, her eyes glassy from tears. She'd missed so many good years with him. Seeing how he looked now made her wish she had at least called him. She wrapped her arms around him, noticing how her fingers met at his back. He'd been a broad, tall man when she was growing up, and she could barely get her arms around him, but now he was so much smaller. He didn't smell the same or feel the same, but it was him. She leaned back to look at his face and smiled, blinking the tears out of her eyes. "I missed you," she said again.

"Have you come back to see Pete?" he asked.

"Um," she wavered. Clearly he was thrilled at the idea, and she didn't want to disappoint him. Pete seemed to read her thoughts and nodded at her as if to say, *Say yes*. "Yes, I have."

Hugh clapped his hands together in one loud motion. "Oh! That's fantastic. Great news!" he said before turning down an aisle and heading toward the packets of nails.

"Pop's making a bookcase today. He needed some supplies."

Together they walked behind Hugh toward the spot where he had stopped to inspect a few small bags of nails. Being next to Pete made her knees feel loose and weak as if she couldn't hold herself up. He wasn't his normal friendly self, but he was pleasant instead of harsh, and she couldn't help but notice it. Was his friendly demeanor because he understood how hard it was for her to explain herself and apologize for her actions? Or was it for Pop's benefit? "What did you mean by 'That's an improvement?'" Libby asked, her arm brushing against his.

"Your outfit. You finally look like one of us," he said, that familiar amusement hiding behind his eyes. "Not that I don't like the other outfits. This just seems more you." The corners of his mouth turned up, and his grin unleashed an unexpected swarm of butterflies in her stomach.

The problem was that it wasn't her at all. Not anymore. She didn't feel any more comfortable in these clothes than she had in the others, but for different reasons.

"You miss Pop," Pete said. "Glad you're not heartless at least."

She could feel the sting of sadness, and she tried not to let it show. "I missed him so much," she said. "I missed you *both* so much." She wished she could sit him down right there and tell him everything she was feeling: how she'd cried about leaving him, how empty she'd felt for so long, how much she'd wanted to be with him.

Pete didn't respond to her comment, but she could see his face become calm, his eyes moving in thought. His jaw wasn't clenched anymore like it had been the other times she'd seen him, and the line between his eyes was gone. Perhaps she was getting through to him.

"Found them!" Hugh scuffled toward Libby and Pete, a small bag dangling from his fingers. Then he stopped and held the bag unusually far from himself and squinched up his nose. "How much are they?"

"It's fine, Pop. I've got it."

"Nope! No, no, no. I can pay for it, son. How much is it?"

"Three dollars and some change." Pete gave Libby a conspiratorial glance, and they both had to hide their grin, for they both knew how stubborn Hugh Roberts could be. With all the other changes in him clearly, that trait had held on. The common ground gave her a floating sensation, as if all their issues were pulled from her shoulders in that one moment. Pete was smiling. At her. There was nothing better than that. Even if, once Pop wasn't there, they still had the same problems, it gave her a chance to feel good, and she hadn't had that in a long time.

Even though she still needed to get the wallpaper stripping liquid and a few things for the cottage, Libby walked with them to the register where Hugh paid for his nails. The same mustached man from the other day handed him his change. "So, my boy, should we leave Libby to her shopping?"

Pete looked straight at her, right into her eyes, and it was as if they were the only two there. "Maybe," he said. The word had come out like *Maybe we should*, but Libby wondered if he really meant *their* maybe. Did he not want to leave her? She kept her face clear of any emotion just in case it was all in her head.

"You'll have to stop by the house sometime," Hugh said, embracing her to say goodbye.

Libby nodded and smiled, unsure of an appropriate response to that suggestion.

"Well, give her a hug then and we'll be on our way!" Hugh said.

Tension zinged through her. Pete let out a nervous-sounding chuckle but took a step toward her, putting his arms around her. Then, to her surprise, he pulled her close just like he had so many years ago, his lips on the top of her head, her face nestled into his chest—it was only an instant, and then it was done. He'd pulled away before she'd even had a chance to really register the feeling. Unexpectedly, all the emotions from the last few weeks flooded her body, and tears surfaced in her eyes again.

Libby had so many feelings when it came to Pete: sadness because she missed his protective nature, the way he made her feel like nothing would ever hurt her; complete joy at seeing him again; anxiety because of how he felt about her now. She didn't want him to hate her, but just that tiny glimpse of how he used to be with her made everything more difficult than it had ever been. The more he let her in, the harder it would be to leave. She wasn't eighteen anymore, and this time she knew exactly what she was leaving. She didn't want to repeat the feeling she'd had the last time she'd left, knowing that she'd never get to be with him again. She couldn't bear it after everything else that had happened. She pushed her tears away.

"See ya," he said. She could tell he had noticed her tears despite her effort to hide them. Hugh patted him on the back. The receipt for the nails floated off the counter and down to the floor where it rested, exposed on the empty concrete. Libby picked it up as Pete and Hugh walked through the door, neither one of them looking back. She folded it and slid it into her pocket. Pete wasn't as angry anymore; she could feel it. That memory needed to be kept, so Pop's receipt was destined for her memory box.

Chapter Ten

"A *firm*" had been a generous description of Marty's business. The only people there were Marty, his receptionist called Janet, and Libby. Marty Bruin was shorter than Libby, had unmanageably curly hair, and twitched a lot when he spoke, making him appear nervous when he probably wasn't. That was the great thing about accounting, however; one didn't have to be a people person. He was pleasant and cheerful, and he'd given her a desk by the window, which was gracious of him since there were only two windows—the other being by the reception area.

"Here are your accounts, he said, handing her a small box of files. The coffeemaker is over by Janet…" The receptionist waved. "And the bathrooms are just down the hall on the left."

"Thank you," Libby smiled.

Marty stood by her desk in silence for an unsettling amount of time, his hand propped up on the wall behind her. She wondered if she should make small talk in an effort to move him along. Before she could offer anything, he said, "I'll be just over there," and pointed toward a small desk with papers haphazardly scattered over it. "Let me know if you need anything else."

"I sure will, Marty. Thank you again for the work. I am very grateful for it. I think I'll dig right in!" Libby slid the box toward her.

Marty clicked his tongue and raised his eyebrows—another one of his gestures. Then, he grinned and waved, heading over to his desk. Libby flipped through the files in the banker's box in front of her. She had accounts for a handful of local store owners, a veterinarian, and a head of a construction company, but piquing her interest was a file labeled Peter Bennett. From his account details, it seemed that *her* Pete had his own web development business, and he was certainly doing well for himself. With a flush of heat to her face, she slapped the file shut and put it back into the box. It didn't matter what their history was, she didn't feel right looking at his yearly income summary.

By lunch time, she'd trudged through the numbers for a few of her clients and created reports reflecting their taxable income. Her stomach growled and she figured that it was as good a time as any to get some lunch, so she let Marty know, out of courtesy, and walked outside into the magnificent sunshine.

Two doors down was The Bay Café, which during the summer months drew in vacationers but today was only moderately busy. The floor was traditionally tiled in large black and white tiles, a handful of tables turned to look like diamonds rather than squares, were covered in red gingham cloths, and sitting in the center of each table was a shiny bucket of fresh yellow and white daisies. Following the note on the chalkboard sign to *seat yourself*, Libby found the table nearest the corner and sat down.

It wasn't until she was settled in her chair and had ordered her iced tea that she saw Mabel Townley, Anne Roberts's best friend, dining alone. She didn't look exactly as Libby had remembered her, but it was clear that it was her. Like Hugh, her age had caught up with her: her light-brown hair was now almost completely silver, her shoulders rounded forward as if the weight of her own body were too much for her these days. Wire-rimmed glasses sat just a little too low on her nose, and she pushed them back up into place. Mabel spotted her and smiled, her lips pressed together. Libby waved.

Seeing Mabel, she wondered if Anne's best friend knew anything about Mitchell or his letter. She sat at her table engrossed in her own thoughts. Could Nana have been unfaithful to Pop? Certainly she hadn't seemed like the type of person who would stray, but then again, was there a *type* for those people? She wondered if Nana had ever been unhappy living in White Stone, if she, too, wanted something more. The letter bothered her considerably, but she knew why. Pop and Nana's relationship had always seemed so easy, so comfortable. It was an unsettling feeling, thinking that their relationship may not have been as perfect as it seemed. Every time she looked over at Mabel Townley, she wondered what she knew. Libby traced the square pattern in the table with her fingernail.

"Libby!" Celia Potter came clacking through the small dining area, flinging her hand up at Mabel in a quick hello. "Why didn't you call me, honey? I'd have met you for lunch." She looked down at her silver bangle watch and twisted it on her wrist to see the time. "Did you just get here?"

"Yep," Libby leaned over and pulled out a chair, trying to sit up a little straighter so she wouldn't have to hear anything from her mother about it. She realized what she was doing and immediately relaxed her body. She didn't have to please her anymore; she was a grown woman. It was time she started thinking like it. "They haven't gotten my drink order yet, so you're just in time. You can join me now," she gestured to the chair she'd pulled out. That was the trouble with a small town; with only one main street and a handful of places to go, running into people was inevitable.

"What a pleasant surprise!" she said, sitting down. "I was just going to pick something up but now we can have lunch together." Celia dropped her handbag under the table and spun around toward Mabel. "Are you by yourself too, Mabel? Come over here and join us if you'd like."

Mabel carefully hoisted herself up, steadying her legs by holding on to the table. Then she ambled over. Watching her mother's ease of conversation there only made Libby wish again for her old life in New York. She didn't feel comfortable at all. People there didn't seem as driven as they did in New York, their pace was slower. It had never worked for her as a kid, and it still didn't work. In her small town there was nothing. And there never would be anything. Just the same thing, day in and day out.

A waitress appeared, transported Mabel's lemonade over to Libby's table, and filled their water glasses with a pitcher of iced water. "Can I take your order?" she asked. "Or do you need a minute?"

"I'm ready," Mabel said, still wriggling herself into a comfortable position. "I'll just have the southern fried steak and potatoes." She looked over at Libby and Celia. "I get the same thing every time I come!" she chuckled. She pulled off the paper band from the silverware and draped the napkin in her lap.

"I think we're probably ready too," Celia said, smiling in Libby's direction. "I'll just have a salad. Do you have Ranch dressing?" The waitress nodded, and Celia turned toward Libby who, until that very moment, hadn't given a second thought to what she was going to eat. She scanned her menu quickly. What should she get? The choices seemed almost foreign to her now: Chicken and Dumplings, Fried Catfish, Pulled Pork Barbeque. "I'll have the same, please." she said in defeat.

"Libby, it's good to see you," Mabel said, squeezing the juice of the complimentary lemon wedge into her lemonade and stirring it with a spoon. "You're living in the Roberts' place, right?"

She nodded.

"It has a lovely view of the bay from the screened porch. Anne and I used to sit out there all the time. I just don't get that kind of breeze on my porch."

"You've known Anne a long time, haven't you?" Libby asked. Had Mabel been at the dinner with Anne and Mitchell that night, she wondered? If Anne had feelings for Mitchell, might she have shared them with Mabel?

"I've known her all my life. We lived next door to each other growing up, and we went all the way through school together." She moved around in her chair, her face showing discomfort as if her sitting position were giving her pain. "We didn't go away to a fancy college like you, Miss Libby," she smiled.

Libby broke eye contact and looked down at her lap, but she could feel that her mother and Mabel were both still looking at her. She didn't want to make things uncomfortable so she pretended to notice something on the napkin in her lap. Heat rose up her neck and onto her face. She hoped they couldn't see it. Did Mabel think she thought herself high and mighty like Pete had? Did she think Libby was just like her mother, too? Libby offered a counterfeit smile and then took a sip of her water to alleviate her drying mouth.

"I'm glad we stayed here, got married here, and lived out our years here... It gave me more time with my best friend," Mabel said, her expression thoughtful. "I remember when Anne and Hugh bought that cottage of yours."

"You do?"

Mabel nodded.

As a kid, Libby hadn't ever considered the lives of Pop and Nana as young people; she'd only seen the end result of their young choices. From her perspective, they seemed happy, settled. They enjoyed their family and each other. What must it have been like for Nana when she'd decided to spend her life with Pop and move into a home they'd bought together?

"She'd spent the whole first month decorating," Mabel smiled. "I wasn't married yet, but I longed to be as happy as she was. I helped her sew the curtains for every one of the rooms. She and Hugh barely had enough money to scrape by, but Anne hadn't let that discourage her. She wanted to make the little cottage into a home, and she certainly did," Mabel chuckled. "Anne had wanted an oriental rug in the living room, I remember—that was the only thing she couldn't make herself—but she never complained that she didn't have it. Never once. We'd look at them at the furniture store in town. Whenever she'd admit that she wanted it, she'd always follow with, 'Ah, it's just a thing. Things don't make us happy; people do.' She and I made table cloths, draperies, and linens… everything we could. Hugh built a lot of the furniture himself.

"Then Hugh's sales picked up and he started making a good living. A great living, actually. Anne and I had gone out to lunch one day, and when we returned, sitting under her living room furniture was the oriental rug that she'd always wanted."

Libby knew that rug. She'd played card games on that rug. She'd watched movies as a girl, on her belly, her head propped up with her hands as she leaned on her elbows on that rug. She'd sat on that rug with Pete as she opened a birthday present that Pop had given her, a birthday present that she still had. Her memory box. The recollection of it caused her fondness for Pop to bubble up.

Mabel's story was a perfect description of Pop. He always tried to make everything better, make it all okay. Nobody wanted for anything when he was around, if he could help it. He'd made Libby the memory box after he'd found out that her parents hadn't been getting along and her dad hadn't been staying at home much anymore. Libby escaped with Pete to Pop and Nana's cottage a lot. She'd spent her birthday that year amidst a broken home, her mother crying, her father absent. With red-rimmed eyes, her mother had baked her a cake, given her a present, and together—just the two of them—they'd sung the birthday song. Celia had tried to keep it together, but it was clear to Libby that their life wasn't together at all.

She looked at her mother across the table now, the lines in her face like battle scars from those trying years, and she felt guilty suddenly for not asking her to lunch. For not trying harder in adulthood to make her happy. Libby had done everything her mother asked of her: She'd worked hard to be successful, to get out of her small town and do something with her life, but it had only occurred to her right then that perhaps she should have shown her mother affection, hugged her a little more. Celia had never been openly affectionate with Libby, and she wondered now if, maybe, Celia didn't know how.

"I'm glad I got to have lunch with you two today," Libby said. She was thankful that Mabel had shared Anne's story with her, and she was glad that she'd had a chance to understand her mother a little more. She wasn't just saying the words. She was truly grateful.

❊ ❊ ❊

Work had been relatively monotonous the entire week. The only excitement Libby had was Pete's file that she still hadn't opened. She knew at some point she'd either have to ask Marty to take the account, or she'd have to let Pete know she had it. She left it on her desk until Monday.

The weather had warmed up just enough by the weekend that she found herself dozing on the hammock under the intermittent shade of the pines, the gentle lapping of the water toying with her consciousness. Her Saturday had been uneventful until the roar of a boat engine pulled her right out of her slumber, the speed of it causing waves to roll in, smacking the shore. The sound of the engine got so loud that Libby sat up, shielding her eyes to make out a white speedboat coming toward her. It slowed as it got closer to the shore. Finally the engine stopped and the boat floated in, right onto her beach.

Is that Pete? she thought to herself, squinting at the all-too-familiar figure walking around on the boat deck. He tossed a tire through the air and it landed with a thud in the sand. Then a very long ladder inched its way along the edge of the boat until it fell free onto the shore below. Libby got off the hammock and made her way toward the boat. The wind picked up closer to the water and she held her hair back with her hand to keep it out of her face. She reached the boat just as a coil of rope came flying at her and hit the beach only a few yards away.

"You almost hit me with that!" she called up to the boat. Happiness fizzled inside her at the sight of him. She couldn't help it. Pete looked over at her, his hair blowing, sunglasses on. Even when his expression was neutral, it looked as though he were almost smiling, as if a smile were the natural resting position for his features, his eyes always dancing, the corners of his mouth turned upward. She walked a little closer toward him just so that she could see it again. As she neared him, it made her feel light and jittery. He moved to the front of the boat and hopped onto the sand.

"What are you doing on my beach?" she asked.

"I'm hanging a swing." He tugged the boat farther onto the shore to keep it from floating away. The water, still rippling angrily from the boat's arrival, rushed in around his ankles. "For Thomas and Matthew. Don't worry. I'll be gone in a few minutes." Behind his sunglasses, his expression was different when he looked at her; it was more rigid, as if he'd pulled his face into a straight position just for her benefit. She willed him to smile at her, to let her see that grin, but it wasn't there.

The miniscule smile she'd seen in the hardware store with Pop, the tiny instance where they'd shared a moment, seemed to be gone. Had he put it on entirely for Pop? Who was she kidding? She didn't deserve his smile or even pleasant conversation from him. Her heart fell. As the tears came again, without warning, she turned away from him.

When they were young, he would've turned her around, lifted her face with his fingers, wiped her tears, but this time, he didn't do anything. She didn't expect him to. It was just one more reminder of what he must think of her now. She blinked in the sunlight, trying to keep the tears from spilling over her lashes.

"I've never seen you cry so much," he said from behind her.

"I'm not happy," she said with a sniffle.

"I know." His voice was quiet and thoughtful.

Once she had swallowed the lump in her throat and pushed the tears back from where they'd come, she turned around to face him.

"I've hurt you by the things I've said and you have every right to hate me, and there's nothing I can do about it. It makes me sad, that's all."

He took in a deep, steady breath and let it out, his eyes on the sand. "It's hard for me too, Libby. You turned out to be someone totally different from the person I knew. A person who left without a care in the world about your family. It's all about you, all the time." He looked out over the water. "It's hard to see you again… You blindsided me when you left. It was as if I hadn't known you at all. I lost the one person I thought I knew best. It knocked the life right out of me for a while. When I look at you, I see everything that made me angry that day. Can you blame me for not wanting to see you?"

Libby shook her head. She didn't blame him. She knew what she'd done. She had to feel that guilt over and over. "I thought you weren't coming back here, anyway," she said.

"What?"

"To my cottage. You said you weren't coming back."

"I never said that."

"But you said 'maybe.'"

He took his sunglasses off and looked down at Libby for an oddly long time as if searching her face for something, a little smirk twitching at the edges of his lips. Was he having the same memory of 'maybe' that she'd had? "You do remember that?"

"Oh. Did you really mean *maybe* and not 'maybe?'"

His face was too close, his eyes not leaving hers. A strand of hair relentlessly blew across her cheek as she tried unsuccessfully to hold it back with her hand. Pete reached out and tucked it behind her ear. It was almost too much, and she felt her limbs start to tremble. He was making her nervous. She worried by his change in expression that he could sense it. He took a step away from her. "I'd better go hang that swing," he said.

Libby nodded.

After he disappeared around the corner of the beach, Libby sat in the sand, hugging her knees, the wind blowing her designer linen trousers around her ankles. *What am I doing getting nervous around him?* she thought. He wasn't right for her, and she wasn't right for him, no matter what their past had been. They'd moved on. The situation was maddening.

The more she thought about it all, the more frustrated she became. She didn't want him showing up anymore, running into her in town. She had to refocus, work on getting out of there. She needed to set things straight with him and make him understand that she wasn't a different person; she was the same driven person she'd always been, she just hadn't made any moves until the one that had taken her to New York. And she needed him to stop… whatever that was he was doing.

With resolve, she got up, brushed the sand off her bottom, and made her way through the woods and down the beach toward Pete. He was at the top of the ladder knotting the rope when she reached him.

"I'd like to make this better, but I can't. Nothing can make it better," she called up to him, her hands balled into fists by her sides from the aggravation she felt with the situation. She felt a catch in her chest as a sob rose from within. "I've always been this person you see before you. Always. I just hadn't grown up yet, that's all. I can't change who I am," she said as the tears returned.

Pete climbed down the ladder two rungs at a time until he was standing in front of her. He looked exasperated, the skin between his eyes puckered, his lips in a tight line. He was quiet for a long while, staring above her head as she tried unsuccessfully to stop crying. When he finally looked at her, he said, "I don't like it when you cry. It makes me crazy, to be honest. But you've done this to yourself. Life doesn't have to be as hard as you're making it. You've made your choices, and now you have to live with them."

"I didn't choose *this*! I didn't choose to come back here! None of this was by choice!" She was shouting at him, but she didn't care at that moment because she had to get it all off her chest. After her outburst, Libby stood, silent, her hands now on her hips to hide the trembling in her fingers. She had nothing to show for her choices, and the reality of it stung her to the point of speechlessness.

"I'm quite aware that you didn't *choose* to come back."

Libby sat down on the beach, the new tire swing suspended beside her. "Even though I didn't choose to come back," she swallowed, her gaze fixed on the sand by her feet, the tears clouding her eyes, "I'm glad I got to see you." She looked up at him, her lips quivering. "I never meant that *you* were insignificant. You were anything *but* insignificant. I'm so sorry. I miss you and your mom and Pop and Nana. I miss everyone so much."

Pete sat down beside her, his expression unreadable. He let out a huff of frustration as he looked out over the bay. The sound of wind was the only sound between them for a long while. Pete was clearly thinking. Then he looked over at her, the corners of his mouth turned up just enough to send her heart pattering. "What are you doing today?" he asked finally. "In that outfit, I'm guessing you aren't working on the house."

Libby huffed out a little chuckle through her tears.

"Want to take a boat ride? I need to go home and check on Pop."

She wanted to take a boat ride, and she wanted to see Pop, but she knew that she probably shouldn't. She needed to get out of the rut she was in and move herself forward. She could rattle off a list of things to do instead: the cottage, Trish's wedding plans, job applications... Plus, there was no reason to get any closer to Pete. It was a ridiculous situation to put herself in.

"Okay," she said anyway.

Chapter Eleven

There was something indescribable about being out on the water, the sun in her eyes, warm air pushing against her, the only noises being the growl of the engine and the sound of the waves against the boat. After a while, the engine slowed and Pete steered toward the shore in front of a secluded cottage, nestled among the pine trees in a clearing of emerald green grass. The cottage was a colonial with bright white clapboard siding, and black shutters. A pair of brick chimneys anchored each side, and the entire front of the house facing the water was screened in, a row of paddle fans whirling around inside. "How long have you lived here?" Libby asked.

Pete reached out and grabbed the dock, tugging the boat over and tying it up. "About eight years." He hoisted himself out and extended a hand to Libby. "Pop'll be happy to see you. He hasn't stopped talking about you since we ran into you the other day. He keeps asking me to have you over."

Libby took Pete's hand and he pulled her up onto the dock. She didn't want to let go, but she did. He led the way up the walk toward the porch steps, opening the door for Libby and gesturing for her to enter. "Pop?" he called from behind her.

She stepped into the house. The rustic interior made her smile; it was every bit Pete's personality. The oak furniture, the mustard-colored walls, oversized windows that filled the room with natural light, the wood-burning fireplace—it all seemed so right for him. She imagined what it felt like to be curled up on the sofa under the plaid blanket that was thrown neatly across the arm of it.

"Pop?" he walked around her and headed into the next room. She followed. They entered the kitchen, a large, open space with maple cabinets and stainless-steel appliances. Pete dropped his boat keys onto the counter and headed down the hall.

"I'm in here," she heard Pop's voice.

A few steps away was a small room with a desk, a computer, a chair, and now—thanks to Pop—a bookcase. Hugh was busy piling books onto its shelves when he caught sight of Libby and stood up. "Libby! I'm so glad you dropped by! Pete," he waggled a shaky finger in his direction, "get my girl something to drink. Show her you know your manners!"

Pete nodded, a smirk twitching at the edges of his lips. "What would you like to drink, Libby? I have the usual."

"I'd love a water, thank you," she said, and Pete left the room.

Hugh set a handful of books onto a shelf and turned toward Libby. He looked so different compared to how she'd seen him years ago, yet his eyes, the curve of his jaw line, the way he smiled at her—those were all reminders of the man he'd been then. "Tell me, dear, what do you think of our Pete all grown up?"

She had all kinds of feelings about Pete *all grown up*. But she couldn't get herself organized enough to formulate a cohesive thought. It would be easy to say how much she loved the way he studied her face when she was talking or how sweet it was to see that little bit of humor behind his eyes just before he was about to say something or how she could tell by his gestures that he'd still take care of her. But the reality of the situation got in the way.

"Do you want an old man's advice?" Pop asked, his hand on her shoulder. She smiled and waited for his answer. "There aren't a lot of people in this world who fit together perfectly, like pieces of a puzzle, so when you find someone who does, don't overlook it just because you think life has something else in mind for you. Life is what you make of it. I surely made mine with Anne." He took in a slow breath. "I miss her so much."

She could see in his face how much Pop missed Nana, and his loss made her chest ache. Involuntarily, she thought again about the letter. Perhaps things weren't as perfect as Pop had thought they were. Maybe Nana had been unhappy with her choice... But whatever had been going through Nana's head, she was perfect in Pop's eyes.

Seeing Pop and hearing him say how he missed her made Libby feel ashamed. She felt guilty for not going to Nana's funeral. Pop had a lot of loving family and friends who supported him on that day, she was sure, but *she* hadn't been there to support him and that made her feel terrible. She should have been there for Nana, and she should have been there for Pop.

"I understand that at my age, I'm not up on all the new things, and I may seem a bit old-fashioned," he smiled. "But when it comes to family, I know," he nodded. "There are two things that don't change over generations: faith and love. And I know both quite well. So at least consider my advice."

Libby nodded and smiled warmly at him. Pop had a simpler way of looking at relationships. He knew he had his one person, and that was all. Libby's life was so different from that. She had so much interfering with her relationships; it was hard to sift out her feelings for anyone because they were clouded by her need to be something in life. But Pop knew—she could tell—that she still felt something for Pete, and it made her self-conscious. Were her feelings for him *that* obvious? She wondered about Pop's idea of two people fitting like puzzle pieces. Was it really true? She'd never known two people to be that perfect for each other before. No couple she'd known had ended up with a happy ending—not her parents, not Pete's parents, not her and Wade. Even Pop, who thought he had a perfect relationship with Nana, may not have. That letter still raised questions in her mind.

She and Pete didn't fit together like Pop's puzzle. If they did, they could be happy together no matter what life offered them. But she knew that Pete loved the small-town life he'd chosen, and Libby needed to be somewhere bigger, livelier, where she could be herself and pursue her goals, free from people's judgment.

She hated the way everyone in White Stone knew all about her. Her mother had told her many times how she'd settled by moving there with Libby's dad. She'd moved there for love, and then the love was gone, and she was stuck in a place where she didn't belong. Libby didn't want that for herself. She wanted to be around people who knew what her day of work was like because they lived it too. She wanted to get back to her real home, where she could live her own life and control her own destiny.

"Here you go," Pete materialized with a glass of water, his eyes darting between her and Pop. Had he heard their conversation? "I also put out some snacks in case you're hungry." Libby took the glass. Looking at him, she could understand how, if her mother had felt for her father the way Libby felt for Pete, she could've dropped everything in Las Vegas and moved to the middle of nowhere. But she knew she mustn't do what her mother had done. She had learned her lesson through Celia Potter's bitterness and dissatisfaction.

"Good boy," Hugh said, nodding toward Libby, picking up another few books and placing them on the shelf.

"Do you like it here?" Libby asked Pete out of the blue, looking straight at him without blinking. She knew the answer, but just in case, she wanted to hear *his* answer. Her heart was beating wildly, her hands clammy. She wanted him to shrug and say it was okay, but she knew he wouldn't. She knew deep down that he loved where he was.

"Of course," he said, studying her face. It was as though he were trying to find answers there.

"You wouldn't ever want to live in a city like New York?"

Pete was quiet for a moment as if he were considering. "Pop, do you mind if I take Libby into the living room so that we can be more comfortable?" Pop shook his head.

Pete led Libby into the living room, offering her a seat on the sofa by one of the large windows. The blue water of the bay filled the bottom two panes of glass. She set her cup of water on a side table and swiveled toward Pete who had sat down closer to her than she'd expected. That wasn't what took her by surprise, however. What startled her most was the way that he was looking at her. It was as if he were waiting, almost willing her to make sense of her question. He looked slightly irritated, almost angry.

"So," she said, wavering slightly, "would you live in New York?"

Pete's face was serious, his eyes appraising. "Maybe," he said without even the hint of a smile, and she knew exactly what that "maybe" meant.

Realizing the disappointment that had most likely made its way to her face, she quickly recovered, straightening out her features to a more cordial expression. She nodded, her hopes dashed. She'd known the answer; it was silly of her to even ask. "I figured," she said.

"Why are you even asking that, Libby? With that one question, you're telling me that you don't know me at all." She'd never seen him look at her like that before, even when she'd told him about Columbia. He wasn't stung, or hurt; he seemed angry and frustrated. "First, I hate New York. I would never want to live there. Second, I wouldn't leave the state when Pop was *healthy*," he hissed in a whisper. "How could you even think that I would leave him now? Don't you care at all? What should I do, Libby? Put Pop in a home, sell it all, and go run off with you somewhere away from everyone I love?"

Humiliation sheeted over her. What would she tell him? How could she ever explain to him why she'd asked about New York? She wouldn't dare admit to him that she was crazy about him, and she had wanted to know if he'd leave everything to be with her. It sounded awful hearing it from his lips. It had been outrageous even to ask. What was she thinking?

Chapter Twelve

While Marty was digging head first into the copier machine, pulling out wads of sooty paper, Libby looked out the window at the late afternoon sky, still thinking about her question to Pete. Their conversation had been mortifying and it had kept her up all night. The conversation went round and round in her head: her motive for asking and what she'd actually implied when she'd asked. She hadn't meant to sound like she had; she had just needed to know if there was any chance they could be together. And there wasn't.

She reached into her newly organized file cabinet and pulled out his file, looking around as if someone would scold her for even having it. The idea of rifling through Pete's finances made her extremely self-conscious. Noting his contact information, she pulled out her cell and sent him a text: *Hi. Just wanted to inform you that I've been assigned as your accountant. Let me know if this is a problem and you'd prefer someone else to look over your finances. If not, I'll have you sign a consent form. Libby.*

Her phone lit up: *You can do my taxes. It's fine.*

She texted back: *Are you sure?*

Her phone pinged again. *I should feel lucky, right? Not everyone in this town gets a fancy New York accountant with a degree from Columbia.*

She stared down at the plant by the window, its leaves drooping and looking a lot like she felt at that moment. She texted back: *I'll send you the form.* She was too tired to text anything more.

She looked around again, still self-conscious about viewing Pete's documents. With a flourish, she opened it up and peered down at the contents. At a quick glance, it looked like Pete had a few separate IT jobs and his own web design company. She turned the page. He'd also invested some money in the winery down the road. *Impressive*, she thought.

She checked her phone but Pete hadn't said anything more, so she turned the sound off and dropped it into her bag before she typed anything else. She didn't want to have to think about him any more than she already had.

❄ ❄ ❄

Libby woke to a stream of sunlight piercing her vision. She couldn't remember the last time she'd slept that well. She'd spent most of the evening planning Trish's bridal shower, and found herself in bed before nine o'clock. Blinking to clear her vision, she pulled her phone over to see what time it was when she noticed a text waiting for her. She sat up in bed to escape the blinding light and opened the message. The number was Jeanie's. It read, *Good morning! I'm picking you up at ten o'clock for a party. This is a two-man mission. I need someone to help me carry food. Wear something a little dressy.*

Libby kicked the blankets off her legs and put her feet on the sun-warmed floor. What if she didn't want to go to a party? Walking back and forth across the hardwoods, she mulled it over. The thought of hanging out with Jeanie did sound very appealing—she needed a friendly face—but she should really focus on the things she had to do at the cottage. Then she wondered, *Will Pete be at this party of Jeanie's?* The idea of seeing him caused Libby's hands to get tingly and her mouth to feel like it was full of cotton. Her phone faded to black and she set it on the dresser.

Throwing her head back and taking in a breath to steady herself, she shook her head. She wanted to tell someone about her predicament, but there wasn't anyone to tell. Her mother certainly wouldn't approve of her feelings for Pete, and Trish was so caught up in her wedding that she probably wouldn't have time to hear her out. Jeanie would just tell her to stay and go for it. She was on her own. She had better get organized and find herself a job before things got any messier. It was only eight o'clock so she resolved to send in a few more job applications over breakfast before she took her shower.

By the time she was ready, it was nearly ten o'clock. As she walked outside, a wad of Trish's bridal shower envelopes in her hand, she met Jeanie on the sidewalk next to her car.

"Hey there! You look nice," Jeanie said with a grin. "Ready?"

"I suppose, " she said, dropping her house keys into her handbag. She slipped Trish's invitations into the mailbox and lifted the flag. "A friend's bridal shower invitations," she explained, noticing her curiosity. Just the mention of Trish caused a pang of homesickness. "Where are we going?"

"Pete's."

"What for?" She could feel energy zing through the palms of her hands, causing unsteadiness in her fingers. She both wanted to see him and run away from him at the same time. Libby knew that spending more time with Pete was not advisable because they were never going to work out their differences, but it didn't stop her from feeling like she'd explode with happiness the minute she saw his face. She opened the passenger door and got in. The salty smell of Jeanie's cooking wafted toward her from the backseat. Nestled along the seat in back was a row of tins, each one covered in aluminum foil.

"It's Helen's birthday. I'm invitin' you to the party because I need someone to help carry all the food," she said as she started the car. "I knew if I told you, you wouldn't want to come since everyone'll be there."

Libby had forgotten until now that Helen Bennett's birthday was only a few days after hers. As much as she wanted to see Pete's mom, Jeanie had been right. She didn't want to have to see everyone else. She worried that people would judge her for having lost her job in New York. Or, worse, that, like Pete, they saw her as a person who thought she was better than everyone else.

"I don't have a gift for Helen," she worried aloud.

"You showin' up will be gift enough, I'm sure," Jeanie smiled.

The closer they got, the more panic slithered through her as she thought about coming face to face with all the people she was about to see.

Chapter Thirteen

It had been a long time since Libby had seen Helen Bennett. Worry had settled in her shoulders, causing them to ache. Libby could put on a good face to hide her feeling of failure, but Helen had a way about her that made Libby feel like she always knew better. About everything. When they were young, Pete and Libby would sneak off to the abandoned field down the road and walk to the water's edge to be alone. When Helen asked where they were going, Pete would say, "We're just going for a walk." Helen would nod, her knowledge clear on her face.

She'd say, "Pete, you had better stay on the road during that walk," like she knew, and Libby felt the need to obey her as if Helen were her own mother. Helen was one of those people who felt like family.

"Helen'll be happy to see you, I'm sure," Jeanie said as if reading her mind. She glanced over at Libby, gripping the wheel around a turn. There was something so familiar and comfortable about taking that drive with Jeanie. It took her back to another time.

The person she had been was insecure and anxious, always concerned about what her mother thought of her. She'd watched her father and his new family carry on, chipping away at her mother's already fractured confidence. She'd had the constant burden of being perfect for her mother's benefit, her successes inflated, her failures hidden.

As an adult, she'd learned how to be the person she'd always strived to become. She was proud of the fact that she'd traveled extensively, had a respectable job with opportunity to advance, and a great boyfriend. Growing up, her mother had measured Libby's worth by her ability to achieve things like those, and Libby felt that she had finally arrived. Without those things, she felt lost, unsure of how to proceed. Being back home was like an indefinite waiting period when her life was put on hold.

"You're quiet," Jeanie noted.

Libby nodded.

"What are you thinking about?"

How much I don't belong here. "Nothing, really," she said instead.

Jeanie pulled onto the extensive drive to Pete's cottage, and they bumped down the rocky path to the front of the house. She turned off the engine, leaving the keys in the ignition. "Ready?" she asked.

"Yep!" Libby said with forced enthusiasm. Her hands began to tingle with nervousness.

They exited the car, piled a stack of food tins in their arms, and walked around to the back of the house where Libby was surprised to find an enormous crowd of people. *Had the whole town come to Helen's party?* she thought. She gazed from face to face, recognizing nearly all of them. A few looked her way, surprise registering on their faces before they settled back into their conversations.

Leaving, with her Columbia acceptance letter in hand, she'd felt unstoppable. She'd made it clear to anyone who'd asked where she was going and what kind of life she'd planned on having. She'd said so many hurtful things about where she'd grown up, she couldn't even remember to whom she'd said what. At eighteen, having grown up hearing her mother constantly complain about White Stone, she didn't realize the enormity of her actions. Now she understood, and that made it worse because the guilt overwhelmed her. And there they all were, looking at her. She felt uneasy, nervous. Jeanie had already set down her tins and took the ones from Libby's arms, leaving Libby standing alone. She looked around for Pete but didn't see him.

"No way!" she heard a booming voice over the chitchat. "Libby Potter?" Ryan Bennett emerged from the crowd, and despite her nervousness, Libby hurried over to him. Ryan was Pete's brother, three years his senior. He was a little taller and broader than Pete, with darker hair, but the two looked strikingly similar—same green eyes, similar smile. "Where have you been, young lady?" he kidded.

Until he was standing in front of her, she hadn't realized how much she'd missed him. Ryan was that classic big brother, not only to Pete but to her as well. He'd looked out for her and stuck up for her when it came down to it.

"I've been in New York," she said, the late morning breeze off the water giving her a chill.

"I'm in Richmond now. Got a little one. Her name's Charlotte." He nodded over to a wisp of a girl with blond ringlets snaking down her back, dressed in a white sundress with a fat, pink ribbon belt and sandals. She was sneaking M&Ms off the table.

"Oh, Ryan, that's fantastic."

"My wife's around here somewhere—Emily."

"Well, I declare..." Libby turned to find Helen Bennett pacing toward her, her dark, shoulder-length hair blowing in the wind, a glass of white wine in one hand and a camera in the other. "My sweet girl, I have missed you so much!" She leaned in and kissed Libby's cheek. Her familiar scent of citrus and flowers sent Libby unexpectedly spiraling toward the memory of Helen holding her when she'd fallen on the gravel outside.

Libby had been just twelve at the time, running as fast as she could after Pete and his friends, but their legs were longer and she couldn't keep up. Her mother had always advised against playing with the boys. Libby wasn't used to that type of play; she'd been taught to be more reserved and ladylike. But she loved to be with Pete and his friends, having some free-spirited rough-and-tumble play away from the eye of her mother.

While trying to catch up to them, Libby had slipped in the dirt and skinned her leg all the way to the top. Helen picked her up and carried her back to the house just as Pete had noticed she wasn't with them. He'd burst through the door, concern on his face, checking to be sure she was all right. Libby remembered being embarrassed because Helen had pulled her shorts up to bandage the scrape, showing her entire leg. That was her awkward age, when she wasn't sure yet what parts of her to show and what not to show, and she remembered that Pete's presence had made her bashful.

Helen got her all bandaged up and held her face in her hands. "You okay?" she'd asked. Libby nodded. "Good," she'd said, smiling, and she kissed Libby on the cheek just as she had right then at the party.

"Want a drink?" Ryan asked, pulling her back into the present. "I can make you a Mimosa. We have champagne," he grinned deviously. "And now we're old enough to drink it in front of people," he winked.

She let out a quiet giggle. Libby had a rule: she didn't drink alcohol before noon. When it was mixed with a breakfast drink such as orange juice, however, that created a gray area, and she was forced to make a judgment call. Given the situation, and the fact that she was about as nervous as she'd been since she'd arrived, with all of those faces staring at her, she accepted Ryan's offer.

"I need to get Charlotte out of the M&Ms anyway," Ryan said.

"So!" Helen grabbed Libby's hands and held them out, "What have you been up to besides runway shows?"

"Sorry?"

"You look like a million bucks," she grinned. Helen's face was endlessly youthful despite her long hours in the sun living along the coast. She had a milky complexion and her face seemed to be incapable of a frown. Her dark auburn hair fell loosely down to her shoulders, and it didn't matter which way the wind blew it, it always ended up looking great. "How's your mama?"

"She's well. She's glad I'm home, I think—although I haven't seen her as much as I should." She thought about her mother's expression when she was pleased—the way she'd almost glowed whenever Libby had done something well—and she wished she could show her that there were other ways to be happy. She wished Celia could find her own way instead of relying so much on Libby.

"Call her over if you'd like. We'll be here all day."

"Thanks. I might do that." She wondered what her mother would think of the fact that she was at the Bennetts' party. While her mother had told her once that she had nothing against them, Libby could sense a sort of tension whenever she mentioned being with the Bennetts. She speculated that her mother worried Pete would distract her—and she had raised Libby to stay focused.

Ryan returned with two bubbling flutes and an unfamiliar woman. She had on a sundress, a thin cardigan, and heels that sunk into the soft ground as she walked. Her hair was piled on top of her head in a curly bunch, with little tendrils falling around her friendly face. Libby knew immediately who she was because she looked almost exactly like Ryan's little girl.

"This is Emily, my wife," Pete introduced them and handed Libby her glass. "This is Libby Potter."

"It's nice to meet you," Libby said.

"Likewise," she beamed. "It's great to finally meet you. I've heard a lot about you."

What does she mean by that? Libby wondered. Had people been talking about her? Was she the laughing stock of the town? Libby wanted to ask about what Emily had been told, but Helen herded them all together for a picture. She straightened her face out, put on a smile and waited for the snap. As Helen turned the camera around to show them the image on her little screen, Ryan grabbed her arm and Emily's and quickly whisked them away, claiming that he wanted to show them something down by the water.

When the shoreline came into view, Libby's breath caught at the sight of what was in front of her. Silver buckets with deeply set burning candles lit a path along the edge of the sea grass down to the sand. Just before the shore, on the grass, there were tables and chairs set up under a large tent. The white tablecloths, which were tied to the table legs with sea-foam-blue ribbons, fought against the wind. Each table had a large, glass bowl centerpiece filled to the brim with seashells and a crowd of people chatting around it. On the other side of the tables, a man with tan trousers, a white cotton shirt, and bare feet tuned a guitar while perched on a stool, a microphone stand and a lone speaker set up beside him. The gentle lapping of the bay water kept time while he strummed and tuned. Standing next to the man was Pete.

"This is gorgeous," she said, glancing from table to table to take in the scenery.

The musician began to play his guitar. Ryan led them onto the beach as a few others farther down the beach started dancing. Pete noticed them and walked over. When he did, Ryan and his wife left, joining the growing crowd, and began to dance to the soft guitar that was playing over the breeze.

"Hey," Pete said, his brows pulled together slightly. "What are you doing here?"

"Jeanie brought me," she said, suddenly feeling extremely nervous. She gave a shiver, pretending her shaking was from a chill, when really it was from looking at him with the wind in his hair. It brought her memories of when they were younger. "I helped her bring food."

There it was. His smile. She felt dizzy at the sight of it. "I didn't need Jeanie to bring food," he chuckled, "but you know how she is. You can't tell her anything."

After the humor about Jeanie had passed, it got quiet between them. Pete became solemn and looked out over the water. They were standing side by side with all those people around them, but it felt like just the two of them on that beach right then.

"This is amazing," she said, trying to remove the obvious heaviness that penetrated every conversation they had.

"Thanks." He smiled down at her. "I got the idea from you."

"What?" she asked, kicking off her sandals to keep them from sinking into the sand. She set them next to an empty chair. The beach was filling with people dancing, the tables emptying out.

"Remember when we were fifteen and Mom was turning forty? She didn't have a party and we gave her a picnic at the public beach just outside of Kilmarnock? It had been your idea."

Libby giggled at the memory. "I do! We packed her sandwiches and a birthday cake that Ryan bought at the supermarket." She had completely forgotten that memory until then.

"Yep," he grinned, and she thought she saw affection seeping out from behind his eyes. Libby didn't want to notice it, but she had. "I thought we could give her a slightly upgraded version of a beach birthday party this time."

"Pete!" Ryan called from the makeshift dance floor. "Bring Libby over here!"

Libby was frozen to the spot. She didn't want to go because if she went over there, they'd probably be forced to dance, and she'd have to feel him against her. Pete looked at her, uncertainty in his eyes. All the tables were empty now, the area by the guitar player full of people. Even Jeanie had found her way down and was doing the jitterbug with a little boy.

"Pete! What are you waiting for?" his brother playfully taunted him. "Get over here!"

Pete nodded toward the gathering of people. "Let's just go over there," he said, clearly not wanting to go himself. They snaked their way through the guests until they reached Ryan and Emily. Just as they neared them, the music changed to something slower and Pete looked at her uncomfortably. Ryan took Emily by the waist and pulled her close, swaying to the music. The guitar player only had to play the first few notes of the song before Libby recognized it. They'd played Helen's Billy Joel album on the old record player hundreds of times, and this had been *their* song.

"*Just the Way You Are,*" she smiled nervously, looking at Pete. He was peering down at her, his eyes gentle but his face serious. He nodded. Just like all the girls she'd known in school with boyfriends, they, too, had a song. The difference was that this particular one hadn't faded with the years for her; it was the kind of song that still made her feel something inside.

As the song played, the notes bouncing around her amidst the sound of the ripples of water against the sand, she felt a different ache. This wasn't an ache of sadness like the one she'd had coming back and having to face everything she'd left; it was an ache for what she couldn't have.

"Be a man, Pete," his brother kidded, clapping him on the back before embracing Emily again. "Dance with her," he said over his shoulder.

Pete took in a slow breath, his gaze somewhere in the distance over the crowd. Then he pulled her toward him and embraced her with one arm, holding her other hand. They were dancing in the sand, his arm around her, the wind rushing in between them. She wanted to clasp her hands behind his neck like she had so many years ago, put her face against his chest, hear his breathing. The feel of him this close to her was making her woozy and she was having trouble knowing where to look because if she looked at him, she worried that she'd fall apart.

Pete didn't say a word as they danced. With the rustling of the pines and the voices of the crowd mixing with the music, she held onto him, wondering what was going through his mind. When she finally looked at him, and he at her, she didn't see the affection behind his eyes anymore like she had all the other times they'd been that close. She silently wished for it, the ache in her chest getting worse.

Chapter Fourteen

The music sped up and Pete let go of Libby. She didn't look at him again because she didn't want to have to try and decipher his expression. She didn't want to know if he was happy or sad or mad… It all hurt too much. With the sun on her face and the soft music gone, she used the moment to try and come to her senses. *My time here is limited*, she said to herself, *and I need to remember that.* Even if she didn't want to ever let him go. It wasn't a real possibility, so she needed to get her head out of the clouds. No more dancing, she resolved. It was too intimate.

The crowd had thinned, some guests now back at the tables. Ryan was dancing with his little girl, Charlotte. Jeanie had found Helen and they were chatting. "I heard you were here somewhere," Pop called from the grassy embankment near the top of the shore.

Libby waved, grabbing both her glass from one of the tables and her sandals, following Pete's lead to meet Pop. With a few wiggles, she kicked the sand off her feet and slipped on her shoes. "How are you, Pop?" she said as she reached him, giving him a hug.

"Very well," he said, looking out over the water. The bay was so large at that spot that there was nothing on the other side but the thin, gray line of the horizon. "Other than the fact that I can't ever take a walk by myself again, life is good. Can't complain."

Her strong, confident, capable Pop was no longer standing before her. Little by little, time was stealing his independence, and it bothered her far more than she let on. She didn't want him to think she pitied him, but the sadness she felt over it was so great. She wished she could rewind time and make it all go away. Clearly, from his comment, Pop was trying to keep things light, so Libby tried to be upbeat about it as well. "There are worse things, I suppose," she said.

His eyebrows went up in thought. "You are quite right," he said, Pete moving beside him and patting him on the back.

"How are ya, Pop? Enjoying the party?"

"I always enjoy a good party. You'd better get back, though. I saw the chefs arrive with the lobster a while back."

"You had the party catered?" Libby asked, surprised. "Fancy." No wonder Jeanie hadn't needed to bring food.

The corners of Pete's mouth turned up and he shook his head back and forth. "I'm sure that's right up your alley," he kidded.

"Oh!" Helen's voice sailed over the lawn toward them. "Wait! Let's take a photo! Pop, you get in the middle. Libby and Pete, get on either side!" She held the camera up to her face. "That's nice!" she said from behind it. "Smile! One, two, three!" As Helen meandered off into the crowd, Libby took that moment to look at Pop and Pete together. It had been a long time since she'd been with just the two of them, everyone happy.

She remembered Pop, when they were kids, leaning over the kitchen table at Helen's while Libby and Pete finished their homework. Pop, who was exceptionally good at algebra, would spend hours going over different rules for solving problems. She'd thought how he could be doing countless other things with his time, but he'd spent many evenings doing schoolwork instead. He was more like a dad than her own father.

She wanted something for her memory box, but there wasn't anything around that she could grab. She wanted to remember that moment by the shore, when Pop was still lucid enough to know them all and when Pete was happy and sweet to her. It was sad to let the moment go without something by which to remember it.

When they got back up to the yard, Pete tended to the caterers, and Libby checked her phone while she was far enough inland to have good reception. A slew of emails that had probably been trapped in cyberspace waiting for a signal pinged into her phone. One of them was from an accounting firm in New York. Her heart leapt at the sight of it. She almost didn't want to open it so that she could maintain her excitement a little longer. She was terrified to read it, fearful that it wasn't everything she'd hoped for: her ticket back to New York, her only shot out of White Stone. She wandered around the side of the house to read it.

In all this bad luck, she'd started to doubt herself. She'd wondered if maybe her Manhattan job had been a fluke. She'd worried that she'd seen the peak of her career. When she had a city apartment, her designer clothes, a fantastic job and a handsome boyfriend, she felt like she could move mountains. Perhaps that had been her mother's coaching, but it didn't matter now. It was a part of who she was. She wanted to get her life back on track.

In the city, she watched mothers push strollers through Central Park wearing Stella McCartney boots and Fendi scarves, drinking lattes as they met the other mothers in the park. She wanted to be one of those mothers, going to the Children's Museum on the Upper

West Side on Saturdays. She wanted to have children to share her years with and a husband to care for and who cared for her. The first step in that journey was to get another job in the city. Once she was back, she'd meet more people, go out, and begin living her life again.

She scrolled through the email on her phone. They wanted to set up an interview, and they left a number to call. *We are interested in finding out more about your skill set… Please call us at your earliest convenience… We'd like to have you in as soon as possible…* The further she read in the email, the more her life came into focus. While White Stone was a lovely place to be, it wasn't where *she* should be.

She read the words over and over, her heart pounding harder with every word. She had to rearrange her lips to mask the grin that wanted to spread across her face. She felt like screaming and running around the yard, waving her phone! Everything she'd worked for her entire life meant something at that moment because it proved that on paper, she was as worthy as everyone else she knew in New York. She had the right experience for the position being offered, and if she played her cards right, she'd nail the interview. She read the email one more time just for kicks.

"You better quit your hidin' and get out here with the rest of us," Libby heard Jeanie say from behind her.

She spun around, clicking off her phone and putting it in her bag. She wanted to throw her arms around Jeanie and yell out, *I got an interview!* "Hey," she said instead.

"I have to admit that I'm glad you're here." Jeanie glanced over her shoulder in Pete's direction.

It only occurred to Libby then that Jeanie might have planned all along to put Libby and Pete together. It would be just like Jeanie to try and play matchmaker. "You didn't have to come with all that food. You knew it was catered, didn't you?"

Jeanie flashed a conspiratorial smile, "I *had* to bring the food. What's a party without my meatballs?" She laced her arm in Libby's and tugged on her to start walking. "I don't care if it *is* catered. That fancy chef doesn't have anything on me."

Libby giggled as they made their way back into the crowd. This time, Libby took a moment to pay attention to all the faces in front of her. Ryan's little girl, Charlotte, went running past holding a party streamer as though it were a kite, the long red paper trailing behind her in the air. Libby recognized the two boys who lived near her cottage, Thomas and Matthew. They were pulling at their shirt collars, clearly uncomfortable in dressier clothing, while playing a game of beanbag toss. Pop was now in a chair under another large white tent that had been erected near the food. He was puffing on a cigar and drinking some sort of frozen drink with a pineapple wedge on the edge of the glass. Helen was leaning on the back of his chair, her glass of wine nearly empty, her cheeks rosy from the wind and alcohol.

"You want a drink?" Jeanie asked, letting go of Libby's arm.

"I think I'll just have water," she wrinkled her nose. "I've already had a Mimosa."

"Oh, go on. Live a little, why don't ya?"

"No, ma'am. I'm having water, thank you very much. I can live again in about thirty minutes. One an hour. That's my max."

Jeanie rolled her eyes playfully. "I'll be back then," she said, leaving her on her own. As she looked around at all the people, the smiles on their faces, the easy way they were with each other, she thought about her mother. She wondered if Celia would enjoy herself if she came. Maybe it was the email she'd gotten or the mimosa, or even the joy of dancing with Pete that had put her in a sentimental mood, but Libby suddenly wanted her mom to share in the moment. Maybe she could loosen up a little, have fun. With Jeanie there, she didn't worry too much about her mother going on and on about her. Jeanie would steer the conversation elsewhere. And she had Helen. Helen was always pleasant with Celia. It was a perfect opportunity to invite her mom. Libby pulled out her phone and texted her: *I'm at the Bennetts'. It's Helen's birthday. Want to stop by? It'd be nice to see you.*

While she was having a nice time, Libby realized she hadn't really gotten much done with the cottage. A lobster lunch sounded much more appealing than stripping kitchen wallpaper. She promised herself that, after the party, Pete and her friends were not going to occupy her time. She had things to get done if she wanted to ever leave town.

Her phone pinged with a text: *On my way!*

Libby shook her head in amusement. She knew that Celia enjoyed being in the middle of the action, surrounded by people. She just hoped that she could help her mother to worry less about appearances and focus on just enjoying herself. She was glad to have time to spend with Celia.

"Here's your water," Jeanie held out the glass, "and I brought you something else." Pete stood beside Jeanie, grinning his crooked grin.

"Everything okay with the catering?" she asked Pete, unsure of what to say to Jeanie's comment.

"Yep. Lunch should be out shortly."

"Mom's coming."

Pete's eyebrows rose in surprise. "Look at you! Inviting your mom. I've never known you to be the family type."

While he seemed to be joking, that comment rubbed her the wrong way. She was still a little anxious about being there, and now Pete was going to throw out a comment like that? Just because she had a slightly odd relationship with her mother did not mean that she wasn't into family. "Why do you say *that*?" she asked. The comment had really bothered her.

"Oh, I don't know. Maybe because I've never seen you with your family out of choice before." Jeanie had shrunk back and was taking baby steps toward the snack table.

"You've never seen me with my mother out of choice, but that doesn't mean I'm not a family person." The words were coming out harsher than she meant them to. She could hear it.

"Why are you getting so edgy over this?" He took a step closer, his brows pulling together, his head tilted to the side. Even that irritated her for some reason.

"I just think that you don't know me anymore, Pete," she said quietly. "You think you do, but you don't. How do you know what I'm like?" she heard her voice rising, and she pulled it down to a more respectable level. Why *was* she so aggravated all of a sudden? She knew why. He was judging her. Just because she'd gone away didn't mean she didn't want the same things that everyone did.

"You're right. I *don't* know you," he said and walked away.

Her whole body stung with agitation, her hand shaking around her water glass. The situation was frustrating. Pete hadn't done anything wrong; he'd only been lovely to her, considering what she'd done to him. What was wrong with her? The whole situation put her in a bad place, and she wasn't herself. She didn't want to yell at Pete, and he didn't deserve that, but she was on edge there all the time, and the slightest thing would set her off because she knew she'd ruined everything by what she'd said before she left, and she feared that she'd never get herself back together. Most of all, she feared that she'd get stuck there like her mother, and her mother had made it quite clear as she was growing up what being stuck there felt like.

"You okay?" Jeanie interrupted her thoughts.

She looked up at the sky in an attempt to calm herself down. "No."

"Wanna talk about it?"

"Not really."

"Want a drink?"

She needed to get out of her head. She needed to loosen up. "Yep."

"There's my girl! We'll have you dancin' by the end of the party!"

Jeanie got Libby a glass of wine just as Pop called out that lunch was ready. She could hear the strumming of the guitar coming from the amplifier near the beach, and a couple of guys dressed like the caterer were taking silver dishes down to the tables. Libby and Jeanie followed the crowd, sitting at an empty table. It was nearly noon now and the wind had died down to a light breeze, just enough to relieve her of the sun's intense rays.

Helen sat down at their table. "Feel like hosting the Birthday Girl?" she asked, her sweet face revealing her resemblance to Pete. She set her glass onto the table.

"We'd love to!" Jeanie said.

Pete walked by and Helen hooked him with her arm. "Sit by your mama, son. It's my birthday so you have to do what I say," she teased. He smiled and pulled out the chair beside Libby, although he didn't look in her direction.

She'd upset him, she could tell. Libby didn't want to hurt him again, and seeing him pull away from her—even subtly—made her tense. They'd been doing so well. They'd been able to enjoy each other without their history coming up. It was there, though, and she knew they both were aware of it. She shouldn't have snapped at him.

Pop came not long after Helen and plopped down beside his daughter. "This looks like a fine bunch. How's everyone? Pete, don't look like you just lost your puppy, young man. Perk up!"

"Can we save a place for my mom?" Libby asked, looking down at her phone to be sure she hadn't texted again. "She's on her way."

"Of course!" Helen said, her bright smile etching very fine lines around her eyes.

Pete was looking out over the bay. Everyone was taking their seats and settling in with the people around them. Libby leaned toward the table as if attempting to view what Pete was seeing, but really just trying to get his attention. She felt awful for snapping at him. Being there, she was so unhappy, and it made her do and say things she shouldn't. She could hear Jeanie making small talk with Helen, but she wasn't listening to their words. She was hoping Pete would turn toward her, hoping he'd forgive her yet again for her actions.

"There's this diner where I like to go and have coffee," she said, bumping him with her shoulder. He turned around and looked at her. "The diner, it has just regular coffee, the kind you would brew at home, and white mugs. It doesn't have anything special and the food isn't great, but it has a window that overlooks a busy side street, and I love to watch all the faces walk past me. I wonder about them: who they are, where they're going."

The sun illuminated the gold flecks in the green of Pete's eyes as he continued to look at her. He was clearly waiting for some explanation of why she'd chosen to tell him this.

"I'm not high and mighty all the time like you think I am. I enjoy the pace of the city, certainly, but I like to take time out and enjoy what's around me too. Relaxing doesn't come as easily for me as it does for you—I've been raised to do without it. But sometimes I do want to relax a bit. I'd love nothing more than to be around people I love, a family. Just like you. It just doesn't show all the time. I need a little practice loosening up." She nudged him again, smiling.

He nodded, his lips pursed in thought. "I remember teaching a young girl to hit balls out at the ball field because she'd never learned to play. You always wanted to play, Libby, you just didn't know how. You'd let me show you, and it was easy. That person in the diner doesn't seem very different from the girl I knew. Although I will say that this immaculately dressed businesswoman *is* quite a change." A man brought by two plates of lobster and set them in front of Pop and Helen. "Makes me wonder if the change is more on the outside than on the inside, but if it's loosening up you need, you've come to the right place."

"Sorry I'm late!" Celia Potter shuffled over, set a gift bag from the boutique down the street onto the table, and sat down next to Libby. "Hi, honey!" she said, slightly out of breath, as she kissed her cheek. With a quick wave, she acknowledged the others at the table before turning to Helen. "Hi, Helen! Happy birthday!" She pushed the bag toward her.

Helen had always been gracious about Celia Potter, and Libby wondered if it was because she knew what it was like to raise a child by herself. No matter how Celia behaved, Helen always knew just what to say. "Thank you, Celia! You didn't have to get me anything. I think this is grand enough," she raised her hands in the air, gesturing at the tables around her.

"Oh, it's your birthday! You deserve something special."

Helen pulled the pink-and-white-striped gift bag toward her and peeked inside. She retrieved a small, gray box with swoopy lettering. A silver bangle bracelet was nestled inside. "That's very thoughtful of you, Celia. Thank you," she said, slipping it on. The caterers finished handing out the plates of food as Ryan stood up from the table behind Helen and tapped his glass with a butter knife.

"I'd like to propose a quick toast—nothing elaborate—to my mother, who has always been there for us. Mom," he turned to her. She looked up at him with doting eyes, "I love you so much. I am so blessed to have you as my mother. Here's to family! Happy birthday." He raised his glass. As Libby raised hers, she couldn't help but think about what kind of toast she would give her own mother. Certainly, she could give a heartfelt toast for Helen or Jeanie, but what she would say about Celia Potter was a mystery. Looking at Celia right then, however, she saw her smiling, the way her eyes twinkled as she watched Jeanie tell a story, and she felt happy for her. Like Libby, maybe she too needed to be taught how to loosen up. As she thought this, it made Libby wish for more time to show her how happy she could be.

Everyone took a drink. The guitar played underneath the chitchat of the guests as they all started eating. The flickering of the candles on the ground, the swishing of the waves in the bay, and the warm breeze made her feel like an outsider, out of place. As she looked at the family gathered around her, she realized, as they talked, that they had shared memories, funny stories, good times together. When she thought of her own mother, her memories were those of emotional survival, determination and hard work. Her mother had taught her a lot, but they hadn't really just *enjoyed* themselves together. For thirty years, she'd missed out on those types of memories with her mother.

Libby knew she had that interview request sitting in her inbox, waiting for her to respond. She had a possible way out. Celia had never had that opportunity. Libby thought about how terrible she'd felt coming back, and she realized that Celia had lived that from the time she was a young lady until now. She'd never gotten out, never gotten away. How sad her mother must feel. Celia probably felt just as isolated as Libby.

"Miss Libby," Pop said from across the table. "Tell us about working for Marty. How's the new job?" Pete stood up, excusing himself from the table, exposing her even more. Now she didn't even have the physical comfort of being situated between two bodies.

"Um…" All eyes were on her, including her mother's. Panic tingled around inside her as she realized that she'd have to ensure that her mother would be pleased with what she said. How could she spin the experience into something positive? Perhaps she could say that Marty was like a mentor for her, showing her how to run a firm so that she could have the experience for future opportunities. Libby ran the words through her head just to be sure, scrambling for the perfect response.

Pete returned just in time to take the focus off her. "Here you are, Celia," he handed her a glass of wine. "I noticed you didn't have anything to drink." He set down another glass in front of Libby. "You're doing great," he whispered to her, his breath tickling her ear. He could always read her face, tell what she was thinking. Pete knew how Libby didn't like being the center of attention. He knew how it bothered her to have her mother there to weigh in on everything she said. He gave her a quick squeeze on the shoulders before sitting down. This only proved to add more confusion to her thoughts.

"Libby's my accountant," Pete grinned, looking at her as if she knew something that no one else did, like they had an insider secret. It made her heart flutter.

Everyone at the table seemed to have something to say all at once, but it was Pop who won out. "Well, son, sometimes it takes a good woman to keep everything straight."

Pete laughed, and his relaxed demeanor calmed her.

"Ain't it the truth!" Jeanie said, and everyone laughed then.

"How's the job hunting coming along, Libby? Any calls from New York?" Celia asked, causing a hush among the group.

Libby felt like sliding off her chair and hiding under the table. Why did her mother have to ruin the moment? She looked at each person in front of her, trying to see on their faces what they were thinking, her pulse in her ears. Even Jeanie didn't have a witty response to that question. How could Libby answer that? She hadn't gotten a job offer, only an interview. She didn't necessarily want to blab that to everyone. What if she didn't get the job? She'd look like even more of a failure.

"Um. I'm still looking," she said, forcing a smile.

"Well, I just know you'll get something soon." Celia smiled, making eye contact with everyone at the table.

"She's a very smart girl, Celia," Helen said. "You've raised a lovely lady." Helen's comment seemed to break the tension, and everyone began chatting again. Libby was so thankful to have Helen around.

By the time lunch had finished, Ryan and Emily had scooted their chairs over to Libby's table, Charlotte bouncing on Ryan's knee. Helen was telling stories about when the boys were little. Jeanie's finger traced the rim of her glass and she seemed completely captivated by the stories. Surprisingly, Celia had managed to listen to all of them without ever once comparing Libby's childhood to Ryan's or Pete's. Libby noticed that she'd even leaned back just a bit in her chair. She'd hoped her mother would relax a little more, take the constant focus off Libby, so this made her smile.

With everyone involved in conversation, she wanted to relax. She was finally feeling like it could be a possibility. She leaned over to Pete. "Want to take a walk?" She knew better than to leave the safety of the party. When they were on their own, they could easily slip right back into who they used to be, getting stuck in that empty space again, but she didn't care.

His chair was turned toward hers. He leaned on his knees with his forearms and clasped his hands, putting him right into her personal space. "Why?"

"It's a nice day. I'd like to enjoy it." She was hoping to be able to enjoy Pete's company as well. Especially after today, when he'd protected her, made her feel okay, been her security at lunch.

She could feel herself letting things with Pete move in a direction that wasn't sensible. She was at his family's party, he'd danced with her on the beach, she'd even admitted she needed to loosen up. She wanted to be near him, but if she did, how would she ever leave him without revisiting that terrible argument again? She was hoping to leave sooner rather than later, given the interview opportunity she'd received. She was making things much more difficult than she should.

When she focused on his face, she realized that he was stifling a laugh, holding it in, the corners of his mouth twitching. "Do you know that every time you're thinking, it shows on your face?" he laughed. "What are you thinking about?"

"Nothing," she grinned. "Let's just take a walk."

When she turned to tell the others that she'd be back in a few, she noticed that Celia was already looking at them, and it was clear that she hadn't just turned around. Libby swallowed and cleared her throat. "I'll be right back, Mom. I just want to take a little walk with Pete." Celia nodded, and Libby knew exactly what she was thinking.

Chapter Fifteen

Celia's reaction had bothered Libby. She was sure Celia worried that she was getting too caught up in Pete again. But even if she was, she wouldn't let it ruin her career. She knew what she needed to be happy, and she was willing to work to get it, even if it meant pushing him away. Yes, she was talking a lot to Pete at the party, but he was easy to talk to, and their history made her time there bearable. And they were just friends.

When she thought about it, however, *friends* didn't seem like the right word to define them. Years ago, they'd been much more than friends. She'd known everything about him. Yet, so much had happened since she'd been gone, she couldn't be sure she really knew him anymore. She didn't know what he did for fun, his hobbies or interests. In fact, she had no idea about his love life—he didn't have a date with him at the party, but that didn't necessarily mean he was single. Was it terrible of Libby to hope that he didn't have a significant other?

"What are you thinking about?" he said, gesturing for her to step first onto the sand.

She kicked off her sandals and set them to the side. How should she answer that? Surely she wouldn't say she was thinking about him, although that's exactly what she'd been doing. She walked down to the water and let the swelling sea foam float over her feet. "Nothing," she finally said as he walked up behind her.

"You're in your head too much." He playfully shook her shoulders. "Loosen up!" he smiled.

She bent over and picked up a seashell no bigger than a quarter, just as the tide washed over her fingers, taking the sand off the shell for her. One side was ridged and white, rough like the sand, but the other side was smooth like a pearl and iridescent pink and purple in color. She ran her finger along the smooth side. She'd seen hundreds of these shells as a kid, she'd even collected them, but she'd never stopped to take in their beauty.

Like her, the shell seemed to be perfect on the outside: strong, flawlessly shaped. That's how it's judged, by its exterior; nothing could penetrate it or mark it. But on the inside, as she turned it to the light, there were an infinite number of colors, all of the shades blending with one another. It was hard to pick out exactly what color was inside. She'd chosen the life she wanted for herself, and so had Pete, but it didn't stop the colors from running into each other, from blurring, going round and round, just like her shell. She slipped it into her pocket.

Pete gently tugged at her arm and she turned around. "I'm sorry about what I said earlier about you not being a family person." He looked straight into her eyes and she could tell he was genuinely sorry. "It must be weird to be back with your mom."

She nodded. "It is strange being back. I feel like I don't fit in here. I've always felt that way."

He took in a large breath and blew it out through pursed lips, seemingly contemplating something. Then he said, "Do you remember Catherine's swing we used to play on? It's just down the beach."

"Of course I remember. I ran into Catherine in town. Do her parents still live there?"

"Yeah. Why don't we go and take a look at that swing?"

Libby walked along the beach, taking in the cottages one at a time as they passed them, thinking about how different the landscape was now that she was an adult. Some of the smaller houses had been torn down for larger ones, and some of the ones that had been lovely as a child were now run down and in need of upkeep.

It was so interesting to see things through the eyes of an adult. There were so many more factors involved now. Cottages weren't just pretty; they were outward expressions of pride and care and investment, years of work. Like relationships. When they were kids, Libby and her friends just coexisted, swinging on tire swings, drinking lemonade, running in the woods. They didn't have to work at social exchanges or pay attention to codes of ethics. They just *were*. But she had been taught to pay attention to the code, not to let the freedom of summer overwhelm her need to focus on her path for success. Watching Pete and her friends as a child, she was able to see a little of that summer magic, even if she hadn't entirely known it herself. As an adult, the magic of the summer wasn't there at all. It was yet another set of days to do work and live life.

After a few minutes' walk, she could see the old swing still hanging from a branch high up in the tree. The beach under it seemed smaller now, narrower. She walked up to the tire and gave it a push, her memories moving with it. She'd been terrified to get on it, but Pete always talked her through it, and after she did, she was glad that he'd helped her to enjoy herself.

"Let's have a swing like we used to," Pete suggested.

"What?"

"Hop on."

"We can't. We'll break it!"

"No we won't. Look at the size of that branch! It'll hold us. Watch." He stepped up onto the tire, his feet inside the center, and held on to the rope. "Get on the other side," he said.

Libby was still afraid it wouldn't hold them. But she wanted to step out of her world for a minute and go back to a time when standing on a tire with Pete had been a perfectly normal reality. Carefully, she wedged her foot between his and, with a quiver, put her other foot on the outside of his foot. The rope was strong in her hands, her fists rubbing against his, their faces only inches apart.

"See?" he smiled. Then, with one foot, he stepped down and pushed off the ground, sending them wobbling toward the woods. He kicked against the tree to get them going.

Libby involuntarily squealed with fright, her stomach full of flutters as they soared the other way toward the water. "It won't break?" she asked, nearly gasping with concern.

"Trust me," he said, pushing off again, his eyes locked with hers. Even his gaze seemed strong enough to protect her from anything. The air moved around her and she felt weightless, as if the whole world were gone at that moment, and it was just the two of them. The lack of control and the lift in her stomach was so out of character for her, she was having trouble knowing how to respond. She kept thinking how silly it all was, wanting to get off, but the memory of it as a child held her in place.

After they'd gone back and forth enough that she was starting to feel less anxious, Pete said, "Do you remember what we used to do once we got going this high?"

"We used to jump."

"Would you jump if I asked you to?"

"What?" He couldn't possibly be serious. "We have clothes on!"

He pushed off again, a suggestive look in his eye. "So you're saying you want to…"

"No! We're not wearing swimsuits." If she wasn't terrified of letting go, she'd have slugged him in the arm.

"Are you worried about ruining those expensive clothes of yours?"

"No!" she said defensively.

"Then why not?"

He was baiting her. He was a grown man now. There was absolutely no reason for him to want to jump into the water. She was ready to hop onto the sand. She'd had enough of this.

"I dare you," he pressed.

"What would everyone say if we showed up at the party soaking wet?"

"Who cares?"

"I do!"

"Why?" He pushed off again, sending them soaring over the water.

This is like having a conversation with a ten-year-old, she thought. "Because normal, respectable adults do not jump into the sea with their party clothes on and then go back to the party. People will think we've lost our minds."

"Who cares?"

"You've said that already." The swing shook beneath them.

"Then clearly I mean it! At the count of three. Ready?"

She wasn't ready! There was absolutely no way she was going to jump into the water. She would be the talk of the town for weeks. No way.

"One…"

It was an utterly stupid idea.

"Two…"

Her chest was getting tight at just the thought of it. She couldn't do it. She *wouldn't* do it. This had to be the most preposterous idea Pete had ever had.

"Three!"

She held on to the rope, the tire becoming light beneath her feet. Her mouth hung open as she saw Pete fly through the air and dive straight into the water below. The tire swung her toward the trees and then out to the sea. She searched for him, finding him quickly. When the swing slowed enough, she jumped off and paced toward Pete now walking up through the waves as they rippled at his knees.

"That didn't go how I wanted it to," he said, wiping the water from his face, one corner of his mouth turned up in a crooked grin. His wet hair curled slightly, and beads of water were dripping onto his temples.

"*What* were you thinking?" she laughed in bewilderment. She tried not to notice the fact that she could make out his physique underneath his soaking shirt.

He took the bottom hem in his hands and wrung out the water. "I said on the count of three."

"Are you insane? What are you going to tell everyone?"

"I'll tell them I jumped into the water, although I don't know if they'll need the explanation really. It may be evident enough." He ran his fingers through his hair and shook the water off his hands.

"You're ridiculous," she said, stomping away from him.

"*I'm* ridiculous?" She could hear him closing the gap between them.

She didn't know why she was so angry with him, but she was. The wet sand gritted under her feet as she turned around to face him, her hands on her hips.

"You are so worried about what people will think of you, about being perfect little you, that you wouldn't let go. Life doesn't have to be that hard. If you want to jump, jump. Don't think about whether or not others will want you to do it or not. They aren't you." He took a step closer. "The only thing that matters is what's in here," he tapped his temple. Then he took her hand and placed her fingers on his wet chest. "And here."

She pulled her hand from his and started walking down the beach. She was irritated and she couldn't explain why. She thought about Wade. He certainly wouldn't have jumped. And, even though he hadn't been the one for her, Wade had been just the type of guy she wanted to date—a non-jumper. She stopped and spun around toward Pete. The sun was on him, making his wet hair shine. "I don't want to jump, Pete. It isn't who I am. I don't know how many times I need to tell you that." She turned back around and started back down the beach.

"Then what *do* you want, Libby? Do you even know?"

Her life seemed to be closing in on her just like it had day after day since she'd come back, and she felt the sting of tears in her eyes. Being near him was messing with her mind. She couldn't think straight with all the old feelings coming back relentlessly. But the truth of the matter was that it was probably only an initial attraction because of their history. They couldn't be happy together. They were too different. Angrily, she wiped a runaway tear with the back of her hand. She *did* know what she wanted. Her mind went to the email on her phone. Right then, it seemed like everything rested on that email, and as soon as she left Pete's, she was going to follow up.

She didn't want to think about Pete and Pop, or Nana's mystery letter anymore, or the fact that she'd not be able to see Jeanie and Helen on a regular basis. None of it mattered because it was all too painful to think about anyway. Why did she need all of this in her life? She'd been perfectly happy in New York and, until recently, things were uncomplicated there.

"I didn't mean to make you cry," Pete said, still dripping wet.

The complete absurdity of it made her laugh.

"What?" he asked, a perplexed look on his face.

The feel of tears still present, she tipped her head back and laughed again. She was losing it.

"What is wrong with you?"

"Everything here is so weird," she giggled and sniffled at the same time. "Look at you! And why do people hang tires from trees anyway?"

He chuckled but looked down at the sand as if searching for something.

Then she sobered a little. None of this was his fault at all. He couldn't help that she was a mess. He'd only been trying to loosen her up like she'd mentioned. He knew her feelings and had been a good friend, just like she'd wanted.

"Well, if you find everything so weird here, maybe you should hurry back to New York." He turned away from her, walking closer to the waves. His back to her, he picked up a shell and skipped it on the water, watching the place where it went under for longer than normal. Libby knew exactly how he felt because she felt it too. Maybe she should've followed her brain instead of her heart and not asked him on a walk. It was easier said than done.

Chapter Sixteen

Libby held the steamer she'd rented from Wentworth's against the kitchen wall with one hand while she attempted to reach the putty knife with the other. She fingered it and pulled it toward her, stretching her arms in opposite directions, sliding on the drop cloth beneath her feet, until she had the putty knife in her grasp. Removing the steamer, she scraped the wall to rid it of the old kitchen wallpaper. It was a slow process and she'd been at it for a good part of the morning, and about half the kitchen paper had been removed. The only benefit to stripping wallpaper was that it gave her time to think about all the things she had on her mind.

She'd set up an interview with Riddick Wiesner in New York. The interview was on the Friday before Trish's bridal shower, at the end of the month. Taxes would all be in by then and work would slow down a little, so she didn't feel too terrible about asking off that day. She'd set it all up the minute she'd gotten home from Helen's party.

She had enjoyed the rest of the party. As expected, the crowd gawked at Pete when they walked up from the beach. Jeanie had yelled, "Libby finally hit her limit and pushed you in, didn't she?"

Everyone laughed, and Pete never gave a straight answer. He went in and changed, and once he returned, the chatter about it died down. The worst thing was that Pete was very quiet the rest of the party, and he stayed far enough away from her, that they didn't have another conversation the rest of the day.

Why couldn't they just be friends? She knew why, but it didn't stop her from asking herself the question. She wanted to try and be friends, though. She wanted to be able to stop by and say hello when she came home for a visit; she wanted to text him when something funny happened; she wanted to see his smile again. She wasn't letting that go. Perhaps, if she could just keep the conversation light, being friends could work.

Libby had spent most of the remaining time at the party with her mother and Jeanie. Surprisingly, Celia hadn't said a whole lot about her new job with Marty or New York after that original discussion, thank goodness. Probably because Jeanie already knew most of the details and everyone else had been occupied in other conversations. After a few more glasses of wine, more birthday toasts, and some great songs, Libby had politely made her exit. She'd left when Pete was talking to someone, so she'd waved in his direction. It occurred to her that perhaps she should have waited, but she really just wanted to get home.

Once she got to the cottage, she pulled the shell from her pocket and looked at it again. She flipped it over in her hand, deciding which side she thought was more beautiful: the hard, rigid side with its perfect lines and symmetrical shape or the swirling colored side where everything seemed to run together, and she couldn't find the end of one color or the beginning of another. Still undecided, she placed the shell in her memory box and closed the lid. It would be her reminder that even though jumping would have been fun, it only made things a mess afterwards.

Now, with the job interview set in New York, Libby had a fresh perspective about the future. It was time to get working on the cottage, spruce it up a bit and get it on the market. If she had any luck left, she'd get the Riddick Wiesner job and leave all of this behind her. The only slightly worrisome feeling was leaving Pete and his family now that they were back in touch. She'd miss them. She would definitely come home more often.

Another strip of old paper came off the wall. She balled it up in her hand just as her cell phone rang. The number was Wade's. "Hello?" she answered, holding the phone with her wrists so as not to get the old wallpaper glue on her phone.

"Hi."

This was certainly a change. *To what do I owe the honor of a "hi" from you?* she thought. "Hi," she said back, grabbing a towel and wiping the glue off her hands.

"I just wanted to see how things were going."

"I'm stripping wallpaper right now. Is that good enough?" she snapped. Everything that had happened to her lately had mentally exhausted her and it made her irritable.

The line was silent.

"I'm going as fast as I can. I have the kitchen torn apart, I've fixed a leak upstairs, and I have an interview in New York at the end of the month, so I hope to be gone soon. Is that enough progress?"

"You have an interview? Anyone good?"

Oh, now he wants to get chatty. "Riddick Wiesner."

"Not a bad firm."

"Yes, it looks promising. Did you need anything else?"

"Nope. Just checking on you." Something in his voice sounded softer, like the old Wade, but she didn't trust her gut since he'd left her like he had.

"Well, you don't need to. I know this is half your house, but I'm taking care of things as quickly as I can." She said goodbye and hung up the phone. Sitting there, she felt uneasy and very much alone. She leaned against the wall and pulled her knees up to her chest. She rubbed her hands. They were sore from stripping paper. As she sat there, she worried that Pete might be upset with how she'd left the party, but she couldn't think how to approach him. She worried about bothering him. Maybe she would send a text. He could ignore it if he wanted to.

Hey! How are you? She began, and then paused. She needed a pretext for contacting him before apologizing for how brusque she had been at the party. *I'm stripping wallpaper and I'm gouging the wall*, she continued. *Do you know how I can fix?*

She put the phone down and resumed stripping the wallpaper when her phone pinged with a message. It read: *Wentworth's has people who can help you.*

It wasn't just because it was in writing, and it wasn't just her reading into it. That text was short and not very friendly. Pete, no matter the situation, would not usually offer such a suggestion; he'd run right over and try to help. The more she analyzed the situation, the more she started to look inward instead of outward. She'd blown it. What was wrong with her? She had just texted him as if it had been twelve years ago. Did she really expect him to drop everything to help her? Suddenly, she wanted to apologize. She tested the waters first. She texted back: *You okay?*

He responded: *Yep.*

No, he wasn't okay. Twelve years ago, he would've been so concerned by the question, that she'd receive at least a two-liner about how fine he was. But, again, his reply was short. She shouldn't have texted. She needed to just leave him alone, but now she didn't want to.

She turned off the steamer and went to the kitchen sink to wash her hands. She was already planning what to ask him, what to say. She wanted to call him or maybe even go and see him. She didn't like this feeling at all. In usual form, she started to run through their last conversation. He'd suggested she hurry back to New York. She'd thought he was just upset with her for not jumping, but was that what he actually wanted? With the water on, she lathered her hands with soap and scrubbed. Her scrubbing became slower as she thought it through, the sound of the tap the only noise in the room. She rinsed her hands and dried them on a towel. Maybe if she made light of her last text it would diffuse things.

She texted again: *Do you want to come over? I won't make you fix my wall. :)*

He responded: *Sorry, Libby. I'm really busy.*

Was there something wrong with Pop? He would've said. It wasn't Pop. And now she'd texted so much that she'd seem weird if she pressed further. She sat on the floor, holding her phone. *What's wrong?* she wondered. Maybe he just felt the same way she did about being friends... that it's too hard. A waste of time.

It was clear that Pete was frustrated with her. As she thought about why he had responded the way he had, she realized that she'd been very selfish. She was so busy trying to convince him that she was someone different, that she hadn't stopped to consider how different *he* may have become. She didn't really have the right to send him such a casual text. It wasn't her place. She was stuck again in that empty space between the past and the present, and she needed to grasp the fact that they were two different people and she couldn't just expect him to drop everything and respond to her. The realization made her feel awful.

❋ ❋ ❋

Catherine had offered to have Libby over to her house for dinner. In the back of the rental car, she had two gallons of canary yellow paint for the kitchen and a bottle of white wine. She'd spent a total of an hour and forty minutes in town with no sign of Pete. Only about ten minutes remained before she needed to be at her friend's house, so the prospect of running into him wasn't looking good.

Libby had asked Catherine if Celia could tag along. She thought perhaps her mother may like to do something with *her* friends for a change. So Catherine had planned a ladies' night, inviting her own mother and grandmother as well. Catherine and her husband, Scott, lived just a few minutes away from town, down a narrow, winding road that allowed snippets of the water through the woods every so often. Catherine lived close enough to the water to allow the humid sea breeze to rush in through the open car windows. Libby pulled the rental onto the gravel drive to Catherine's house, the bottle of wine tinkling against the paint cans in the back.

Catherine had been one of the few people Libby had kept in touch with sporadically over the years. She never seemed to judge her, she never questioned why Libby had moved to New York, and she seemed to completely accept who Libby was now. Since their lives had moved in different directions, they hadn't ever initiated more than the correspondence they had, but there was a mutual fondness and respect there that Libby really loved. She always thought how nice it would be to spend time with her, so she was glad to be visiting for dinner.

When the car slowed to a stop, Catherine's thin frame came into view. She was on her porch, barefoot, waving with one hand, a glass of wine in the other. Celia was already there, getting out of her car. Libby reached into the back and pulled the bottle of wine from the floorboard. As she got out, she held it up. "Just in case you didn't have enough," she smiled.

"One can never have too much," Catherine said.

"Hi, Mom," she said as Celia pattered up to her, an enormous grin on her face. She was wearing a matching silk tank and trousers set with sandals, clearly spruced up.

"Hi, honey," she said, kissing her cheek. The smell of musk perfume nearly overwhelmed her. "Hello, Catherine! It's been so long since we've had a chance to chat! How's your mom?"

"She's well! She's inside," Catherine said, opening the door and allowing Libby and her mother to enter. Catherine's home was the type of house that made her want to curl up with a mug of hot chocolate, even in the summer. Two large denim sofas flanked the room, a whitewashed table in between them, and everything sitting on a shaggy area rug. Her mother and grandmother were already chatting and both looked up to wave at her.

Esther Mullins was Catherine's grandmother. She was a hefty woman with white hair that was pinned back on each side, and large, jade earrings that matched a ring on the ring finger of her right hand. On the other hand, she wore a single gold band. She looked exactly the same as she had so many years ago when she would visit Catherine. Esther was chatting with Catherine's mother, Leanne.

Leanne stood up to say hello, her long, thin arms reaching out toward Celia. "How are you?" she said, her cheeks naturally rosy and her eyes almost squinting as she smiled. Celia embraced her and said hello.

"Want a glass of wine?" Catherine asked Libby and Celia. "It's from the winery." *The* winery meant Sandy Grove Winery down the road. It was the only one in town. It was also the one in which Pete had invested quite a bit of his money.

"I'd love one. Thanks," Libby said.

"Yes, thank you!" Celia agreed, as she sat down next to Catherine's mother, Leanne. "Anyone else need anything from the kitchen?" The other ladies shook their heads, already involved in a discussion of the local bank's new hours.

"I'll come with you," Libby said, following her.

Catherine handed her a glass and set the bottle on the counter. "So, what's *up*?" she said, pulling another glass from the cabinet as Libby filled her own glass with Pinot Grigio.

"Still getting the Roberts' cottage ready for sale. I bought it with my ex-fiancé." She took a sip of wine.

"Ex…?"

"Well, he wasn't my ex at the time," she grinned.

"Girl, I don't care about the cottage!" She poured wine into a glass for Celia. "What's up with you and Pete? I heard y'all have been hanging out lately! Anything exciting happen?"

How did she hear that? The mere thought of people discussing her and Pete gave her a queasy feeling. That was exactly why she wanted to get back to New York. Didn't people here have anything better to do than stick their nose in her business? In New York there was plenty to do, so no one bothered with anyone else's lives. "Who told you about that?"

"Pete told Jason that you came to his mom's birthday party, and Jason's still good friends with Scott." All those names together pulled her toward the memory of a colder day, fifteen years ago. Even though it had been cold outside, the memory was as warm as any she had.

On the first full weekend of every November, things began to change. In the town of Urbanna, a few towns over, no-parking signs and other festive decorations suddenly appeared. On the Friday night, sirens blared, lights flashed, and standing there, she nearly had to cover her ears from the sound of it all. Fire trucks from everywhere in Virginia paraded down the main street, and people with unrecognizable faces began filling the whole town. They'd come from all over the state. The Oyster Festival had begun.

So many people showed up, that the school buses couldn't get through the streets, so every year on that Friday, school was closed. When she was only fifteen, Libby and Catherine had spent the whole Friday getting ready just so they could meet their friends behind the fire house after the parade. That was where the beer garden was, and, although they weren't old enough to drink, they liked to hang around near the older crowd; it made them feel mature. So, with a brand new sweater and her favorite jeans, a fresh haircut and paint on her nails, Libby waited for her friends. Pete, Scott, and their friend, Jason, had shown up not too long after the girls had gotten there.

It was that night of the Oyster Festival that the five of them had stayed up until the wee hours of the morning in Catherine's living room. Later that morning, Libby had awakened next to Pete, curled up in his arms. As she looked at his face, it was the first time she'd felt what it would be like to be Pete Bennett's girlfriend.

Five years later, Catherine had married Scott in a small family ceremony on the beach. Catherine had dated Scott about as long as Libby had known Pete.

She remembered Jason very well. He'd been one of the boys she'd chased after that day that she'd hurt her leg when Helen had to bandage it.

"Jason still lives around here?"

"He owns a siding company now, and he bartends at Rocky's on the weekends. He and Pete like to restore boats together sometimes. You know how they were as kids. They aren't much different now," she grinned.

It was true. That very conversation could have happened when she was fifteen: *Pete told Jason, and he knows Scott....*

"I'm aware that they aren't much different now." Libby took another sip of wine and peeked in to check that her mother was still chatting with the other ladies. "Did you know that Pete jumped off your tire swing the other day?"

"What?" she said over her shoulder as she took Celia her wine. After a quick moment, Catherine returned, a look of confusion on her face, but a smile on her lips.

"Would you believe he got me on that thing?"

"Want to go ahead and start dinner, Catherine?" her grandmother, Esther, called from the other room. "You and Libby get the crabs and cook while we enjoy a little conversation amongst ourselves."

"Okay," she called back. "When were you even near that swing?" she giggled, pulling out a bowl of fresh green beans and an empty bowl. She washed at the sink, grabbed a fistful of beans, and set them on a plate in front of Libby. She started snapping ends off the beans, her face full of interest.

Libby walked around the bar to the sink and turned on the water. "At Helen's party. We went for a walk. He actually wanted me to jump in fully clothed!" She flicked water in the basin and dried her hands on the kitchen towel. "I wouldn't do it, but he did! Stupid man." She grabbed a bean from the plate and snapped off an end.

Catherine laughed, holding beans in both hands. "What did everyone say?"

"You know how this town is. I'm sure they had more thoughts than what was actually being said. No one said much of anything at that moment." Her mind moved to the end of the party and how distant Pete seemed. Perhaps it was best that he was being distant.

Catherine pulled out a large pot, filled it at the sink and put it on the stove to boil.

"Where's Scott?" Libby asked, snapping another bean.

"He's out with the guys since you were coming over. I think they're all coming back here later tonight."

She wondered if Pete was with him. *Will Pete be coming back tonight as well?* she asked herself. *Don't even think about it.* She took another drink of wine.

Chapter Seventeen

"So, other than Pete jumping into the sea fully clothed, is there anything else interesting going on between you two?" Catherine said as she dropped the beans into the pot of boiling water. "Sorry. I'm being nosy—but I can't help it." Catherine took a sip of wine, pulled a small bowl out of the refrigerator with some sort of homemade dressing in it and whisked it with a fork. "There hasn't been anyone in Pete's life since he dated Allison Bradley."

Libby had to keep her mouth from dropping open. It was as easy as light conversation, but Catherine had just dropped a bomb on Libby. She'd always wondered about who Pete may have dated, but now she had a name, and it was someone she knew, someone she could visualize. Jealousy smacked her right in the face.

"Allison Bradley?" She had been top of their class. She was very pretty with long, dark brown hair, a heart-shaped face, and deep brown eyes. Libby shouldn't care one way or the other whom he dated, so why did it bother her? It did, though. A *lot*. Although he'd probably dated all kinds of people, seeing Allison's face in her mind, her hand holding Pete's, made her stomach feel queasy.

She didn't want to think of his smile, the warmth in his eyes—any of it—directed at someone else. So many times when she first got to New York, and the nights brought her feelings of loneliness to the surface, she'd imagined the way he used to look at her. Had he been looking at Allison when Libby had been thinking about him? It made her shudder.

"Now that you're back, he's been out and about all over the place. I see him everywhere!"

"Is he coming tonight?" She couldn't help herself. The wine on her empty stomach was causing her to voice more of her thoughts than she usually would. And she wanted to see him. His behavior since the end of the party was troubling her. She didn't like it at all. Being near him and getting to experience that again made being without it a lonely feeling. He made her feel happy, and she hadn't felt happy about much lately.

"Probably not. I don't think he can leave his grandfather alone that long. Scott said Pete really worries about him." She strained the steaming beans and added the dressing, tossing them around until they were coated in it. Then she set the bowl in the refrigerator and pulled out a silver bucket from the bottom shelf.

"Well, it's time to go and catch our dinner. Follow me."

"Are we going crabbing?" Libby asked, nearly unable to contain her excitement at the sight of the bucket. She had loved crabbing as a girl. She used to go to Pop's pier and crab with him. He'd taught her how, and she'd never forgotten. There was nothing like it. Catherine's mere mention of it caused reminiscence of those days: *Don't let it pinch ya*, he'd said. *You need all those pretty little fingers. Tap it like this…*

Catherine refilled their glasses to the very brim. "I'm hoping Scott gets home by the time we have to get them into the steamer. He's already put the crab bucket and things out on the pier for us. Get your wine. I'll take the bait." She grabbed her own glass and opened the door.

After they'd waved to the ladies in the living room, they left the house and walked down the drive toward the road. The sun was beginning to set, painting streaks of orange in the pale blue sky. "The weather's been warm, so I hope we get lucky and catch a ton."

Libby looked both ways down the winding road at the end of the drive. There was nothing for miles; the double yellow lines stretching out as far as she could see. They crossed and made their way through a path in the woods, walking carefully, Libby's wine sloshing slightly in her glass. Through the last thin line of trees, the pier came into view.

It looked like so many other piers she'd visited with Pop. She could still remember the hat he wore to keep the sun off his face, the black-rimmed sunglasses he had, and the large white bucket he used. She could see it swinging from his hand, his strong fingers wrapped around the handle.

She hadn't thought about crabbing in years, and reflecting on it now made her sentimental. She had been raised differently than her friends, and when it came to activities around town, she didn't always know what to do, but Pop had been so gentle with her, so patient, coaching her one tiny step at a time until she got it right. She always felt perfect around him, even when she was trying something new. She didn't feel like she needed to please him, she just needed to listen to him and she'd be okay.

She took another sip of wine and stepped over a branch on the ground just before climbing the steps to the pier. The crickets were just starting to chirp in the woods as Catherine set down the bucket next to a net, a box with some weights, a ball of string, and other odds and ends. Catherine unrolled a very long piece of string and snipped it with a pair of scissors. Libby sat down next to her, slipped off her flats and hung her legs over the edge, her feet dangling above the rippling water. She took a sip of her wine and she felt the heat in her face from the alcohol and the setting sun.

"So how's the cottage coming?" Catherine asked, reaching into the smaller bucket she'd brought from the refrigerator, retrieving a small piece of chicken and tying it to the end of the string. She handed it to Libby.

"It's going well. I'm painting and taking down wallpaper."

"Once you get it all done, won't you be tempted to stay?"

"I can't."

She worried. How could she explain to Catherine why she wasn't staying? It was so difficult to put into words what she enjoyed about the high-pressure environment in New York—particularly when she considered how calm and peaceful Catherine's life was there by the sea. She took a sip of wine just as she felt a tug on her string.

"Can you hand me the net, please?" Libby pulled the string straight up, pinching it hand-over-hand until a crab dangled above the water. Carefully, she grabbed the net and scooped it right in. She still remembered the way Pop had taught her to tap the net against the bucket to get the crab off the string. Then, with a plop, it let go and fell into the bucket.

"Do you like living in White Stone?" Libby asked.

"I love it. I wouldn't live anywhere else."

Libby was happy for her friend. It was nice to hear that Catherine was content and settled. The two of them were so similar in many ways, but as Libby looked around at Catherine's surroundings—the rough wood of the pier, the sun glistening off the water—she realized how dissimilar their worlds were.

"Once you sell the cottage, what will you do then? Move back to New York? Can you hand me the net now? I'm feeling a pull." Libby gave her the net, and Catherine drew another crab from the water.

"That's the plan." She wished she could steer the conversation elsewhere.

"I hope you aren't leaving too soon," she said, turning the net over and dropping the crab into the bucket with Libby's.

"Well, I hope we can get together again before I do. This has been so nice! I'm really enjoying it," she said and took another sip of her wine. It was true. As much as she was itching to get on with her life, she loved seeing Catherine and Jeanie, Helen and Pop… and most of all Pete. Even being with her mother was getting better. But, she reminded herself, she needed to be back in the city, with a purpose, a focus. Without that, she felt out of sorts.

After they'd caught enough crabs for everyone, they carried the two buckets back with their glasses of wine. "Scott'll pick up the rest of our things when he goes fishing in the morning," Catherine said, which was good because they were out of hands.

When they got back, Catherine started the steamer in the garage. She looked at her watch. "Let's just cook these up, and I'll put some away for Scott when he gets home." She tipped the bucket and dropped the crabs in. "Let me tell the ladies we're back. I'll get us some more wine and a pile of newspaper, and we can eat outside."

"Well, look at that!" Esther said, holding the railing and making her way down the three stairs to the garage. "Y'all caught a bunch of crabs, didn't you?" Celia and Leanne followed. They walked outside to the picnic table and sat down, the warm sun bearing down from its spot on the horizon. Without the proximity of the water, the air didn't move as much, and the humidity hit them like a wet towel. Celia tugged on her blouse, fluffing it out, the air flowing in and around it.

"It doesn't get this hot in New York, does it, Libby?" Celia asked.

"No," Libby said cautiously. She didn't want to have to talk about New York with a bunch of people who probably didn't care a bit about the city. Her mother was always asking those kinds of questions. It made Libby feel so uncomfortable. She'd dealt with it her whole life and still had never gotten used to it. At eighteen, she hadn't cared what people thought because she was leaving and never planning to return, but now that she was there, she realized how her comments could hurt people.

"Libby hopes to sell the Roberts' cottage soon," her mother said as Catherine returned with the newspaper.

Leanne took a bundle of newspaper from her daughter and began spreading it over the picnic table. That was one of Pop's tricks: always crack crabs on newspaper so it can be wadded up at the end for easy cleanup. She could hear him saying it in her head, and it made her smile.

"Oh, yes! I knew Anne Roberts very well," Esther said. "We were good friends all the way through high school."

Libby perked up. She couldn't help but wonder if Esther had known Mitchell. This could be the perfect opportunity to find out more about him. Who *was* the man who had propositioned Nana? Had Nana been sure about her love for Hugh at the beginning of their relationship? Had she ever been interested in Mitchell? Had Nana given Mitchell a reason to hope she might run away with him? She had so many questions and no answers.

Anne had been offered a life in a different place, with a man who had a fantastic job in a big city, and yet she'd stayed in White Stone, with Hugh. Had it just been the fact that she was married that had stopped her from leaving? Having seen Nana and Pop together, it was hard to imagine. They'd seemed so happy. Nana didn't seem like someone who was trapped.

"Living in her house, I've become so curious about Anne and Hugh. I knew them as adults, but I find it fascinating to hear stories about them when they were young. What was Anne like as a girl?" she asked, hoping to shed some light on the letter, and glad to be off the topic of New York.

"Ah, she was the queen of the town. She was so pretty. Everyone loved Anne. But more than that, she was so kind. Did you know, at only twenty she helped raise money to restore the church in town? It's a historical monument. She didn't want to see it in decay, so she'd organized bake sales and car washes, as well as soliciting donations—door to door—with the area businesses to pay for its renovations and upkeep. I think she was probably known for her kindness more than her beauty."

Libby knew exactly what she meant because, while Nana was a beautiful woman, Libby remembered her kindness most of all. She remembered her tender smile, the way she looked up at the sky when she laughed, and how she would sing whenever someone was upset. If Libby had come over after a particularly stressful day when her mother had argued bitterly on the phone with her father, or when her mother had pushed her too hard that day, Nana would pull out a chair, make her something to drink, and quietly sing while she moved around the kitchen—sometimes singing the words, sometimes humming a tune. She'd always known how to calm her.

"Do you know how Hugh and Anne met?" she asked Esther.

"I do! I was there!" she smiled, her face lighting up. "It was our first day at high school. The three area middle schools emptied out into our one high school, and I still remember putting on my pink lipstick because I wanted to look nice for all the new people I may encounter. I met Anne before school, and we walked there together. She saw Hugh going up the steps into the building and she grabbed my arm, stopping me right there on the sidewalk. 'Who's that?' she asked, knowing I didn't know either. She was instantly captivated by him—and thrilled when she realized they had Science class together."

"They'd known each other that long?" Libby asked, wanting her to go on for hours with her stories.

"Yes. They only started dating, though, their senior year. Hugh was too traditional to ask her out before she was eighteen."

Libby smiled at the thought. It was just like Pop.

Catherine set the crabs and the bowl of green beans onto the table along with a bottle of wine in a bucket of ice. "Time to eat!" she said, pulling Libby back into the present.

"This is lovely, Catherine! Thank you!" Celia said, pulling a paper napkin from the roll and placing it in her lap. The other ladies nodded.

To Libby's relief, Celia didn't say anything embarrassing as they had their dinner. She'd let Leanne dominate the conversation with discussion regarding organizing the summer bonfire. As she watched her mother, Libby was surprised at how relaxed she looked sitting at a picnic table in the hot sun, cracking crabs. Celia even laughed loudly at something Esther said, covering her mouth and looking around as if she'd done something wrong. It made Libby smile. She was glad to see her mother having a good time. In a way, Pete was right. There was a lot of Celia in Libby. She could understand how difficult it was for her mother to open up, and she knew what that worry and awkwardness felt like. Watching her, it made Libby feel a sense of closeness to her mother that she'd never felt before.

Chapter Eighteen

By the time Scott arrived at Catherine's, Libby'd had so much wine that she'd decided it best she didn't drive home, so Scott had driven her, and a friend of his had followed in her rental. After they left, she sat in the cottage with a swimming head and the quiet buzz of the lamp beside her, feeling very alone. She knew better, but with the help of the wine, she decided to text Pete. Catherine had been lovely, but she felt as though Pete was her best friend there. Her fingers moved unsteadily across the letters: *I've been thinking about you. How are you? I'm bored. What are you doing right now?*

She stared at the screen, her little blue text bubble the only thing on it. The minutes seemed like hours. She got up and got herself a glass of water. When she came back to the small sofa in the living room where her phone rested, she picked it up to be sure she hadn't missed the ping. Nothing.

She sat for quite a while, drinking her water and holding the phone. As she diluted the alcohol in her body, she came to the conclusion that she shouldn't have texted him. He knew as well as she did why they couldn't be together, and it seemed that being friends was as hard for him as it was for her, so he was distancing himself.

She knew him well enough to know that. She'd told him over and over how she wasn't the same person anymore, so she had no right to text him as if she were still that girl who'd loved him.

After an hour of clicking through the shows on television and coming up empty, Libby decided to turn off the TV and call it a night. She picked up the remote just as she heard a knock at the door. She peeked out the window but she couldn't see the person, so she stood there, deliberating. Another knock. She looked out again and this time she could see who it was. Pete was shifting impatiently from one foot to another. He ran his fingers through his hair, looking back and forth behind him. Libby opened the door.

"Has Pop come by here? I can't find him," he said. There was a tiredness in his eyes; the usual spirit that she'd seen in his face was absent tonight.

"No," she said, suddenly worried beyond words. She glanced down the dark drive toward the street looking for him, hoping to see him wandering along.

"Damn." He looked around again, his shoulders slumped, defeated. "I thought that if he'd forgotten again, he'd come back here, since this was his home with Nana, and if he did remember where he was, perhaps he'd come to see you on the off chance."

Libby slipped her flats on and grabbed her keys. "I'll help you find him." She locked the handle and shut the door behind her. "Leave your car; we'll look for him on foot. We can split up."

They paced briskly down the walk and out to the street where the darkness wrapped around them like a woolen blanket. "Which way should we go?" she asked, her stomach filling with anxiousness.

"Let's head toward town."

As they headed down the road in silence the loose gravel of the asphalt beneath their feet, she felt more terrible with every step. There she was, telling Pete how different she was as an adult, how much had changed for her, yet she hadn't stopped, yet again, to consider his point of view. Look how much had changed for him. He'd lost his grandmother, who was as close to him as his own mother, and now, in front of his eyes, he was losing his grandfather. Like Libby, there were remnants of who he was, but he, too, was someone else now. They continued down the street toward town, two people who used to know each other, bound by only memories, walking along in the empty space.

They arrived at the first intersection and Pete started looking in the windows of all the shops. Libby followed his lead, searching the faces of everyone she saw, willing Hugh to come out of one of the doors. *Where would he have gone?* She racked her brain for an answer. The intensity behind Pete's movements was making her even more nervous. He knew more about Hugh's prognosis than she, and if he was this worried, there was reason. She wanted to find him, if anything to take the concern out of Pete's eyes, because it was killing her. He'd never looked so vulnerable, so unsure.

"How long has he been gone?" she asked, cupping her hands on her forehead and peering into the market window.

Pete looked down at his watch. "About two hours."

Libby worried for Hugh. It was dark, the spring air was a little chilly. There was so much water and dense forest around them. If he had forgotten, would he know where he was when he became himself again? Only a few hours ago, nothing was wrong except her circumstances—which seemed so silly now that she'd been struck with the worst worry she'd ever felt, apart from the worry she'd had as a child as her daddy drove away to start his new family.

"Go down by Lucky's and meet me back at the park," Pete said, looking more frantic with every move. Libby nodded and headed toward Lucky's gas station about two blocks away. She looked between buildings, on benches, around every corner she could think of. No Pop. The dark streets were so familiar that she didn't need the store lights to know exactly where to go. She knew all the places in which to look, and still she couldn't find him. As she raced toward the park, she glanced down the street that took her to Jeanie's, but it was empty.

Her hands were starting to tremble from apprehension just as she caught sight of a familiar figure. When she saw the man coming out of the corner store, she blinked several times to be sure it was really the person she thought it was. "Pop!" she called out, and the figure turned around. "Pop! What are you doing?" She ran toward him, feeling as though the happiness would burst right out of her chest.

When she reached him, she threw her arms around him. "Where were you?" she asked, out of breath from the whole ordeal, a lump forming in her throat. She'd never been so glad to see anyone before.

"I sat down at Joe's and had a cup of coffee and a chat with the folks in there. Then I picked up a loaf of bread. We were out." As he said the words, Libby could tell by his eyes what he was probably thinking: that he couldn't even go out for something that simple anymore without worrying everyone to death.

"Pete's probably at the park by now. We were looking for you. We'd split up." She linked her arm in his. "Let's go meet him. He'll be so happy you're okay. And Pop," she stopped walking and waited for him to make eye contact. "Next time, would you leave us a note?" He nodded, and she could tell the suggestion bothered him. He didn't like his predicament any more than they did.

When they got to the park, Pete was waiting under a street light, his arms folded, his gaze up near the tops of the trees. "Pete," she called out quietly, approaching him from behind. He turned around, and she could see the worry leave him as if it were some foreign being in his body. His shoulders fell, the tightness in his features left.

"Pop. Where have you been?"

Pop's cheerful demeanor was replaced by one of annoyance. Lib- by had never seen him that way before. "I've already accounted for my night with Libby. Do I have to say it again just for your benefit?" he snapped. Libby looked at Pete, concerned again. Hugh hadn't ever spoken to anyone like that before, that she'd ever heard. "Here," he held out the loaf of bread tied in a plastic bag with a twist tie. "We were out."

The three of them walked back to Libby's to get Pete's car. None of them uttered a word. Libby was too busy thinking about Pop's behavior. *It's the disease*, she thought. It had to be terrible not re- membering basic things like where one lived. Even worse, it must be hard knowing that a time may come when Hugh wouldn't even know the people around him. She wondered if he was irritable like that on a regular basis.

Pete must have a lot on his mind. Her presence was probably making it worse. He didn't need her to get in the way with her insen- sitive texting. She thought again how selfish she'd been to send that text tonight.

By the time they got back to the cottage, the silence between them was deafening. The situation was too heavy to make small talk, yet none of them had anything to offer regarding the issue at hand. When they got onto the patch of grass, illuminated by the porch light, Libby finally said, "Pop, I'm glad you were just getting coffee and bread." She hugged him, and she was happy he hugged her back. "Have a good night," she said to Pete.

"You too," Pete said and then left her on the grass. He and Hugh climbed into his Bronco. The engine growled as Pete looked one last time in her direction. Then they drove away into the darkness of the night, his red taillights shrinking in the distance. With the sound of crickets singing in the woods nearby, Libby stood, thinking.

Her worries about Pete's shortness with her, the wine, seeing Catherine, and then the frantic search for Hugh had exhausted her. She tried to make sense of her thoughts, but her fatigue was knotting them all together, and she couldn't even get one entire thought to process. She'd never been that tired in New York. Things had never been that hard. Even losing her job, leaving her apartment, and breaking up with Wade hadn't exhausted her like that. She thought again how she needed to get a move on with the cottage, sell the thing and get out of town as soon as she could.

As she got inside and got settled, a text showed up on her phone. She opened the screen and read: *Still bored? Didn't think so. :) Good night.* Libby smiled, feeling the fizz of happiness at the sight of his text. But then, as reality sank in, she realized there was a sadness to his message; she could feel it, and it made her remorseful for even sending such a flippant text in the first place. What had she been thinking? The only thing that made her smile again when she reread the text was that she'd gotten a smiley face. That was enough to make the rest of the night okay.

Chapter Nineteen

"Do you think you can continue the hardwoods into the kitchen, or would tile look better?" Libby asked Bert from the flooring shop on Irvington Road as he snapped his measuring tape against a wall. She could hardly hear his answer above the banging of the cabinetry guys doing the kitchen remodel. She'd been busy all week, setting appointments and getting work done to ready the cottage for sale, and she was nearly finished. The kitchen wall had been repaired and painted a canary yellow, cabinets were being hung, and a new countertop would be installed by that evening. Bert was getting final measurements for a quote on the new kitchen floor, and that would be her final decision of the day.

Libby had been so busy with the house, she hadn't seen Pete after the night he'd lost Pop to a loaf of bread, except to get him to sign his tax paperwork. When he'd come into the office, she didn't ask him to lunch even though she'd wanted to. She kept it all business, like she should. He'd signed and they'd filed the taxes. Job complete. He hadn't texted, and she hadn't texted him either. Losing Pop that evening had been a wakeup call for her. She'd realized that Pete had his own life to live and she shouldn't interfere with it, especially if she wasn't planning on staying.

And she wasn't staying. After work tomorrow, she was boarding a plane for New York. She couldn't wait to see her friends at the shower, find out the latest from Trish, and maybe even go out for drinks. Her bags were packed, her tickets on her dresser, and the bridal shower gift purchased online and in transit. But there was a part of her that felt a little sad to be leaving. She'd made so many relationships stronger in her short time there, and as much as she'd tried to escape it when she'd arrived, she'd miss White Stone's calming atmosphere and friendly people.

"Let's go with tile in the kitchen," she called out to Bert over the racket. "It'll look best since you can't match the hardwoods perfectly. Why don't we do that white and gray tile that you showed me?" Bert nodded, scribbled a few things onto his clipboard, and then stepped over cabinetry to get to the front door.

The kitchen remodel had been going on all day while she was at work, so she'd called her mother and set up a supper date. She'd really enjoyed having Celia at Catherine's house. It had marked a change in their relationship; it was a start to understanding her mom better. She was glad to be going over to her childhood home, and she was happy to be spending time with Celia. Their relationship had been difficult over the years, certainly, but she loved her mother and she wanted to spend time with her before going back to New York. Conversation was still a little difficult between them, but Libby was willing to give it a shot. Other than her father, who wasn't ever near enough to her to have any kind of real relationship, Celia was Libby's only family.

She left the cabinetry guys to finish their work, asking them to lock up as they left—one of the perks of a small town: knowing everyone enough to leave them to lock up her house. Then she went to her mother's.

She pulled the car into the drive just as Celia stepped onto the front porch, waving like someone leaving port. It made her giggle, which felt good. She got out and shut the door. "Hi, Mom. How are you?" she called up to her.

"Great! Great. Come in and relax with something to drink." her mother beamed, as they entered the house, Celia scuttling off to the kitchen.

Libby stood next to the curio cabinet by the front door, noticing her swimming trophies inside. She went through the small entryway that led to the living room and dropped down onto the sofa. A candle burned on the mantle, just in front of a massive oil painting of Libby at the age of five. The overwhelming display of her achievements right at the front door, the pictures of her all over the living room, it all hadn't seemed odd until she'd seen it as an adult. It occurred to her that her mother's sense of worth rested on her achievements, and it made getting that job in New York feel even more important. Not only was her own happiness riding on it; her mother's was as well. The tense feeling she'd had as a child came back even with her efforts to rationalize it.

"Hope you like lemon in your sweet tea," she said, handing Libby a glass. "It's not homemade. I got it premade at the market. It was some new brand. Thought I'd try it." Celia took a sip of her own and set the glass on the coffee table.

"Thanks," Libby smiled. In adulthood, her mother seemed to want to please her, to make her happy. It occurred to Libby that Celia's own insecurities and need to please people had probably been instrumental in her choices in raising Libby. Her mother seemed as anxious as Libby did most of the time, and Libby understood that now. "I got an interview in New York," she said, knowing how delighted her mother would be with the news.

Celia clapped her hands together loudly. "Oh! That's fantastic, Libby! I'm so proud of you!" Then, as quickly as her smile had emerged, it faded. "Be sure you tell Marty. Give him enough time to get organized before you leave."

"I haven't gotten the job yet, Mom. And Marty did tell me in our initial phone interview that it could be temporary, so it shouldn't be too much trouble for him."

"Well, I just know you're going to get it! Won't you be so happy to get out of here?" She took a sip of her tea.

"Can I ask you something?" Libby said, setting her glass down and turning toward Celia. Her mother waited, her eyebrows raised, an expectant look on her face. "If you're so glad for me to get out of here, why did *you* stay all these years?"

Celia's face became serious and she sat for a few silent seconds without responding. She frowned, her chest rising and falling with her breath. "Your father and I moved here for his job when we were young. I didn't necessarily like it here, but we had to go where he could work. Then, like anywhere else, we started to make a life." She paused for a long time, then took a sip of tea before continuing. "Your dad left *me*, Libby, and I couldn't afford to go anywhere. I'd left my career far behind. That's why I worked so hard to get you where you are. I didn't want you to fall into the same trap."

Libby had never heard her mother be that candid before, that honest, that open. She'd always said, "Chin up," whenever Libby failed, and she'd pushed her harder. Now, Celia was showing Libby that she didn't always have her chin up. She was letting Libby see her vulnerable side. For the first time in her life, Libby saw someone in front of her who was just like her, who understood her like only family could.

"I figured, but I've always wondered. Thank you for telling me."

Celia smiled. "Now you know." She stood up. "I've got chicken parmesan in the oven. Let me go check on it."

Libby watched her leave, still thinking about her mother's words. Now, looking at Celia Potter, Libby saw someone completely different. She saw a woman who had been heartbroken, who had spent her whole adult life trying to overcome the misery of a failed marriage. Her mother had lived so many years there, stuck where she'd never wanted to be, most likely hoping to find that happiness again, but knowing she wouldn't get it. So she'd pinned all her hopes on Libby. She didn't want Libby to get caught there, trapped in a relationship that may be doomed to fail. She'd made sure Libby's life didn't look a thing like hers. The whole time, Libby had thought she'd been protecting her mother by trying to make her happy, when really it had been Celia who had been trying with everything she had to ensure Libby's happiness. Celia struggled with showing love—that much was clear. But Libby finally understood that by raising her the way she had, Celia was trying her best to show that love. Libby felt a warmth for her mother that she'd never felt before.

"It's steaming hot, but dinner's ready," Celia called out from the next room.

Libby took her glass and headed into the kitchen.

"Grab your plate," Celia said with a grin, "Let's eat like we used to, just us girls."

So many nights it had been only the two of them eating exactly like that. All of those nights, Libby had tried her best to relate to her mother but always struggled. Tonight was different. She finally got her.

During dinner, conversation was easy and enjoyable. Libby only wished she'd figured her mother out sooner than the day before her interview. If she got the job, she'd be moving back as soon as she could, putting distance between them once again. She promised herself she'd come home more often. She'd be sure to stop by Catherine's and say hello. She may even try to get around to visit some of the people in town if she could. But most importantly, she'd come and visit her mom and Jeanie, Helen and Pop. And Pete. She'd never stay away that long again.

Chapter Twenty

Libby wondered how Pete fit in her life. She wanted to talk to him, let him know her excitement at getting the interview, tell him how eager she was to get back, but she knew that he wouldn't share in the thrill of it. She wasn't the girl anymore that he wanted to hear from. She'd spent the whole day at work, her mind alternating between thinking about Pete and how things had changed with her mom. With her mother, Libby felt she was in a good place; she felt like she could finally communicate with her. With Pete, things weren't that clear.

With a deep breath, she checked one last time for her tickets, grasped the handle of her suitcase, and headed for the airport.

❊ ❊ ❊

Riddick Wiesner was every bit Libby's dream job. She'd have an actual office—no cubicle—a solid number of vacation days, and a better salary than the one she'd had at her last job. All she had to do was nail the interview. With her best Tom James power suit on and her highest heels clicking along the pavement, she crossed the busy Manhattan street toward the address on the screen of her phone.

It was glorious to be back. The sun was shining, the morning was crisp. In the air she could hear the sound of traffic, honking taxis, and the movement of commerce, all of it filling her with an inexplicable excitement.

She entered through two glass doors—both taller than the oak trees back home—and made her way to the reception desk. A woman about her age sat at a sleek, fifties-inspired wood-grained desk, a brass plaque behind her with a list of the businesses in the building. Libby caught her eye and the woman smiled. "May I help you?" she asked pleasantly.

"Yes. I'm here for an interview at Riddick Wiesner."

The woman reached over the desk to direct Libby to the elevators where she would get off at floor fourteen. She walked the blindingly shiny white floors to the elevator and hit the button just as her cell phone alerted her to a message. While waiting for the doors to open, she took a look at her phone. She was surprised to see a text from Wade. It read simply: *Can we talk?* Why did she have to get a message like that just before going in? Now her mind was wandering to all the reasons Wade could want to talk instead of focusing on her interview. Wade would not distract her. She was there for one purpose and one purpose only: to get that job. Nothing was going to get in the way of that.

The elevator doors swished open and she stepped aside to allow a few people to exit. When she got on and the doors had closed, she quickly texted a response: *Can't talk now. About five mins out from interview with RW.* Then she turned the sound off on her phone and put it in her handbag. She wasn't even going to look at the response if there was one. She didn't want to know if he was checking on the sale of the cottage or if he was wishing her luck on the interview or anything else.

He'd left her at her lowest moment, dumped her—just like that. As she thought about it, she wasn't sad anymore. She was angry. How dare he be that insensitive after all the time they'd spent together? She deserved more than the sad excuse for a break-up he'd offered. She shook the thought from her mind, trying to clear her head for the interview. He was *not* getting in the way of her success on that interview. She was giving it all she had.

When she arrived at floor fourteen, she stepped off the elevator into the hallway, still trying to clear her mind. She needed to be there, in the present, not thinking about anything else. Time to get to work on real life. She could sort out her muddled love life later.

After a quick call to Steven Wiesner, Libby was ushered into the Riddick Wiesner conference room where she met her potential new boss. He was tall and thin with a tailored, navy suit, a heavily starched blue pinstriped shirt peeking out from under his jacket, and a blood-red tie, but his face was friendly, his eyes warm. "Hello." He held out his hand.

"Hi. Libby Potter." She offered a firm handshake.

"Have a seat." He pulled out a chair, the castors rolling toward her. She sat down across from him, the gleaming table empty except for a leather-bound legal pad and a pen on his side. "Thank you for coming today," he said as he looked down at his notes.

He began to ask her all the right questions and she was firing answers back with ease and skill. There was no better feeling. Her mind went back to that tire swing, soaring toward the water, knowing the thrill of her fate. This was it. Like that perfect, splash-free dive, she was gliding along, completely free. The entire interview felt right, like she was meant to be there, and she could tell by his responses to her that he was impressed—the raised eyebrows, the eye contact, the smiles at just the right moment.

"Well, Miss Potter, normally I give it a day or two, but I have to say, you are the right fit for this job. I'd like to have you on our team."

Like a bolt of electricity, excitement zinged through her. "I'd love to join Riddick Wiesner," she said, standing and offering her hand across the table. Mr. Wiesner shook her hand, nodding.

"Thank you for a fantastic interview." He walked around to her side of the table. "I remember you had some things to tie up, and I know you'll need the obligatory two weeks' notice for your current employer. Would you be able to start, say, in a month's time?"

"Certainly."

"Excellent. It was very nice meeting you. I look forward to working with you."

"Thank you so much. It was a pleasure to meet you," she smiled, trying with every ounce of energy she had not to burst into fits of screaming and laughter. She'd done it. She was back in the game. As she walked out of the office, Libby took in a deep breath and let it out, all her insecurities and worries lifting right off her like helium balloons. The warm sun was shining down on her like a ray of hope, and she knew things could only go up from there. She'd never been more focused, never more willing. She was going to sell the cottage and move as soon as she possibly could.

As luck would have it, Riddick Wiesner was only a couple blocks from her favorite diner, so she paced along the sidewalk outside, with her fellow New Yorkers, driven, focused, and with no time to waste.

When she entered the diner, she didn't recognize any of the staff and they didn't seem to notice her. She sat down at the table near the window that overlooked her favorite street. A waitress took her order, and within a few minutes she had her coffee in the white porcelain cup. With her hands wrapped around it, she looked out the window, the sun streaming in on her face.

She'd gotten the job.

She wanted to share her news with someone. Usually, when she had big news, she'd call Trish. *But I don't want to call Trish*, she thought. *I want…* She didn't want to admit it because it didn't make any sense. *I want to call Pete*, she thought against her will.

She wished she could tell him in person, and he would share in her happiness, that she could see the laughter behind his eyes as she jumped up and down over it. It was selfish of her; she knew that. Telling Pete would be awful because when she told him, she'd lose him all over again. Getting that job meant leaving White Stone, but it also meant leaving him.

She called her mother instead. If anyone would share in her joy, it would be Celia. As soon as she answered, Libby gave her the news. The phone pressed against her ear, Libby caught herself smiling alone with only her cup of coffee to keep her warm, while her mother went on about how proud of her she was. Without a doubt, this had been a low point in her career and in her life. She knew her mother understood that. In some ways, however, it had been good for Libby. It had given her a chance to stop and think about what was important—understanding her mother, setting things right with Pete, seeing everyone again. It also made her realize that the people in her town had welcomed her back with open arms. No one had flinched when she returned; in fact, they'd made her feel… special.

❋ ❋ ❋

Libby sat in the hotel room flipping through the TV channels, staring at the television against the opposite wall. She finally clicked it off and buried herself in the covers. She'd spent the day in Central Park by herself, thinking about how nice it felt to get her life back on track. The weather was unseasonably warm, and the sun was shining through the trees. It was amazing how long she could just sit and take it all in. It felt so good.

Her phone pinged. She reached an arm outside the duvet and felt around for it. Pulling it under the covers, she opened a waiting text: *Can you talk yet? How'd the interview go?* In all the excitement, she'd let Wade's text go unanswered. Even a few months ago, she never would have dreamed that after finally getting a job, she'd call people back home before she even thought to call Wade.

She swam out of the covers and dialed his number. "Hello," she said when he answered.

"Hi," he returned, an awkward silence trailing behind. There was something different about that "hi." It was softer, quieter, as if there were some sort of significance behind it.

"What did you want to tell me?" she asked suspiciously.

"Where are you?"

"The W on Lexington. Why?"

"Can I see you?"

"It's after ten! What's going on? Just tell me."

"Nothing's going on. I don't have anything to tell you," he said. "I just want to see you. I miss you."

Those last three words hung in the air as she felt the sting of heat crawl up her neck. She thought about all of the times they'd snuggled together, watching television or reading books, the times they'd laughed during drinks in the evenings, the way he looked at her… and then how easily he'd left her. Anger bounced around inside her like a runaway ping-pong ball. Her stomach felt acidic, her head beginning to pound. He had some nerve thinking he could call her and tell her that he missed her and expect a reaction that was anything other than complete rage.

There was a time when she'd been sad about it, but not now. Now she was incensed that he'd not been there for her. Things were good now; she had a job opportunity. Now he thought he could slide back in, avoid the hard times. Well, he was completely wrong.

"Say something."

"What do you want me to say, Wade? Do you really think that I'll jump with excitement at your admission that you miss me? That I'll come running back to you after you've hurt me like you have? Who are you kidding?"

There was silence on the other end for quite some time before he said, "Libby. I just realized how much I missed you once you were gone. That's all."

A loud laugh escaped her lips, and she tried to calm her drumming heart. She could hear a buzz in her ears as the anger rose up inside. Wade had lived a very sheltered life, he'd always had the best of everything, and he'd been denied nothing. That was going to change right now. There was no way she was going to take him back.

"Can we at least talk about it?" he asked.

"I'd rather not."

But he started talking anyway. "I was terrible to leave you when I did. I was scared. You'd lost everything. I didn't know if I could be everything you needed me to be in that moment, and I wondered if maybe I wasn't strong enough and you needed someone stronger than me."

For some reason, she thought of how Pete took care of Pop. It was an odd thing to think about, given the conversation, but she couldn't help it. Pete would never give up on anyone. He was one of the strongest people she knew. He was kind, like his grandmother, happy, like his mother, and loyal, like Pop.

"You're right," she said. "I do need someone stronger."

Chapter Twenty-one

"Eeeee!"

Libby spun around to the sound of heels against the bare floor and the whine of her friend coming toward her. As she did, she was nearly knocked over by Trish, the scent of her Bois perfume assaulting Libby's senses. She only recognized it because they'd shopped for it together.

"I have missed you so much! How are you?" Trish pulled back. "You're tan!"

Libby was in her element. She had a job and she was coming back. She felt strong and happy and full of energy. No more one-to-one if she could help it. "I'm fantastic! Can't wait to hear all about you," she said, pulling Trish's arm in the direction of a waiting taxi. The benefit of meeting at the hotel was that there were taxis available since they were always waiting for potential travelers. "Let's go so that we can get you there on time."

"I'm so excited!" Trish said, sliding into the taxi. "How many are coming today?"

"Twenty-six of your closest friends."

"You are a doll! Love you!"

As they made small talk—mostly Trish chatting about the drama surrounding the planning of a wedding—Libby took in the musty scent of the taxi, the gray buildings darting past her window, the sun on the faces of pedestrians as they stood at the corners of intersections waiting for their turn to make their way through the city. It all felt exhilarating. It was good to be back.

The taxi pulled along the curb outside a small bistro where Libby had reserved a room for the bridal shower guests. She handed the fare to the driver and led Trish inside. The staff had set up a small table for presents; a few gifts, exploding in silver and white ribbons, were already on the table. A handful of women she knew from around town waved from their seats, the wait staff dutifully filling their champagne glasses. Their clothes, their hair, the way they sat straight up in their chairs—the slight formality of it calmed her. This was what she was used to.

A few at a time, the ladies arrived and took seats at the tables, and after a couple of bridal shower games, everyone had settled into friendly chitchat. Libby sat next to Trish, and Trish had been telling her about how difficult it was to get china patterns years down the road unless one opts for a very well-known pattern, which was why she had chosen Mottahedeh, a word that Libby had to phonetically butcher just to try and say it. It would cost her wedding guests more money, but in the end it would be easier to replace, and thus a better investment in general and worth the money paid. When there was finally a lull in the wedding planning conversation, Libby decided to share the news of her new job.

"Oh! My goodness!" Trish threw her arms around Libby. "That's fantastic news! When will you be moving?"

"I start in a month. I wasn't expecting to be back so quickly! I'll need to find an apartment very soon."

"Wait! Janice has an apartment she wants to sublet on the Upper East Side." Trish leaned over to the table beside her. "Sorry to interrupt. Janice, do you still have that one-bedroom you're trying to rent? Libby needs an apartment."

"I do!" Janice bent around the other ladies to make eye contact with Libby. "It's three thousand a month. It's small but very clean. Hardwoods throughout, new appliances. It's only for a few months while I'm overseas. Interested?"

She couldn't believe her luck! A few months would give her time to go apartment shopping and find something permanent. "I'd love to take a look." Everything was falling into place. It was a sign that this was where she belonged.

"Here," Janice tapped her phone a few times and passed it to Libby via Trish. "These are the pictures."

Libby scrolled though them. It was a basic apartment: white walls, small galley-style kitchen, relatively roomy living space for the area. "I'll take it," she said, handing Janice her phone. "When can I move in?"

"I'm leaving in two weeks."

Libby settled back in her chair with a grin as the wait staff served enormous slices of cake to the guests. It had been a life-changing weekend for her. She'd gotten a great job and a new apartment. It didn't get much better than that. Now, all she had to do was get the cottage ready for sale in the month that she had. With persistence, she knew she could do it, and the good news was that even if it sat on the market a while, with her new salary she could afford her half of the mortgage payments.

Despite all of it, there was something in the back of her mind lurking there, a sadness about leaving it all behind—everything she'd learned about her mother, all the relationships she'd built with the people there, her feelings for Pete, they all held her in place and made part of her feel heartbroken to leave it.

※ ※ ※

Once she'd arrived back in White Stone, Libby decided to stop off at Wentworth's the very next Saturday to get the last of the paint for the living room so she could get started as soon as possible. She wanted to wrap things up as quickly as she could so maybe she could leave in two weeks, get her things moved in, and give herself a little time before she started work. The silver bells tied to the door handle jingled with her entrance and the now familiar man waved from behind the counter. "Hello!" he called out to her. "How's the house coming?" he asked, coming around to the front of the counter.

"It's going well," she smiled. "I've moved on to the living room. I need some paint. Can you help me out?" It occurred to her that she'd never asked the man's name. "I'm Libby Potter, by the way," she said, holding out her hand in greeting.

"Bruce Coleman. Nice to meet you." He shook her hand and led the way to the paint aisle. "What color were you looking for today?"

"I thought perhaps a light mossy green or something."

"I've got these." He pulled three paper paint samples from the wall display and handed them to Libby.

"How about this one?" she said. "It's really nice. I'll take a gallon."

"Good choice. I'll just mix it up for you."

As she waited for the paint, she had to look twice before she realized that she was seeing Pop through the shop window. He was walking alone. Libby understood enough about his condition from what she'd seen to know that he would not be walking the streets alone if Pete knew about it. "Do you mind if I step outside for a minute?" she asked Mr. Coleman. "I'll be right back." She grabbed the door handle and sent the bells into a ringing frenzy.

"Pop!" she called, jogging up beside him. He stopped and looked at her blankly. "Pop." She noticed his eyes first. They didn't look right; they looked confused. "Pop, are you okay?" Hugh wrung his hands, the dry sound of them like wadding paper. "Oh, hello!" he said.

It was clear that he didn't know her. His blinking eyes, his unsure smile, it all made her feel unsettled. The man standing in front of her was very far from the man who had taken her to swim practice and played cards with her on the porch of the cottage. That man was gone, and she didn't know if she could get him back. She felt as though she wanted to mourn him while his body was still there. What an odd feeling, like having her prized possessions stolen right out from under her nose.

"Hi, Pop. Where are you headed?" The sun was setting, sending their shadows sliding along the sidewalk. Libby noticed how different his shadow was to the man she used to know. It was slightly hunched, large at the shoulders, but also at the waist. Hugh hadn't answered, so she reworded the question. "Where are you going?" she asked gently.

"I... I..." He looked around at the various storefronts.

"Will you walk with me?" she said, gingerly taking his arm by his shrunken bicep. "I need to pick up some paint from Wentworth's. Perhaps that's where you were going? To get paint with me?"

Hugh nodded.

"Excellent. I'm so glad you found me." She pulled out her phone and texted Pete, telling him that she'd bring Pop back and not to worry.

Hugh insisted on helping Libby carry the paint and put it in her car. He had yet to call her by name, and she wondered if he could remember anything about her at all. It was bad enough that he had gotten lost; she didn't want to burden him with making him remember her name, so she just opened the door of the rental without saying a word and allowed him to get in.

In silence, they made the short drive to Pete's house. On the drive, she thought of those five nails jutting out of the cottage walls. On that wall had been a collage of photos, one nail for every person in the family: Pop, Nana, Helen, Pete, and Ryan. She remembered the pictures. They were snapshots that had been blown up to a larger size. Each one was a different occasion. She remembered the one with Pop in the middle. It was on one of his birthdays. He was in a chair, a silly, paper cone hat on his head opening a present while Ryan and Pete watched on the floor beside him. She wondered where those pictures were. Were they packed away somewhere unreachable like Pop's memory?

"I remember now where I was going," he said as she pulled into the drive. "I was going to get a cup of coffee." He looked down at his lap.

"I'll get you a cup. You just go on in and relax," she smiled, but her insides were turning over. He was so much worse than when she'd first seen him, and it was terrifying for her. It must be doubly terrifying for him.

Pete opened the door as Hugh walked up the few porch steps. Libby noticed how tired Pete looked. She met him on the porch after Hugh had gone inside. "I'll get you a cup of coffee, Pop. You just kick back," she called inside to him.

"Thank you," Pete said. He had his hands in his pockets, his shoulders slumped as if in defeat. "I was working in the office. I didn't even hear the door open."

"He looks bad, Pete," she worried aloud.

"It comes and goes."

The idea of living with Hugh and never knowing when he'd snap into that state or snap out of it had to be exhausting. How long had Pete been dealing with that stage of the disease?

"I promised him I'd make him a cup of coffee. Do you have any here?"

"Yeah," he said, placing his hand on Libby's back and walking her inside.

She put her arm around his waist in return. It wasn't entirely an embrace, but more a support, as if she were keeping him from crumbling. He looked so drained. She wanted to stay there and help both him and Pop.

Pete pulled a bag of decaf ground coffee from the cabinet and set it in front of the coffeemaker. He followed it with filters and a measuring spoon.

"Want some for yourself?" she asked.

"No. I think I'll have a beer. Want one?"

"You twisted my arm." She tried to sound cheery to lighten the mood.

As she filled the coffeemaker and set it to percolate, Pete popped the tops off two bottles, setting hers down with an empty glass. She smiled, knowing he remembered how she only likes to drink from a glass, and poured it in.

Libby thought about the man she'd known in Hugh Roberts. He was spectacularly charismatic, funny, generous, strong. She could string adjectives together all day long about him. He was so smart that she had felt she could ask him anything and he'd have the answer on his lips. Pop had always made her feel safe and cared for.

He'd been a supportive husband to Anne, showing his wife affection, sneaking up behind her as she cooked, putting his arms around her and kissing her cheek right in front of Libby and Pete. And now, she'd seen a hollow man, a lost soul in and out of reality, his brain and body failing him.

"You're quiet," Pete noted.

"Just thinking." She sipped her beer as she tried to put her thoughts together. "Can you do this alone? I mean, can't Ryan help? Or your mom?"

"I thought I could. I'm the best one for him. I work from home, I have a spare room for him, a yard for walks. It's getting harder though," he said quietly.

Libby nodded. She knew Pete probably hadn't asked for help. When it came to his independence, he was about as stubborn as Pop. Looking at Pete's face, she could tell it was taking a lot out of him, and she worried that he wouldn't be able to continue at that pace.

She leaned around the corner and called out, "Pop," once the carafe had enough coffee in it to pour a cup. "Coffee's ready."

"I'm just lying down for a rest," he called from down the hallway. "Leave it in the pot for me, would you?"

Pete took his beer and gestured toward the living room. "He gets tired a lot. That's why I lose him. I keep thinking he's sleeping, but he gets up and wanders." Libby sat down in the exact same spot she'd been when she'd asked if he'd ever live in New York. Now, it seemed like a preposterous question. So much had changed in such a small time. As she sat there, knowing her future and how in only a few weeks she'd be back to her old life, she felt different, a little nervous.

She wanted to be there to help with Pop. Would Pete be able to do it alone? She knew he was capable, but the extra set of hands that she could provide might be helpful. Would she be able to see Pop again before he slipped away completely and didn't know any of them? She would lose precious time with him by leaving. The conundrum put her in a very perplexing position. She'd never had anyone emotionally pulling her one way or the other before. She'd always focused on her goal no matter the cost. She knew she needed to go back to New York, but the situation was tugging at her heartstrings.

"What are you painting?" he asked, attempting to make small talk.

"The living room."

Pete was leaning forward on his knees, his hands clasped. The beer sat on the coffee table, sweating from the heat that even the paddle fans couldn't push out of the room. He wasn't looking at her; he was looking down at the floor, and she thought again how exhausted he seemed. That wasn't the Pete she'd known as a girl. She'd lost him as much as he'd lost her. They were just two strangers who shared common memories.

"Is there a facility in the area?" she asked quietly, her thoughts moving back to Pop. "Somewhere he could live where he could get help when he needs it?"

Pete finally looked up. "I don't want to do that to him." He rubbed his hands back and forth on his trousers for a moment before turning toward Libby. "Why punish him for his failing memory? He needs his family. We're all he's got. Take that away and who knows what he'd be like. He may slip further from us."

She didn't know if Pete was right or not, or what the safest method of care was for Pop, but she understood what he meant about family. Her family wasn't perfect, but, in a quirky way, his was, and now with Nana's death and Pop's illness, it seemed to be taking all his strength to cinch it together and keep it from falling apart. Her worry for Hugh and his family took her far away from her life in New York, but at that moment, there was no place she felt more needed than right there in White Stone.

Chapter Twenty-two

The sun's warmth was just starting to seep in, burning off the morning dew. Libby scraped the porch's wooden floor with her bare foot, nudging the swing as she rocked with Jeanie, listening to the sound of the waves swishing about in the bay. She would certainly miss this. It was so calming and peaceful.

"I wonder how Helen's handling it all, " Jeanie scowled in concern.

"I don't know. I haven't talked to her since the party."

"How's Pete?"

"He looks tired, Jeanie. I don't know if he can keep up the pace for much longer. I think I'll go check on them today," Libby said, apprehension pecking at her. She felt an unease that was indescribable after having seen Pop. She hadn't wanted to leave him and Pete last night but it seemed strange to ask to stay, so she'd gone, taking her worry with her.

"That might be a good idea. Is Pete eatin'? I could make him supper and bring it over."

"I'll let you know."

"Please do. I'd be more than happy to help, you know that." A smile spread across her face—the smile that Libby knew well.

"And I make a mean potato casserole." Always trying to lighten the mood. Libby could have guessed it before the words even came out of her mouth.

"Why don't you just make that anyway," she grinned. She was glad to see Jeanie. Sitting there with her, she wondered how she'd gone all those years without being in touch. She would miss Jeanie's easy way about her, her lighthearted jokes and mothering care.

"Jeanie," she turned on the swing, tucking her leg under herself, "I'm sorry I left for college and didn't ever call or anything."

"Aw, honey." Jeanie patted Libby's knee. "I'm glad to hear that. You know, God didn't offer me what he offered your mom, and I'm okay with that. I love you as if you were my own child. Here or not here—I still love ya."

A knock at the screen door stopped them rocking. With the wind in her ears, she couldn't ever hear when people came up to the screen door. When Libby stood to open it, she recognized Tim Mathis from the flower shop. She'd grown up with him. He was two years younger than her in school. His parents owned the local florist, and it seemed he'd carried on in their footsteps. Tim was holding a vase with at least two dozen red roses.

"Hi, Tim," she said as she accepted the arrangement.

"Hey there! It's been a while."

"Sure has!"

"I heard you'd come back from New York."

She nodded.

"Well, New York is following ya. Got the call for these this morning," he pointed to the flowers.

"Thank you so much." Libby said goodbye and plucked the card from the flowers.

It read: *I miss you. Give me another chance. Love, Wade.* Looking at the flowers—those perfectly arranged, identical, red roses—she realized how unoriginal they were. Wade knew what he was supposed to do, but he didn't have any heart behind it. There was no passion there, and she just hadn't realized it until right then. Certainly, it was nice to get red roses, but in Wade's case, it had been a box to check: *Bad Breakup: Red Roses.* She didn't want the perfectly arranged bouquet; she wanted something with heart. She set them on the table.

"Hello? Don't just leave me sittin' over here! Who're they from?"

"Sorry," she smiled. "They're from a man named Wade. He was my fiancé…"

"Was? Looks like he wants to be an *is.*"

"Yes. He does." She pinched one of the stems and pulled it toward her to take in its scent. As she maneuvered the large, glass vase on the small porch table, it occurred to her how out of place and formal they seemed there.

"What happened?"

"We dated for a year before he proposed. Then, a year after that, not long after I lost my job, he broke it off. He said he was scared."

"You gonna give it another shot with him?"

Libby shook her head. "I don't think so."

"There are plenty other fish in the sea. This sea in particular," she winked. "Well, honey, I'm gonna head out." Jeanie opened the screen door, the porch swing still swaying from her exit. "You need to check on our boys anyway."

❊ ❊ ❊

After Jeanie had gone, Libby had a chance to be alone in the cottage. The reality of leaving finally hit her. Her plans were coming together

Jenny Hale

and she was heading for the life she'd spent so long building for herself, but there was so much here she could still do. She would miss the new friendship she'd started with her mom, Jeanie's wit, Helen's kind nature, and she still felt she could help with caring for Pop. Then there was Pete. She felt it in her soul: he could make someone so happy. If only it could be her.

She wanted to spend every minute with Pop and Pete until she left so, after much consideration, she'd decided to go over to see him. It was an odd feeling, wanting to be there for Pop. Nothing had changed. She still wanted to move on with her life, but it was as if the past were creeping up on her, pulling her in. It muddled her thoughts and made her chest ache.

She pulled the car up the drive and parked it next to Pete's Bronco. He opened the door before she could even get up the steps.

"Hey," he said, leaning against the doorframe.

"Hi." She noticed the gold flecks in his hair. His hair had always turned golden in the summer, and, as the weather got warmer, the gold was showing up again. He had a heavy stubble today—she'd never seen him unshaven like that before—and he had his glasses on. It made him look older.

"How's Pop?" she asked.

"He's okay today. He's taking a nap. He's been awfully tired lately."

"As are you, I'm sure."

"Ah, I'm fine." He waved a dismissive hand in the air. "I just have to keep my head on a swivel with him around."

"How long has he been like this?" she said as he shut the door behind them and led her to the living room.

"A few months. I've noticed it coming on gradually. It started when, one day, he couldn't do the math to settle his checkbook. He was at the desk, punching numbers over and over on the calculator. That was the first thing. That same week, he was out of his favorite pancake mix—the blueberry kind. He'd gone with me to the store to get more, and that afternoon he didn't remember going."

"Pete, I'm so sorry. I feel just terrible that this is happening to him."

"I'm okay with all of it as long as he remembers us, but when he starts to forget who we are, it's going to be very hard to handle."

"You don't have to talk about me like I'm not here," Hugh snapped from the doorway, and both their heads turned in his direction.

"We weren't, Pop," Pete said, standing. "I'd say the same thing to you if you were sitting with us."

"You'd better. Don't sugarcoat things on my account. I know what's going on in my head, and I can't stand it any more than you can."

She followed both of them into the kitchen. Libby had never seen Pop that ill-tempered. He'd always been the calm, cool one. He could outsmart, outtalk anyone in any argument, and he never even had to raise his voice. That's what had made him a great salesman. But now he seemed paranoid and frustrated. She could only imagine what it must feel like to not have control of her own thoughts.

"Is there anything to eat in this house?" Hugh asked, rummaging in the fridge.

"Jeanie said she'd make you a casserole," Libby smiled, trying to lighten the atmosphere.

"That would probably be a good idea since no one else seems to be cooking," he barked.

Libby's eyes went right to Pete, her cheeks burning with protectiveness. It wasn't Pete's fault. He'd been doing a wonderful job with Pop. Now Pop was spitting insults at him. Pete's face was stoic, emotionless as he watched him putter around the kitchen huffing and puffing. He caught Libby's eye, and nodded as if to say, "It's okay," but she didn't feel okay. She felt awful. How could Pop speak to his grandson like that after he'd nearly exhausted himself over his care?

"Pop, Libby and I are going outside on the beach if you need us," he said.

Pop didn't answer. He just continued to pull dishes from cabinets and food from the pantry.

Pete took Libby's hand, and reluctantly she left Pop in the kitchen and followed him outside. "How dare he speak to you like that," she said once the door had shut behind them. The sun was in her eyes, making them water.

"It isn't him. It's the disease. It makes people touchy. Don't worry. When he's just Pop again, he's very agreeable."

"My gosh, how can you stand to hear that, though?"

"I have this memory of him at the beach when we had one of our family parties. He and Nana were sitting under the umbrella in their beach chairs. He had a Bloody Mary in one hand and a cigar in the other, and he was wearing a straw hat. I can't remember the joke he told, but it had made everyone laugh, including him. I just recall that image every time this disease takes him over. It's my way of coping, I suppose."

They made it to the beach and stepped onto the shore. The warm sand beneath her feet and the sea air did its best to block out the heaviness of the state of affairs. It was nice to just be with Pete. It was an awful thought to have, but she was glad to have a reprieve from the situation.

At the edge of the beach, where the sand met the grass, Pete had built a circular, stone fire pit. He began tossing twigs into it and Libby thought to herself how it would be perfect for roasting marshmallows. There he was with this massive cottage with extra rooms, a large yard, a fire pit for marshmallows, and a hundred trees with large branches just waiting for a swing. He had everything he needed to have a family there, yet he didn't have anyone but Pop. The sadness of this hit her in that moment. What was he waiting for? And what would he do when Pop passed? What good was all of it if he had no one with whom to share it?

With a spark, he lit a match and threw it in, the fire consuming the kindling inside. Then he pulled two wooden Adirondack chairs over next to it, the heat from the fire dancing into the sky. Libby sat down and watched the flames shimmy upward and then dissipate.

"I'm glad we're not taking a walk today," she said, holding her hair back with her hand to keep it from blowing into her face.

"Why?" he said as he took a seat beside her.

"I don't want you anywhere near that tire swing," she huffed out a laugh.

He smiled, the lines around his temples just starting to show, his eyes on her as if he were waiting for a response. "I'll be honest: I imagined both of us in the water, just the two of us, like we used to do all those years ago… Silly, really." He shook his head, his thoughts clearly occupied.

Libby felt as though a weight were pressing on her chest. She did care for Pete. She just couldn't imagine how they could fit in each other's lives. What would she do if she didn't have something to work for, a goal to reach? In New York, she was never still, always moving from one thing to the next. She didn't know how to slow down. For so many years, there was no other choice, no other option but to move fast and push harder. Now she'd taken the new job and the apartment was ready. It was done. She had to return to the only life she knew. The sadness was welling up, against her will.

"But it was good that you didn't jump, because it helped me to focus on the truth of the situation." A log popped, the kindling glowing bright orange, embers popping into the air like lightning bugs. "Do you know what I realized that day on the beach?" He seemed to be waiting for a reply, so Libby shook her head. She could feel a lump in her throat at the thought of not seeing him every day, and shaking her head was all she could manage. "I'd forgotten that I was no different to you than this town. You *think* you can do better," he said with a huff she took as cynicism.

His words chased each other through her mind like a runaway train. She *didn't* think she could do better than Pete Bennett. He was everything she ever wanted in a person. It was true; she used to think she could do better than White Stone, but she had realized that she wasn't choosing something better, just something different. She hadn't told him yet about the new job or the apartment. She knew she had to bring it up, as painful as it was.

"I don't think I can do better than you," she said. She couldn't help it; she put her hand on his knee. He fixed his eyes on her hand for a second, and then they moved up to her face. "But my life is somewhere else. I'm leaving for New York in two weeks. I got a job."

Pete nodded, his eyes now on the fire. She waited a long while for him to say something, but then she thought, *What could he say?* She wanted him to be okay with it, but it was too complicated to be okay, so they sat in silence, together, the screech of birds overhead the only sound among them.

Chapter Twenty-three

Libby sat at her desk among three cards, a cake, and a small bunch of Mylar balloons that smacked the wall as the air conditioning vent blew them around. "We sure will miss you," Marty said, leaning on the other side of her desk.

"Thank you so much for this. I'm sorry my stay here was shorter than I'd anticipated."

"Well, it was only temporary work. You got us through tax season." His eyebrows bounced up and down as he said, "I'm glad we had you as long as we did."

Libby got up and gave him a hug. She'd miss that quirky office and its clients.

"We're taking you to lunch," he said. "I won't take no for an answer."

"Thank you," she grinned. As different as that job had been from her old one, she really enjoyed it. She'd miss the little, wooden cubbies where everyone stored the coffee mugs they'd brought from home, the plant that seemed to brown no matter how much or little water was put on it, and the supply closet where Marty had them log the pads of sticky notes they took so he'd know when to order more.

"We'd like to take you to Miller's, if that's okay."

Miller's was a nice gesture, but it was quite expensive and Libby didn't want Marty forking out that kind of money just for her. "I'd be just as happy somewhere less formal, if you'd like," she said, trying to get the point across without being rude.

"No, ma'am. We're going to Miller's," he said. Janet grabbed her car keys and slipped her purse onto her shoulder. "No arguing," he said with a very broad smile and a wink.

They piled into Marty's sedan and headed to the restaurant. As they pulled up, she noticed all the familiar cars parked along the curb. She saw Sophia's and then her mother's. A little farther down the street, she could swear it was Jeanie's blue Civic, and even Helen's car was parked in front.

When she got inside, she was led to a small dining room where, to her complete surprise, she found a few familiar faces waiting for her. "Your mom helped me plan this," Marty said as all the recognizable faces smiled in their direction. Celia was front and center, batting her eyelashes with a big grin on her face.

The sight of them filled her with happiness. She knew all of them so well now, and she'd enjoyed seeing them as an adult. It had given her perspective that she hadn't had before. There they all were, coming to see her off. It was enough to put tears in her eyes. They weren't mocking her or judging her for everything that had gone wrong for her. They were celebrating with her, sending her off with love and smiling faces. For anyone else it wouldn't be such a big deal, but for Libby it was huge. For the first time, she felt accepted, like one of them.

"Hi, honey," Celia said, coming forward and kissing Libby's cheek. "Marty called, and I helped him plan this. They're all really sad to see you go, so they wanted to do something special for you."

"Thank you," Libby said. Then, she turned to the crowd and said in a loud voice, "Thank you to everyone for coming. This is too much!" She waved her hands in the air. "Please, have a seat!" A short time ago, she'd have been mortified at being the center of attention like that, having people coming to see her, but now, she saw friends. She saw Sophia laughing at something Jeanie was saying, Mabel wiggling herself comfortable in her chair, pushing her glasses up onto her nose and looking around to see who else was at her table. Helen was talking to Scott and Catherine, Catherine nodding vigorously, Esther and Leanne beside her. She did wonder about Pete and Pop—they weren't there—but she tried not to let it bother her. Everyone else was there to say goodbye; she needed to focus on that.

After the waiter took their orders, Helen came over and leaned on the back of Libby's chair. "Pete wanted to come," she said near her ear, "but Pop wasn't himself today."

It was easy to say—Pop wasn't himself—but those three words had new meaning to Libby. She knew the severity of them, and it concerned her. While she was enjoying a nice meal, Pop was struggling with keeping himself together, and Pete was having to deal with it all. It made her want to cry right there at the table. She wanted to be there, to help in some way, but she had to stay to say goodbye. "I'm so sorry to hear that," Libby said. Helen put her hand on Libby's shoulder and rubbed back and forth.

They were interrupted for a moment as the waiter made an announcement. "Everyone gets one drink from the bar compliments of Marty," the waiter called out over the chatting. "You can all go out to the deck and sit by the water while you're waiting for your food to come."

"I'll see him tonight," Libby said, resuming their discussion. "I'm taking Jeanie's supper over to them."

"Pete's having a tough time," Helen said, her expression indecipherable. "This is all so hard for him."

❋ ❋ ❋

Their lunch had lasted most of the afternoon, but Marty let Libby go right at five, which made her happy because she could meet Jeanie in town to pick up the casserole for Pop and Pete. It had been a few days since she'd been to Pete's, and she felt apprehensive on many levels: she worried about Pop, of course, but she also wasn't sure how to act with Pete. She wanted to comfort him, protect him, make him happy, but she knew she couldn't achieve any of those things. She decided that the best she could do was to help out.

Jeanie rounded the corner, carrying a warmer that resembled an enormous rectangular oven mitt. "Hope it's still warm. I just took it out of the oven about fifteen minutes ago," she said, handing it over to Libby. "Hugh doin' all right?"

"I don't know. I hope so. I'm sure he'll be glad to have this though. It smells divine."

"Dish yourself some before you leave there then. I made enough to feed an army."

"Okay," she smiled. "Thanks, Jeanie."

"Have a good night," she said.

Libby set the dish gingerly in the front seat of the car and headed down the quiet road that led to Pete's cottage. She wondered what she would encounter at Pete's. It had to be so frustrating to never know if the day would be good or bad, hard or easy. Guilt washed over her as she pondered the life she was about to have for herself:

the apartment overlooking the busy city streets, the busy social life, the new job. She wished Pete could be in that life. She had nothing pressing there, nothing consuming her time other than work. She wished she were closer so that she could lend a hand with Pop.

She parked the car and carried the dish up to the door. With her elbow, she knocked. The sun was staying out later these days and the sky was still bright. Libby noticed freshly chopped logs at the end of the porch and smiled to herself as she thought of Pete's stone fireplace in winter, when the logs would be used. How warm it would probably be. It was odd to think that by then she'd have her regular life again, and everything would be back to normal. She knocked a second time.

After a few more knocks, she tried the knob, and it was unlocked. "Pete?" she called inside, holding the dish against her side with one arm. "Pete? Pop? Anyone home?" She'd told them she was going to stop by. Where had they gone? She felt the trepidation start to filter through her as she wondered if perhaps Pop had gone on one of his walks.

She let herself in, shut the door and went over to the kitchen where she slid the dish onto the counter. The house was completely silent. She looked out the window at the backyard but saw no one, anxiety now flooding her. Was Pete out running the streets looking for him? She walked through the kitchen and into the hallway. She'd never been past the office before, but she kept going, looking in rooms, concern creeping in on her by the second. Her heart was beating so hard, it felt like her whole chest was moving, and her hands were trembling. *Please, please be okay*, she chanted to herself.

She passed a bedroom. Empty. Then the next... She stopped, and her shoulders fell in relief. The room looked like it must be

Pop's. He was sprawled across the bed, asleep. Pete was on the floor, his head on the bed, resting on his forearms; he'd dozed off as well. Gently and carefully, so as not to startle him, she caressed Pete's arm until he came to. He blinked a few times and then looked around.

Libby raised her hand in hello.

Once he'd gotten oriented, Pete stood up, put his hands on his back and bent backwards in a stretch. Then he followed Libby to the kitchen.

"Everything okay?" she asked quietly so as not to disturb Pop.

"Yeah." Pete rolled his head around on his shoulders. "He couldn't remember anything from today at all. It terrified him so much that he didn't want me to leave. I sat with him until he fell asleep. What's this?" he peeked into the giant oven mitt.

"Jeanie's sausage and potato casserole."

Pete raised his eyebrows in excitement. "Want some?" he asked, sliding it out and retrieving a serving spoon from a drawer.

"Absolutely!" she smiled, an attempt to change focus from Pop's dementia to something positive. It worked because Pete's face broke out into a smile. It was good to see, although his eyes were dark from lack of sleep.

Once the food had been dished out, Pete poured the two of them a glass of sweet tea, and they sat down across from each other at the small, circular kitchen table near a window with a view of the bay. She wondered how much worse Pop's condition could get, how much more Pete would need in terms of help. Her time there seemed to be shrinking right in front of her eyes.

"Thank you for coming, Libby. And I'll have to thank Jeanie for this fantastic food," he said, smiling again. The sight of it sent happiness zinging through her like an electric charge. It was so good to see him smile.

"You're welcome. I had to come. I couldn't imagine not helping, even if it is only dinner." She wanted to grab him, bury her head in his chest and stay there all night. Even in his weakest moment there was something so protective about him, so strong. It was going to be hard to leave him. She took in a deep breath to try and clear her head, and focused on his smile. It's funny how when they were kids, smiles were so frequent that they took them for granted. Now, when she could see Pete's face brighten, it had significance, because she knew that waiting just behind it was a whole lot of pain and anguish.

"That's the girl I remember. The caring, sweet girl. You haven't changed as much as you think you have," he said, still grinning. "What do you have planned tonight?"

"Nothing really. The cottage is done, and it's too late to pack anything. Why?"

"Pop sometimes gets back up—usually around nine or so. Would you mind staying? …just in case I need you."

"Of course I'll stay."

❀ ❀ ❀

By ten o'clock, Libby found herself wrapped in the throw that had been draped on the sofa, watching a movie with Pete. Pop had yet to wake. The movie was funny and she was glad for that, because it made Pete laugh. Once, he'd laughed and it had come out like an explosion—one giant "Ha!" that had sent her nearly falling off the sofa. He probably thought she was laughing at the movie, but she had laughed in response to him. Hearing him happy was the best sound—more calming than anything else, even better than the sound of the sea.

She watched the film wrap up, knowing that in any minute the credits would roll. She hoped for some unexpected second plot to emerge to keep her there, but, as expected, the credits did roll and she found herself looking at a black screen. Pete turned off the television.

"That was good," he said, his face still showing amusement.

"Pop's been sleeping like a baby."

"Only because you're here," he teased. "Ever since Nana passed, he hasn't slept an entire night. Maybe today just took it out of him. It was a tough day."

"I'm sorry."

"I'm not tired at all after my catnap on Pop's bed," he said, wriggling to a straighter position. "Want to have a drink?"

"Yeah." For the first time in a long time, she hadn't had to think about that answer. There was nothing to ponder, nothing to decide. She knew without a doubt she wanted to have a drink with Pete Bennett. It wasn't just because she felt bad for him or because he'd asked her; it was because all she wanted to do tonight was stay with him. She started to unwind herself from the blanket.

"No, don't move. Stay right where you are. I'll bring it in to you."

After Pete left the room, Libby looked around. She'd been there long enough that a feeling of normalcy had fallen over her. It wasn't strange anymore to be back, or to be there with Pete. It was... like home. What a strange feeling: two places that were totally juxtaposed both felt perfectly comfortable to her.

What would it be like when she got back to New York? Work would certainly consume her hours, and she expected to fall right back into the swing of things. But that one niggling feeling kept coming back: she'd miss Pete. She'd miss a whole lot of other people too, but most of all, she'd miss him. And there was nothing she could do about that.

"Here you go." He handed her a glass of beer.

"Thank you."

He sat down right next to her, draping his arm along the back of the sofa, and making her feel as if he had his arm around her. "Remember how we used to watch movies at Pop and Nana's," Pete said, "and she would bring us soda, telling us we were the only ones she allowed to drink in her living room?"

"Yeah," Libby chuckled. So many memories...

"And she acted like soda was part of some sort of prohibition, getting skittish when Mom picked us up and asked what we'd been up to. She was always uneasy about giving us too many treats."

"Nana was a funny lady." She could feel the tips of his fingers on her shoulder. She didn't want to look, but it felt almost like a caress. *Please don't put me in this situation*, she thought. *I don't have the strength to push you away anymore.* She began to rationalize: Pete was someone she'd known a very long time—like family; that's why they could be snuggled up under a blanket drinking beers together into the night, right? Whatever chemistry she was feeling was because of their long history together, nothing more—right? She kept repeating it, attempting to convince herself.

Trying to stop thinking of Pete, she let her mind wander to Anne and the letter from Mitchell. Was there really such a thing as a perfect relationship? She welcomed the doubt that was sneaking in because it helped her validate moving away from Pete. She only had a matter of days, and she'd need all the help she could get because there wasn't a bone in her body that wanted to leave him.

Chapter Twenty-four

The first thing Libby felt was soft cotton on her face. Whatever she was sleeping on was moving almost in time with her own breath. Suddenly she became aware of her limbs, tangled up, a hand on her side, the all-too-familiar scent at her nose. She opened her eyes. The sun coming off the bay was nearly blinding through the window as she blinked, trying to register where she was. Pete stirred on the sofa under her.

The night had been so enjoyable, he'd said last night, that he wanted her to stay a little longer. She remembered talking and Pete putting on another movie, but then she had no memory, so she must have fallen asleep.

For a while he didn't open his eyes, but she wondered if he was awake. His arms were wrapped around her, his head above hers just slightly. With one tiny movement, she could twist her body and be face to face with him. At that moment, though, she just shifted her eyes to see his face from her resting spot on his shoulder.

Pete touched her face, his finger trailing down her cheek, so she turned over and faced him, propping herself up on his chest. "Good morning," she said. He smiled but didn't say anything. "Do you remember falling asleep?" Her hair fell forward into her face and he tenderly tucked it behind her ear. She knew that look he had in his eyes. She knew what he was thinking. No matter how old they were, that look was exactly the same. It was the same look he'd given her when she'd told him, back in high school, that she didn't want to date anyone else; it was the same look he'd had whenever she'd told him she loved him.

Right away, her mind went to the new job, the apartment waiting for her. She couldn't make leaving harder than it was. Seeing him like that was killing her. There was no way to leave nicely once they'd gone to that place. She didn't want to leave on bad terms; she didn't want to hurt him again. "Pete... I need... I have to go." She pushed herself up, the blanket falling to the floor. "I'm sorry I fell asleep last night," was all she could get out. Her thoughts, once again, were racing through her mind, making it difficult to pinpoint the words for what she wanted to say. She wished she hadn't stayed and they hadn't woken like they had. It was too intimate, too much like it had been so many years ago.

She had everything she'd worked for her entire life right in the palm of her hand. She couldn't give up everything she'd accomplished for a gut feeling. Her mother's life kept flashing before her like a neon sign. She saw her mother's red eyes, her fake smile. She knew what would happen if things didn't go as planned, and one thing Libby knew about herself was that she was a planner. She couldn't afford anything to go awry. She had to follow her mind, not her heart. It was the only way. She couldn't stay. It didn't make any sense.

"Morning!" Pop came in and sat down between them on the sofa, smiling as he looked back and forth between the two of them.

"I feel great today!" It made both Libby and Pete laugh despite the heaviness of their thoughts.

"Libby was just apologizing for sleeping," Pete said, tilting his head around Pop to make eye contact with her.

Pop stood back up. "Oh, dear," he said. "I can tell by the look of you two that I shouldn't get involved in this conversation. Continue… whatever this is." As he left the room, he called over his shoulder, "The bonfire's tonight. Perhaps you can go together if you can get along with each other long enough."

After Pop left the room, Libby said, "I really need to go. I planned to see Mom today."

He took in a breath and let it out. "You need to go?" he repeated, a slightly irritated look on his face. "You don't need to do anything. You *want* to go."

"I'm sorry." She combed her hair with her fingers and straightened her clothes as best she could. She stood up and folded the blanket, setting it back onto the arm of the sofa. She wasn't just saying the words. She truly was sorry.

"Look, I only have a few days and I'd like to spend them with friends. Can we do that? Can we put this…" she wagged a finger between them, "behind us for now?"

Pete stood up, sighed and looked down at her. "I'm going to the bonfire tonight. Want to go?"

"What time?" she asked.

"I'll pick you up at seven."

※ ※ ※

"I still don't know why they advertise the bonfire every year. It's busy enough without all the summer visitors finding out about it," Celia said as she leaned out the window of her car. Libby had spent the entire Sunday afternoon with her mother at the cottage. Celia hadn't boasted or gossiped or anything. They'd just talked. She enjoyed it so much.

She wanted her mother to relax, to enjoy the festivities without worrying about showing off or making sure everyone thought she had a successful life. She wanted her mother to see that she could be happy and that people would like her whether or not Libby went to New York or her mother had gotten dressed up in a showy outfit. The one thing Libby had seen in town was that people there genuinely liked one another. They looked out for each other. If her mother stopped worrying about appearances so much, she may see it as well.

"Are you going to go?" Libby asked.

"Absolutely!" she said, and they laughed because they both knew that whenever there was a social event in this town, Celia would certainly be in attendance.

"Silly question."

"Parking's going to be a bear. Are you riding with someone?"

"Pete's picking me up."

It was fleeting. The look didn't stay on her mother's face very long and she straightened it out. Probably not to cast any shadow on a perfect day. But it was there—the slight disapproval or annoyance, she couldn't tell. The flutter of her eyes told Libby that Celia knew she'd seen the look.

"Why don't you like Pete?" It felt good to have the courage to ask her mother about it directly. She was family after all—she should be able to do that—but for so many years she hadn't. It made her feel stronger, like she'd finally grown up.

"It's not that I don't like him. I just want to be sure you don't waste your life because of silly emotions you had as a girl."

She wanted to tell her mother not to worry about her anymore, that she didn't have to worry about anything anymore; Libby would be there for her and she could finally relax. "Believe me, Mom, no matter what I choose in life, it won't be wasted. You have to trust me to make the best choices for myself. Plus, I've got a new job! And I found an apartment for the time being. It's all going to be fine." She was trying very hard to make Celia happy again, but then she realized she didn't need to do that anymore. "But no matter what I choose, Mom, it'll be what's right for me. You've done a good job showing me how to make choices for myself. Don't worry. I'll make the right ones."

Celia looked thoughtful for a moment and then, with a smile, she said, "I'm your mother. I will always worry about you. But I know that I no longer have to worry about your choices. You've shown me time and time again that you know what you're doing." Watching Celia's reaction, Libby was excited for what was to come with their relationship.

Once Celia had made her way down the drive, Libby went inside to freshen up for the bonfire. It was a yearly tradition in the area, marking the beginning of summer. All the businesses contributed, the public beach exploded with vendors in brightly colored booths selling their wares, and the sidewalks were overrun by townspeople and tourists alike as they balanced locally made gifts, area produce, and cotton candy in their arms.

She'd had just enough time to freshen up when she heard the grumble of Pete's Bronco outside. She opened the door. "Hey there!" he said with a grin that told her he'd left all of his worries at home tonight.

"Hi," she smiled back, genuinely happy to see him. "Do you mind coming inside for a second?" she asked. "I just need to put on my jewelry."

He followed her into the cottage. It took a minute before she realized that she was still walking toward her room but he wasn't. He was stopped in the entryway, looking around. His head turned toward the kitchen door, and he was still for longer than he should have been. His face showed no emotion, but she could see something in his eyes. He was definitely processing something. He'd seen Wade's roses. She was ready to discuss it, to explain them. She wanted to tell him how they didn't mean anything, how they weren't from anyone special. She wanted to let him know that phone-order red roses from someone who didn't care about her enough to stick by her weren't her thing. She wanted something better than that, something meaningful. But Pete didn't ask, he didn't say a word. He just turned and met her in the short hallway leading to her room.

It seemed like such a long time since he'd helped her move her boxes to the house. The old memories had been painted over, remodeled, made into something different. She took a hoop earring off the bedside table and put it on.

Pete stepped toward her dresser and flashed that crooked grin of his. He slid her memory box toward him. "You *still* have this?"

"Yes." His question had made her feel a little sad. *Why wouldn't I?* she wanted to say. Would he expect her to just leave her memories behind once she'd gone to New York? As she gave the question more thought, she realized that it probably was what he thought. She'd left everything else behind, why not her memories too?

He opened the lid and peered inside. It didn't bother her. Her memory box wasn't like a top-secret diary that needed a lock to keep her most inner thoughts hidden. They were already hidden because no one but her knew the true meaning of the items inside. It didn't matter if he saw a piece of paper or a pebble or a twig. The significance of them was lost on him.

He unfolded the pink flier and read the words. Then he creased the paper and put it back. He picked up the white shell she'd gotten on their walk and traced it in his hand. He sat there for what seemed like ages, staring at it, and she could feel the heat under her skin as she thought of that day. She knew he recognized it, and it worried her. In truth, she'd kept the shell because it reminded her of who she was, but it had come from the day of Helen's party, the day he'd jumped and she hadn't. Why did *he* think she'd saved it? Did he think that she wanted a reminder of how she had refused to be the kind of person he was? She didn't want the shell to ruin his mood. Before she could say anything, he put it back.

"I think I recognize some of the things in this box," he said closing the lid. "Is it still full of your memories?"

"Yeah."

"You have a few new ones in there. Anything interesting?" he smiled.

"If there is, I'm not telling. They're *my* memories."

"You're just as tight-lipped about them as ever."

"Yep," she grinned back at him.

"Well." He walked over to the door of the bedroom. "Ready?"

She followed him out, walking toward his truck and hopping in on her side. "Where's Pop?" She didn't really want to bring it up, afraid she'd bring him back down to reality, but she was genuinely curious and wondered how Pete had been able to slip away without him.

"He's with Mom. She thought I needed a night out."

"Smart woman," she smiled.

"If he feels like coming, she said she'd bring him."

Pete pulled down the drive toward the road, a gust of warm wind blowing in on them from the open windows. The feeling of summer was in the air: the marshy grasses along the road bending with the breeze of the passing cars, the large, orange sun hanging low on the horizon, and the crescendo of festive clatter filling her ears as they neared the town. The streets were full of people walking toward the beach for the bonfire—all in their shorts and T-shirts with straw bags to carry the treasures they'd found at the open-air market and craft stalls.

Libby looked across Pete to see who had set up closer toward the beach, but she was also taking in Pete out of the corner of her eye. He, too, had a T-shirt on, the soft-looking cotton of it reminding her of how it felt lying on his chest, his warmth radiating from underneath, the quiet thumping of his heart and the rising and falling under her from his breathing. She turned and looked out her own window.

"Looks like a good crowd," he said, pulling up and parking the car.

"Yeah," she said, but her head was swimming. As she looked out at all those people, she realized that she knew so many of them. She remembered them from when she was young, and some of them she even knew now. She could see Sophia in the distance, looking at the wooden crafts made by a man she swore had been her mailman. She saw Jason! How he'd changed. He wasn't quite as thin anymore—same face, though. Marty was walking toward the beach with his family, and Leanne was parking her car. Thomas and Matthew went running toward them, flying kites with the other kids on the stretch of grass beside the tents. Nostalgia crashed over her like a stormy wave, pitting in her stomach, and she suddenly felt very sad that she wouldn't see them anymore after she went back to New York.

"You okay?" Pete asked, suddenly on her side of the car, concern flooding his face. She hadn't even noticed him get out.

"I'm fine," she said, coming out of her thoughts. She opened the door to join him.

Pete swung a bag over his shoulder and took her hand. "Let's have a lot of fun tonight. Don't think too much, and I won't either." Together, holding hands, they started to walk toward the beach.

Chapter Twenty-five

"Well look at you two!" Jeanie called out as they walked toward her. Live music from down the street nearly overtook her voice. "Y'all look so sweet walkin' up, holdin' hands." Holding Pete's hand felt as normal as breathing, as if the last twelve years hadn't even happened. Knowing it could be the last time she'd be able hold his hand, she didn't let go.

"Hey, Jeanie," Pete greeted her, and then looked down at Libby, a thoughtful look in his eyes. He seemed so much like the same boy she'd known all those years ago. The smell of caramel apples and burning embers, the sound of the band in the background among the chatter of the crowd, the sea air, it all took her right back to the years she'd been to the bonfire as a girl with Pete.

She'd loved that night every year. It had been one of the few times she could escape and enjoy herself. As she looked around at all the happy faces, all the children playing, she wondered if her mother realized what she had there. She'd been so bitter about her life; had she ever taken a moment to see what was in front of her? There was no monotony there tonight. There was laughter and celebration, family and friends. It was enough to make her question whether her mother might have been wrong about White Stone after all.

"Your mama's comin'. I talked to her this afternoon after she left your house," Jeanie said.

"She said she was coming," Libby affirmed. Maybe tonight she'd see her mother relax a little more. Celia had been doing so much better. Perhaps Celia just needed time before she could see that she could be content without relying on Libby's achievements for her own happiness.

"Well, I'll wait up here for her. Y'all go on down to the bonfire and enjoy yourselves," Jeanie said.

On the way, they passed the stalls of games. She couldn't even count how many stuffed animals Pete had won her over the years. Pete stopped, and Libby followed suit. Each game booth had teddy bears the size of toddlers nestled along the shelves at the back. The stall closest to them had a line of baskets. The gist was to throw a baseball into the basket to win a prize. It seemed simple enough, but it must have been rigged in some way as not one person had been successful. Pete was bending sideways to peer down the aisle at the various games. Then, without warning, he started pulling her down the walk.

"Where are you going?" she asked, shuffling along beside him.

"I see a game I want to play," he said over his shoulder.

They came to a halt in front of a child's game with yellow ducks floating in a tiny stream of water on the table in front of them. The goal was to choose a duck and match the number on the bottom with a corresponding prize number. Pete pulled a wad of cash from his pocket, separated two dollars, and handed them to the attendant.

"Which duck do you want?" he asked Libby.

With a deep breath, Libby looked down at all of the smiling yellow ducks jiggling past her. There were so many—all the same. She looked at each one, trying to find some sort of significance, some marker on it that would give something away, but their treasures were hidden. Even though they looked like nothing special, each one completely ordinary, there was something different waiting under every one. She just had to pick. Would she get something big and shiny or something smaller? Carefully, she plucked one out of the water.

"Twenty-two," she read aloud.

"Twenty-two!" the man behind the ducks repeated with too much enthusiasm. She followed his finger to the board of prizes. Twenty-two was a child's pretend fashion ring with a stone the same blue as the ocean. The attendant pulled one from a box containing a couple hundred more rings inside and handed it to Libby. She giggled, slipping it on her finger.

"Thank you," she said to Pete, still giggling, as they turned back down the aisle leading to the beach.

"Well, you leave tomorrow. I wanted you to have something for your memory box and I didn't think any of those…" he pointed to the giant bears, "would fit."

"Thank you," she said again, peering down at the toy ring.

The water sparkled like golden butterflies, the gentle waves fizzing at the shore. An enormous orange blaze popped and crackled on the sand in front of the water, the crowd lounging in chairs and on beach towels. The band music had picked up and was louder on that part of the beach. Pete reached into his bag and pulled out two foldable camping chairs. He shook them until they had their chair-like shape and set them in the sand.

"Hey!" Catherine came running ahead of Scott. "How are you?"

"Great," Libby stood up and gave her a quick hug. "How about you?"

Scott caught up with them and waved at Libby. "We're really well! I have a little news!"

"You do?" she said. Pete sat down beside her in his chair, the roar of the fire sending an intense heat through the bay breeze.

"Looks like you and I shouldn't have had that wine the other night." Her face was pinched into a colossal smile, eyebrows raised, eyes darting from side to side. Libby could only guess what her news was with a face like that. "We're expecting!" she squealed.

"Oh, Catherine, congratulations!" Libby hugged her again. This time it was a long hug, the type of hug that says, *this is how happy I am for you.* Libby was thrilled for her. Truly. But it sent a quiver of sadness through her at the same time. She wouldn't be there to see Catherine's baby, to go crabbing, to enjoy the summer air outside. There would be a lot she would miss once she was back in New York.

"We found you!" a familiar voice soared over the crowd. Ryan and Emily came trudging through the sand with their chairs hanging on their shoulders from straps. Charlotte bounded ahead of them, stopping abruptly to examine a shell that had revealed itself in the sand.

"I didn't know you were coming!" Libby walked over and offered another hug.

"I haven't missed a single one!" Ryan said, setting up their chairs near Pete's.

Before they could even get settled, Helen and Pop were coming toward them. "Pop!" Libby nearly squealed with excitement. It was so nice to see him out. His eyes were bright and shiny, and she could tell he was himself. "Hi, Helen!" she said, so happy to see her.

Pop handed his chair to Pete, who set it up for him, and they all sat down together like a big family. "I didn't want to miss this with everyone here. I don't know how many more of these I'll have, so best I make sure to attend."

Libby hated it when elderly people spoke frankly about their ending years. She didn't want to think about how fleeting life was or life without Pop. The thought took her by surprise, and she didn't want to ever leave him, knowing his condition. What if it worsened when she was so far away? What would she do?

"You look so serious," Pete said quietly against her shoulder. For a moment, he looked out at the fire, the thumping of the music in her ears as she watched him. Then, without warning, he looked right at her and stood up. He pulled her off her chair by her hands and spun her around to the music. She kicked off her shoes as Pete whirled her out and in, their arms moving together like the waves in the sea. She couldn't help but smile when he did that. He had always danced with her, ever since they were young. They'd danced together so many times that moving with him was as easy and graceful as her long-practiced strokes in the water.

Thomas and a few other kids went running past as Pete pulled her into an embrace, their feet kicking up sand with each movement. Libby got a glimpse of Helen, and her eyes seemed to be saying she missed this—the laughter, the dancing, the feeling in that moment that nothing could go wrong.

"I want to dance, Uncle Pete," a tinkling voice sailed over the music from behind them, and Pete let go of Libby so they could turn around to face Charlotte.

"You do?" he kneeled down and took her hands, her fingers lost in his giant grip. Then, a squeal of laughter escaped her lips as he stood up and spun her around, her entire body lifting off the sand. Her striped sundress puffed out as the wind caught it, the gold of her hair catching the light from the bonfire, her ringlets trailing behind her. He set her back down onto her bare feet. Then Pete got on his knees again and started dancing with her, dipping her and spinning her, her giggles like bubbles in champagne.

"I love you, Uncle Pete," she said, throwing her arms around his neck.

"Love you too," he smiled. "Do you mind if I dance with Libby now?"

"Okay," she said, dropping down onto a towel that Emily had filled with toys.

Pete grabbed Libby's waist, but he didn't dance. He leaned in toward her. "Want to walk around a little?" he asked in her ear.

"You're not going to make me jump into anything are you?" Libby grinned.

"Ha ha." He took her hand, fingering her duck-game ring. "We're going to take a walk," he told the others. "We'll be back." Libby noticed Ryan's grin and the darting glance he gave Emily. She wondered again what Emily had meant by her comment about having heard a lot about her.

"You're holding my hand a lot tonight," Libby noted.

"Well, you're leaving tomorrow. I need to get all my hand-holding in before then," he kidded. There was so much familiarity in his face. When he looked at her, it was as if they could talk without saying anything. His gaze was so pensive every time he looked at her tonight, and she wondered if he felt as sad about her leaving as she did about leaving him.

Walking along the beach with him, with the sounds of the crowd and the band and the waves, Libby went right back to the smell of chlorine in her hair after a swim meet so long ago, the feel of the wind against her face in his Bronco, the taste of the strawberry wine they'd smuggled onto the beach, the laughter of friends, and the feel of his warm, salty skin as they sat, his arms around her, the moon shining off the bay, the pines towering behind them.

"Pete. I…" She knew that when the night was over, when the sun brought new perspective, she'd have a clearer head, and she would go to New York, but it wouldn't change what she felt for him. "I'll miss you, that's all."

"I know." He looked out at the crowd of people walking through the stalls. He turned back to her, his eyes searching hers. The breeze blew her hair back away from her face as she waited for a response. After a long silence, he said, "I'll miss you too. I just enjoy being with you. So tonight, can we do that—just be together and not think about tomorrow?"

Her chest ached with uncertainty and fear and longing all at once. "Yeah," she said in nearly a whisper.

"Libby!" her mother's voice tore through the moment. She was pacing along the sidewalk in short, clipped strides, Jeanie barreling along beside her. "I didn't think I'd find you in this crowd!" she said from too far away.

"You found us!" Libby said, pulling away from all the thoughts that were slamming the inside of her head. She was thinking about Charlotte's little curls and what having children there would be like. She was thinking about Pop and how nice it was to see him lucid. She was thinking about Helen's face as she watched them dancing. But most of all, she was thinking about Pete, his hand still in hers, that contemplative look in his eyes, the way her heart hurt at the idea of leaving. It was all making her head pound with anxiety.

"Good grief!" Jeanie said, slightly out of breath. "Your mama'd have us walkin' the length of the county lookin' if we hadn't found you." Then, as if just now noticing them, their close proximity, the way Pete had moved his arm around her waist almost protectively, she said, "Where are ya'll headed?" her eyes darting between the two of them as if she wanted to know more than just the answer to her question.

"We were just taking a walk," Pete said.

"Lordy, don't let him near the shore. We know what happened last time," Jeanie teased.

Pete rolled his eyes. "Libby already made that joke, thank you very much." The corners of his mouth twitched as he attempted to hide his amusement.

"Why don't y'all take your walk? We'll go find somewhere to sit," Jeanie said. "I'm dyin' to unload this bag." She squinted toward the beach. "Hugh end up comin'?"

"Yep," Libby said. "They're all here." And as she said the words, her heart was full. Never before, and probably never again, would everyone be together like that.

She and Pete walked silently through the crowd. Every person there had their own view of that night, but Libby's was one of reflection. Jeanie's words kept coming to mind: *Not everyone wants to leave this town. There's a lot of good here, you know. Some people like it enough to spend their whole lives here.* She finally understood what Jeanie had meant.

Chapter Twenty-six

Libby marveled at the changes she'd made to the cottage as she tidied the last few things in the bathroom. The For Sale sign was in the yard, and at least four cars had driven slowly by. Things were looking good. Summer's arrival had brought warmer air and the first of the season's tourists, making it the perfect time to sell. She secretly hoped that a family would buy it to give Thomas and Matthew more children to play with. Would they all pile onto Pete's swing like she had done at Catherine's house so many years ago?

Since her time there was limited, she'd woken early, and decided to take a swim and enjoy the beach while she still could. Grabbing her towel and her beach bag, she padded out of the cottage and down the lawn toward the sand.

She'd eaten her breakfast on the porch, watching the sun in all its orange glory peeking over the edge of the bay little by little until it was suspended in the air. By the time she cleared her breakfast dishes, the purple sky was bright blue, and the orange sun had burned away to a golden color. She stepped onto the sand that was already warm and dropped her things.

The morning wind was blowing very softly, causing the water to seep onto the shore, crawling along it like spilled milk. She put her toes in. The cool of it was a perfect complement to the record high temperatures. Libby waded in a little at a time until she was waist deep, taking care not to get too close to the rocks at the shore. They liked to hide on the bottom, and they were very unpleasant to find with one's feet. She lay on her back and moved her arms along the surface, the sun warming her face, until she could barely touch. The only sound was the movement of water beneath her body and the wind in her ears.

So much had changed in the short time she'd been there. She kept thinking about it. The town had a way of romanticizing life. But she had to be levelheaded. That's what her mother always taught her, it was what had gotten her to where she was, and it was what would keep her going. Success came from hard work, and she had spent a whole lot of her life working hard for her future. She had been given a second chance in New York. It would be ridiculous not to take it.

There was definitely something there with Pete as well, an easy relationship. She didn't have to try with him; she just understood him in a way that she didn't seem to understand anyone else. They shared the same opinions most of the time, and what made him laugh made her laugh too. Libby worried for Pop and his family—they'd been through so much with Nana's recent passing and now with Pop's problems. She would have loved to be able to be there for them. For Pete. In another time, another place, things could have been different for them.

She'd miss Jeanie. Thinking of her made Libby smile as she turned over onto her stomach and pushed herself under the water. She moved her arms and legs in the strokes she'd been taught so many years ago, making her way out into the gray-blue of the bay. Jeanie was someone with whom she'd always had a connection, but it wasn't until adulthood that she realized how lovely a person Jeanie really was. The way she treated everyone as if she'd known them for years, the way she cared for people, bringing them dinners, stopping by.

She'd miss her mom as well. She thought about how her mother was alone most of the time. She wished that she could fill some of those empty hours for her mother, especially as she aged. She'd have to visit more, have her come to New York more. Libby came up for air, turned back toward the shore, and went under again.

All the people in town she'd been with these past months—Marty, Catherine, Mabel, Esther, Leanne—they all had a place in her life, and she felt as though she were leaving them too. But there was no other way to do it.

She reached the shore—her head still a jumble of emotions, despite her effort to sort everything out—and pulled the towel from her bag, wiping herself dry. She'd said goodbye to everyone at the bonfire except for two people. This time, her mother was taking her to the airport, and she wasn't going to peek in on Pete through his window. She'd already planned to say a proper goodbye.

The bonfire was still on her mind. They'd danced, roasted hotdogs, talked, and enjoyed themselves until the fire had died down and Charlotte was beginning to get fussy. It was only due to necessity that they'd all packed up. They could have gone on like that all night.

Pete had driven her home, and, sitting in his car, she'd struggled to find the right words before getting out. She wanted to say something to convey how much she thought of his efforts in taking care of Pop, and how glad she was that he'd forgiven her after so many years. She wanted to tell him how much she cared for him and how she never wanted to lose touch again. But instead she'd said only,

"Thank you," because if she tried to say the rest, the tears would come, and she knew she couldn't go there. Not that night.

As she dried off, she took in a deep breath of fresh air to calm herself. When she'd first come to that beach, she'd been battling sadness, and now, when leaving it, she still was. This time, though, it couldn't be fixed with a new job or a plane ride. This sadness was formed by people and family and a charming place that she'd miss very much. She went inside to get dressed so she could see Pete one last time.

※ ※ ※

Libby opened the door to the cottage to find Pete leaning against his Bronco out front with that crooked grin on his face and a bunch of wildflowers in his hand. The wildflowers made her happy because they were so unexpected, so full of life, each one with its own personality. Some of them drooped over his hand while others were tall, their blooms bursting from the center of the bouquet. He'd picked them, she could tell. The stems were wrapped in a little brown paper at the bottom to keep them together.

"For you," he said as she came closer.

She took in the sweet smell of the flowers as he handed them to her. "Thank you," she said quietly. She didn't want to think about the fact that the entire cottage had been packed as quickly as she'd unpacked it, and that she didn't even have a glass to put the flowers in. She probably couldn't take them on the plane, so she'd have to leave them there, like everything else. When she climbed into the bronco, she set them on the seat beside her. Pete shut her door for her and then went around to the other side and climbed in.

"I know you don't have a lot of time, but I wanted to show you something."

They drove for a few minutes until the cottages gave way to woods, and the street narrowed into one lane. Pete turned onto a dirt road, the truck bouncing beneath them, causing her flowers to rustle. Libby held on to the door handle for support. Finally, they came to a stop in the woods. Something about that place was very familiar. Even though it was nothing but a patch of trees, there were memories lurking there, she could feel them.

"Where are we?" she asked when he opened her door.

"It looks different now than when we were here last. The paths are overgrown." He took her hand to help her out of the car. "Watch your step," he said, pointing out a large limb, probably knocked down during a storm.

As they walked through the woods, the memory of it was coming back in cloudy bits. The night hadn't been anything special, she remembered. It had just been a normal night. They spent most of their childhood outside, and when they'd gotten older and started dating seriously, that didn't change. One night, Pete had taken her there because it was quiet, and, like most teenagers, they liked being out of the sight of their elders. She did remember that path...

Pete took her hand again and led her down the path that was so full of underbrush it was barely recognizable from the path they'd taken as kids. She was glad she'd slipped on her sneakers today. The branches and leaves had nearly covered the path, and Libby wondered how Pete even knew where he was going. She looked over at him. He was clearly focused, determined on getting wherever it was. Even though it just looked like woods to her, it must not to him.

Not too far down from that, there was a clearing that overlooked the water at a distance. She remembered that clearing. But, in the clearing, there was something new. Sitting all by itself was a rustic bench made from the trunks of trees, the bark still intact. Libby walked over to it and ran her hand along the back of it. Then, with a tiny gasp, she turned her head sideways to read the inscription on the center tree trunk on the back of the bench. There was a heart carved, and inside it read "Pete & Libby." She'd never seen anything more beautiful. The imperfections of it gave it so much character. The sight of it brought tears to her eyes.

"Do you remember when we carved that on the tree?" he asked, walking up behind her.

She did remember. It was evening and the woods were aglow with lightning bugs. It was after he carved those words in the tree that he turned to Libby and kissed her for the very first time. From that moment on they were inseparable.

"I come here sometimes to be alone," he said.

"Whose land is this?" she sniffled, blinking the tears away as she stood beside him, her emotions overwhelming her suddenly.

"Pop's. He's owned it for as long as I can remember."

"When did you make this?" She patted the seat of the bench.

"A little while after you left." He turned to her and smiled. "I don't have a memory box. This is it for me."

The breeze blew in through the trees, making the leaves crackle. Libby thought about that first kiss they'd had so many years ago and how happy it had made her. As she looked at him standing in front of her now, she still felt the same way about him. Never before and never since had anyone made her that happy. He *was* her puzzle piece. He was The One. This time, she didn't try and talk herself out of the feelings. She didn't push them away.

She took a step toward him, the brush snapping beneath her feet, and she grabbed his pockets and pulled him to her. He looked down at her, his brows furrowing in confusion. She reached up and put her arms around his neck, pushing herself onto her tiptoes. His face was only inches from hers, his eyes unblinking, his expression still. Her heart was beating so wildly that she was sure he could feel it against his chest. She couldn't believe she'd pushed away her feelings for so long.

Libby closed her eyes and pressed her lips to his. She could taste his salty, sunburned lips, feel the softness of them against hers, the scratch of stubble making contact with her skin. She ran her nails lightly through the short hair at his hairline and down his neck, as she recalled what it felt like to drag her fingertips along his bare chest. His spicy scent mixed with the lotion he always wore to keep the sun off him—it made her lightheaded. There was nothing better than this feeling. She wanted to have it forever and never give it up. They fit perfectly together. All the overthinking and rationalizing she'd done meant nothing in this moment because she knew without a shadow of a doubt that this was the person she wanted to be with.

Then, just as a plate shatters the minute it hits a tile floor—it was that fast—*crash*, he pulled away from her, her thoughts like pieces of pottery scattering out in broken bits.

He turned toward the woods for a moment before facing her as she scrambled to pull herself together, to make sense of what was happening. Pete's face was serious, preoccupied. The sound of the bay barely made its way through the trees. She hadn't noticed it before. It was the only sound between them as she waited for an explanation even though she didn't want to hear it.

She watched his face, suddenly realizing how overconfident she'd been. She tried to swallow, but her mouth had dried out as she waited the excruciatingly long time that it took him to offer a reason for not kissing her back. She'd been so busy thinking about what *she* wanted, that she didn't consider what he wanted. Or *didn't* want.

"Libby, I'm worried that you've misunderstood why I've brought you here. I wanted to show you this bench to let you know how much I value what we had together, the memories we made so long ago. They've stayed with me."

He took a step closer but maintained enough distance to unnerve her. She didn't want to be that far away from him anymore. She wanted to hold on to him, have his arms around her. She could feel the ache in her throat and the distress moving through her body like a heat wave.

"I understand that, for whatever reason, New York is where you need to be, just like I need to be here." Libby took in a slow, conscious breath to keep herself together. Her breath wanted to come in uneven heaves but she wouldn't allow it. "I'm happy you came back," he said. "It gave us a chance to set things straight. Now I can say goodbye with no hard feelings, and I'm glad for that."

She didn't know what to say. She didn't want to say goodbye. Her chest felt icy, hollow, as if she couldn't get a breath without falling over into a coughing fit. This wasn't what she wanted at all. She was so confused by what she knew now that she wanted. It wasn't what her mother had always said she'd want. It was so much better. But she couldn't have it. Pete didn't want her to stay. She'd blown it, *again*. She wanted to let herself cry, to plead with him, but she knew better than to do that. He didn't want her.

Suddenly, the things that she'd worked so hard to achieve all came tumbling down around her as she realized that she'd put them all above everyone else in her life. She felt silly now, small. Did she really think she could just waltz in and throw her arms around Pete and expect him to fall at her feet? He had his own life now, and it didn't include her. End of story. She didn't know how to live with that. How could she go on with her daily life knowing that he was The One, and she'd ruined it?

How could she think that she could reject everything about the choices he was making in life, and then come back and expect him to want her on her terms? She was starting to realize the audaciousness of that kiss, and the more she thought about it, the more she grasped how arrogant she'd been. No wonder he didn't want her. What she'd done just now—practically throwing herself at him with no regard to his wishes—was almost worse than the way she'd left in the first place. She felt an angry throb well up behind her eyes as the mortification set in.

She watched him for a reaction but there were no tears hiding in his eyes, no contemplation anymore. He'd made his choice. He wasn't waiting around. Maybe he never was. All of the troubles she'd had recently didn't even compare to this. This *hurt*. It hurt more than anything she'd experienced.

The wind and the engine were the only sounds between them as they drove back to the cottage. If she dared to speak, she'd lose it and make a spectacle of herself. Instead, she looked straight ahead, watching the possibilities trail behind them with the scenery outside. She was leaving this life behind, and there was no turning back now. Libby thought about Pete's words the rest of the way home.

Chapter Twenty-seven

Libby's new apartment was nice. The living area was about as spacious as she could get for a one-bedroom in the city, the galley kitchen was just enough for her to move around, and the bedroom was dark at night and bright in the morning. She could hear the sound of traffic on the street below. To others, it may be an annoyance, but to her it had always been exhilarating. She hoped that the exhilarating feeling would return soon because she didn't feel it just yet.

Already her calendar was filling up for the week. She'd spent the last few days unpacking her things, decorating the new space, and trying unsuccessfully to clear her head. She kept replaying the events in her mind from that day at the bench in the woods, trying to find some way not to blame herself, but in the end, she kept coming back to the fact that Pete's rejection was all her fault. She'd never considered what he wanted, and now he wanted a life that didn't include her. Every time she thought about it, she felt like she couldn't breathe. She wanted to crawl into bed and stay there—cry into her pillow and never get back out.

She had Trish's bridal brunch today and the wedding on Saturday. She'd had a haircut, a manicure, and half her wardrobe had been dry-cleaned. It was Libby's last weekend before starting her new job at Riddick Wiesner, and she wanted to be at the top of her game, but she felt so low that she didn't know how she was going to think about anything other than how she'd wrecked her life by her selfish behavior.

Since the shower, she hadn't seen Trish. She'd wanted to get herself together before jumping back into her old life. As she stood in front of her reflection in the full-length mirror, it was difficult to see past her own thoughts. She looked the part; everything was the same as it had been before she'd gone back home. On the outside, she was just as she'd always been, but on the inside something had shifted, changed.

She thought about seeing Trish and being prepared to keep up with her, but the more she thought about it, the more she didn't really care about one-upping her friend. Perhaps all those times, Trish had been genuinely concerned about her, and maybe she hadn't been trying to be better than Libby at all. She found herself feeling happy for Trish, glad she was having the wedding she'd always wanted.

Pop's issues had put the little things into perspective. In the end, she may not have all the things Trish had, or be married with a family, but she was healthy, and she still had time to do everything she wanted. The wedding dresses, the honeymoon locations—it all seemed unimportant now because what she wanted the most was to be with that one person who made her the happiest. She didn't care anymore where they lived, what they'd do, where they were going. She just wanted to be with him. She tried to push away the sinking feeling of knowing that she wouldn't get to be with Pete. She needed to make this day about Trish, even if it took all the energy she had to make herself smile.

The yellow taxi pulled up against the curb outside and she took the stairs down to the lobby and out to the street. It was a magnificently bright New York day so she slipped on the Gucci sunglasses she'd gotten herself as a reward for getting her new job, and slid into the backseat of the taxi. With everything now in place, it was time to try and get back to her regular life.

"West Houston Street, please," she said. Off they sped. The towering structures slipped past her window. They were a definite change from the pines back home. The diesel fumes, the traffic, the vast expanses of concrete, she saw them all in a different way now. She paid more attention to them. The taxi idled at a stop light and she looked over at a man walking his dog, and wondered why Pete had never gotten a dog. She envisioned a Labrador bounding past them into the water to retrieve a tennis ball. He should definitely have a dog. But then again, maybe it would be too much with Pop there.

Tears were clouding her eyes as she thought about how she'd never get to see whether Pete got a dog. He was moving on without her, and it made her feel like her feet were stuck in cement, every movement she made taking all the effort she could muster because she really just wanted to crumble to the ground. She shook her head to break free from the thought, and her vision cleared, the man and his dog now behind her as the car began to pick up speed toward her destination.

The taxi pulled up at the restaurant. Libby paid her fare and headed inside.

"So glad you're here!" Trish came over to her, wearing the most stunning outfit Libby had ever seen her wear—clearly one of her wedding purchases. "How are you?" Trish nearly squealed. She kissed Libby on both cheeks.

"I'm very well!" Libby lied, pushing her sunglasses on top of her head.

"I was worried you were going to fall in love with that cottage and never come back! Weren't you thinking about staying?"

The comment caused her to make a tiny gasp as she felt her chest tighten to the point where she couldn't get enough air. She cleared her throat to play it off. *It wasn't the cottage I fell in love with*, she thought. She remembered her one-to-one comment to Trish when she'd first gotten to the cottage. She could see the empty house in her mind, the For Sale sign in the front yard. The mental picture was hanging somewhere between reality and a memory, still so fresh that she could close her eyes and smell the salty air. The sun on the horizon, the sand on her feet, the crickets at night…

"You look like you might be considering that cottage," Trish said.

"You know," Libby forced a smile, "I absolutely love it there, but New York was calling. I couldn't stay away."

"I'm so glad. And you did a fantastic job with this brunch! Everything looks gorgeous."

"Well, it only took a few phone calls. Let's have a seat so we can chat before everyone arrives."

Libby and Trish sat down at the table as a waitress poured iced water into their goblets. The sun was streaming through the over-sized glass windows at an angle, its rays catching on the dark wood floor. The interior of the place was so different from the little restaurants back home—the columns, wood tables, trendy staff, and glossy decor. She sipped her water and took in a deep breath. Everything she'd wanted for so long was right in front of her now—the new job, being back in New York, the apartment—but she couldn't see any of it. All she could see was what she'd lost, what she'd never have, and Libby realized that it was more valuable than anything she'd ever worked for.

She thought a lot about her mother. Celia had been both right and wrong, and it had knocked Libby sideways once she realized it. Her mother was right in that Libby could be successful, eventually wealthy, and have opportunities to advance in a big city. Celia knew what it took to have that life, and she'd done an excellent job grooming Libby to do it. But she'd been wrong, too. She'd painted a picture of back home that wasn't accurate. No one was judging her; they were interested, concerned. More people had gotten to know her there than in all the time she'd lived in New York. They could've just passed by like people do in the city, but they hadn't. They'd asked her questions, made her laugh, brought her into their lives. She already missed them all. Where in the city would people call her by name when she entered a store, or wave at her just for walking by?

"So! Are you bringing a date to the wedding? I gave you a plus one," Trish said.

In the past, this would have felt like a one-to-one comment, but now, it was just a question to Libby.

"No one yet!" she smiled. She told Trish about how Wade had tried to get back together again, and she told her what she thought about him and his roses.

It didn't take long before she and Trish were talking like they always had. Trish dished the latest on all the gossip she'd missed, and got Libby caught up on the wedding drama involving two caterers and a sick florist. Little by little the guests arrived, and brunch was served.

❋ ❋ ❋

The next morning, Libby sat on the edge of her bed with her phone in her hand. The sound of honking and engines outside did nothing to calm her thoughts today. She'd just gotten an email from the real estate agent. A family with a little boy had put in an offer on the cottage. Perhaps he would find his way over to Thomas and Matthew. What kept coming back to her was that Pop and Nana's house was gone. It would belong to someone else now. Part of her was nostalgic for all of the memories she'd had there, but another part of her was ready to let it go so another family could enjoy it. She had nothing tying her down anymore. She was free to carry on with her life.

Although he probably knew already, just because word spread so quickly in White Stone, she decided to text Pete and tell him the news. Her fingers tingled as they moved along the screen of her phone. She typed: *Morning. Wanted to tell you Pop's house sold.*

Almost instantly, he responded: *Sorry you're homeless when you come for a visit. Good thing you have your mom. How are you?*

She typed: *I'm well.* She wasn't well. She was heartbroken. Just seeing his words made the hurt of not having him come back. Who would have thought that at the young age of eighteen, she'd have already had everything she needed in life? Pete had loved her and he was making plans to move forward with her then. They could have gone to college together, and who knows where they'd be right now—maybe as perfect as Pop and Nana. But she'd blown it. She'd lost her chance because she couldn't see what was right in front of her until it was too late. He'd moved on with his life, and there was nothing she could do about it. She felt her bottom lip start to tremble, and she closed her eyes before the tears could start.

She missed him. If only she could see that grin playing at the corners of his mouth, the friendliness in his face, the warmth behind his eyes. She missed the way his head turned to the side just slightly when she was talking, how he leaned forward a tiny bit in interest. She missed the sight of him with his hands in his pockets whenever he was standing. She missed the feel of his hand in hers. Those things weren't hers to have anymore. They weren't ever meant for her. Would he look at someone else with doting eyes and that smile of his? Her stomach burned with the thought.

She typed back: *How do you think Pop feels about the sale?*

She looked up from her phone. Her apartment seemed more sparse than it had in the past few days. And quiet. No one stopped by to say hello, she didn't know her neighbors and, while coming and going, she'd only seen a handful of people more than once.

As she waited for Pete's response, she remembered the way it felt lying on his chest that morning, his arms around her, his hand on her hip, the feel of his steady breathing. She could lie like that indefinitely. She'd been so quick to get up, to move things along, that she'd missed out on more of that feeling. What if the best moments of life were spent being still? As she sat in her apartment, trepidation settled inside her because she knew the answer already. Being in New York wasn't as important as being with people she loved.

Just like Nana's story about the rug: All the earnings and accolades were just things; things don't make us happy. People do. Now Pete didn't want to be with her, and she was miserable in New York because she couldn't be with him. A wave of fear swept over her, prickling her skin from the inside out because she realized in that moment that she didn't have a plan for this, she didn't know how to fix it. And what worried her most was that she didn't know if it could ever be fixed.

Her phone pinged. Her heart fell as she read Pete's answer: *Honestly, lately, he doesn't even remember that house. He's losing it, Libby. A few days here and there, he didn't remember my name. The good news— if you can call it that—is that he hasn't wanted to take walks lately. He spends most of his time in his room.*

She stared at his words until the screen on her phone went black. She sat in silence, tears welling up in her eyes and then spilling over. She felt so far away. She wanted to talk to Pop—about anything—so she could have those last few moments of the real him before the disease stole him from her. She knew there probably wasn't much time left, and she felt guilty for not being there. A runaway tear chased another down her cheek, and she wiped them with the back of her hand.

If it weren't for Trish's wedding, she'd be on a plane immediately. She wanted every minute with Pop, so she wouldn't miss a single moment when he was lucid.

I want to be with him, she typed. The tears were coming faster, one after another, with no end in sight. Her heart ached for Pop.

The phone pinged again. *The minute he's himself again, I'll be sure to tell him that you miss him. Promise.*

She needed Pete's hug. She needed him to hold her hand. No one else could make the hurt any better. But she couldn't have any of it. The reality of that was like a boulder on her chest. The sound of engines outside began to make her ears ring as she sat, alone, trying to figure out how to get herself together. She had to get ready for work, and she hadn't been there long enough to take a day off.

Another ping. She opened the screen and read: *Libby, I know you want to be here and you can't. I'll give him enough love for the both of us. I'm right at the other end of your phone if you want to check in on him. Go get ready for work. You're going to be late.*

The last bit made her smile, her unremitting tears still falling. How did he know she wasn't getting ready? With a deep breath, she got up and walked into the bathroom for a shower.

Chapter Twenty-eight

L ibby put the last of the day's files into the basket on her desk and looked up. Her office was a far cry from the small desk she'd had at Marty's. She hadn't bought any plants yet, and the walls were still bare. Libby rested her forearms on the dark mahogany-stained desk, her eyes roaming the top of it. She'd put her name plate in the center, a lamp on one corner, and her computer on the other, but the emptiness was still apparent. There were no framed photos of children or loved ones, no family to display. Not even a pet.

She'd thought about Pop all day, wondering how he was and if Pete was doing okay. She knew that even if she were there, she couldn't make the disease go away, and there was nothing she could do right then anyway, but it didn't ease the worry she felt. She wondered about whether Pop was scared all the time, or if he'd felt anything when his mind had been gone. She was frightened for him, worried that he wouldn't be able to say goodbye when the time finally came because he wouldn't be lucid.

On her way home after work, she contemplated her life. She wished she lived closer to her friends, that people would drop by unannounced the way Jeanie had done back home. She missed Pop,

Helen, Jeanie and her mother, and wished they, too, could be there with her.

The one person she tried not to think about, but he kept rising to the surface every time she had a thought, was Pete. She'd made such a fool of herself in the woods that day at the bench, when she'd been too caught up in her own feelings to take Pete's feelings into consideration. He'd been quite clear that day. The sadness that she'd had when he'd told her how he felt was as fresh as the day it happened. She played the conversation over and over in her head, and every time she thought about it, she felt more terrible about her own behavior. No one had caused this sadness but her.

Libby unlocked the door to her apartment and went inside. With a thud, she dropped her bag onto the floor, went into her bedroom and plopped down on her bed. For a few minutes, she stared at the ceiling, not letting any thoughts at all into her mind. Her eyes moved from the window to the heating vent to the dresser. Across the room, on the dresser, sat her memory box. She got up and opened it, pulling out the little blue-stoned ring Pete had won her at the bonfire. She slipped it onto her finger.

Then she lay back on her bed, buried her face in her pillow, and allowed herself to cry like she had after she'd left so many years ago. This time, however, she felt worse. She felt as if she had a hole in her chest that she couldn't fill. *Get yourself together!* she thought. *You have Trish's wedding tomorrow!* She bunched the covers up over her head and tried to clear her mind, her tears unrelenting.

* * *

"Do you think they're too much with the veil?" Trish asked Libby, holding up a pair of teardrop pearl earrings to her ear in front of the church mirror. "Should I have kept it more basic?" Her chestnut hair was swept up, tucked, in hundreds of curly strands, into a simple headband with a veil attached. The deep shade of her hair contrasted beautifully with the antique white of the veil.

Trish had talked a whole lot about the planning of her wedding, but Libby wondered if her friend realized how lucky she truly was because, after the wedding, she'd have the start of her own family, the one person she wanted to spend the rest of her life with right there when she needed him. As much work as weddings took, it was really the moments after the wedding that would be the happiest, in Libby's opinion.

"They're gorgeous," Libby said. She pulled Trish's train out from under the table and fluffed it along the floor. The heat from outside seeped in through the old window frames and doorways of the cathedral, flushing the faces of the bridal party. Thank goodness their dresses were strapless and their hair was up. Libby ruffled the skirt of her pale green satin dress to allow some air to flow under it. There was no breeze like back home to relieve the warmth in the air. She couldn't slip her shoes off and walk under the shade of a large tree, the cool grass beneath her feet. Outside there was just more sunlight and pavement, making the summer heat seem worse.

"About two minutes," the wedding planner said, her eyes darting around the room as if to ensure everything was as it should be. "Take your places."

Libby helped Trish turn around by lifting her train as Trish fastened the last earring. The organ began through the large double doors. It was time.

Trish twisted toward Libby. "I'm so glad you could be in my wedding." In the past that would have felt like the ultimate one-to-one:

I'm getting married and you're not. This time, however, it didn't bother her one bit. She didn't feel competitive about it at all.

"Congratulations," she said, feeling genuinely happy for her friend.

Libby walked down the aisle, holding a bouquet of roses, the stems wrapped in wide, white satin, an Austrian crystal broach holding the whole thing together. As she walked to the front of the church, she thought about the meaning of the day. She was struck again by the fact that it wasn't about the dresses or the flowers or the church. It was about celebrating that one person that you love more than anyone else in the entire world. She turned, walked to the right and took her place next to the center of the church where Trish would stand with Kevin to say her vows.

❋ ❋ ❋

It seemed as though the entire room were made of glass. Windows stretched from the floor all the way to the three-story ceiling, the flickers of candles reflecting off their surface. The tables were covered in white linen, and summer blooms cascaded down vases the size of baseball bats. Everything about Trish's reception, down to the hand-calligraphy on the place cards, was perfect. The reception was in full swing by the time she had finished her bridal party photos, and Libby was ready to relax.

She sat alone at her table as the other couples meandered onto the dance floor. She wondered what Pete was doing at that moment. Was Pop okay? Was Pete tired, or had he managed to have a good night's sleep? With no one to talk to, she pulled out her phone from the tiny clutch that had been her bridesmaid's gift, and checked to be sure there weren't any messages. Nothing. Would he text her if Pop was having trouble?

"Libby!" she heard Trish's voice and turned around. Libby had helped her remove her veil and pin up the train of her dress before the reception, so Trish was swishing toward her easily, an unfamiliar man on her arm. "This is Clyde Williams. He works with me. I told him that you may like to dance." She winked at Libby. "Clyde, this is Libby Potter, the girl I told you about." Trish dropped his arm, smiled at both of them, and swished away into the crowd, leaving Clyde in front of Libby.

"Hi," he smiled, sitting down next to her.

"Hello," she returned weakly.

"How do you know Trish?" he asked, clearly unable to come up with something better. Weddings were full of that sort of conversation. Libby had already had it about five other times that day.

Clyde seemed like a nice guy. He had a genuine smile, and his face showed interest, but she didn't even want to give it a shot. Normally, she'd have perked up, smiled bigger than usual, crossed her legs at just the right time, gotten a drink, and made light conversation. She didn't want to do that right then. The idea of it was exhausting.

"I'm just a friend of hers," she said with a smile. It wasn't Clyde's fault she was in the state she was in.

"Would you like to get a drink?"

"Actually," she feigned a tired look—although the conversation was making it a reality—"I'm really tired and I don't feel well. I'm going to head out soon. Sorry. Thank you, though."

"No problem. Maybe we'll meet again sometime."

"Maybe," she said and smiled to herself, knowing which "maybe" she meant.

Chapter Twenty-nine

Libby's alarm clock went off, the sound registering, but she kept her eyes closed. It was still strange being back in New York. She was finally getting settled, but she kept thinking about White Stone and the people in it. It was strange the way going home had changed her. She wondered about Pop and how he was doing, if Catherine was feeling okay at the start of her pregnancy.

She wondered about Pete, about what he was doing, about how he spent his day... She'd never be able to feel his arms around her on the boat, watch her toes dangle off the edge of the pier next to his, lie on a hammock as the weight of the two of them rolled them into one another, forcing their limbs to intertwine. She looked around at the stark walls, the gray of the buildings outside casting the only color in the room, as tears clouded her vision.

Pete had said she could text any time, so she decided to type a text to him: *Hi. How are things?* Her finger hovered over the word *send*. Did he care to hear from her? Would she be bothering him? She could feel the weight on her shoulders as she pondered it all. She'd never had to think so hard about sending a simple text before, but she wanted to be sure that Pete was okay and that Pop was managing. Without thinking anymore, she hit the button, and it was done.

The coffee pot had just finished percolating, so she poured herself a cup and sat down at the tiny table she'd set up in a corner of the living area. Her phone was still quiet, so she opened the newspaper and started to read the *In Style* section.

When she thought back to her days in the city before going home, she'd spent them having coffee with friends, doing charity events, finishing up work, things like that. Now, because she still hadn't completely gotten into the swing of things, her days were very quiet when she wasn't working. It wasn't the first time she'd thought something was different since she'd come back. She was still capable of working hard, but the drive she had for success had been replaced by something else. She just wanted to go home and be with the people she loved.

Libby closed the newspaper when she realized she'd read the last three sentences a few times and still hadn't internalized them. Her thoughts were somewhere else. *Where is Pete?* she wondered. She looked at her phone. Nothing. Out the window, a few people were walking briskly down the sidewalk. She'd been one of those people once. Now, she found herself walking more slowly, looking up, taking in the things surrounding her, thinking. Now, she was in her head all the time.

Her phone pinged and she nearly scrambled to get it. The excitement that had fizzed when she saw Pete's number quickly dissolved as she read his words: *Hi, Libby. Things are not good. Pop's not well. Can I call you?*

Panic stung her insides as she dialed his number. "What's wrong?" she asked when he answered.

"Hi," Pete returned, his voice quiet.

"Tell me what's going on."

With a deep breath, he started in, "You know how stubborn Pop is, don't you?"

"Yeah."

"His bones are getting brittle. He refused to go to the doctor, but I'd noticed that things weren't right—he kept limping—so a couple days ago, I made him an appointment and dragged him there. He'd been walking around with a broken leg. He's in a cast right now because he fell trying to get down the stairs outside. He hadn't told anyone."

"Oh, I'm so sorry." She wanted to leave right then, just get her keys, lock up, and head for the airport.

"He barely remembers recent events anymore," he said, his voice sounding tired. "He's cranky most of the time because of the dementia. I'm doing my best, but it's getting really hard. He'll have only a day, maybe two at a time where he remembers. His mind's gone more than it's here these days."

Pop was starting to leave them more often now, and Libby didn't want to miss a single lucid moment. "I'm coming home. You need me, and Pop needs me. I can help you." She didn't care about work or her responsibilities. She needed to be with them as much as they needed her help.

"Libby, you don't have to."

"I want to. I want to see Pop. I'm coming."

* * *

She'd caught the last flight out of New York, her mother was picking her up at Richmond International, and she'd told her boss,

Mr. Wiesner, that she had a family emergency and had to return home immediately. She wasn't lying. Pop was family, and he needed her.

"It'll be okay, honey," her mother said as they drove down the narrow, two-lane road toward home. Libby hadn't wanted to talk the whole way there. If she had tried, then the sobs would come, and she was scared that she'd not be able to make them stop. "It'll be okay," her mother said again, patting her arm with her free hand. It's funny how people say that when something goes wrong. It wasn't going to be okay. Pop wouldn't magically get better; he couldn't make his brain work again.

Her phone pinged in her bag and she pulled it out, her mother glancing over at her with concern as she drove into town. Pete had texted: *How far are you from home? Pop's himself!*

She texted back: *Not far. Be there in five.*

"Mom, can you take me straight to Pete's and drop me off there? I'll get him to bring me home," she asked.

"Of course," her mother said, and Libby noticed that this time there wasn't any sideways look, no flash of disapproval. Just concern. It was a relief to be back, to know she'd get to see Pop and talk to him at least one more time. Seeing Pete would take a weight off her shoulders that had been so heavy, she could hardly stand it. She'd wanted to see him, be near him, help him in any way she could.

The five minutes seemed like fifty. Libby nearly jumped from the car before it had come to a stop in front of Pete's. His front door opened as she leaned in the car window and thanked her mother. With a quick wave, she ran up the stairs to see Pete. He stood with his hands in his pockets, his glasses on, a small grin on his face. Seeing him was like coming up for air.

"Hey," he said. It was one word, but his eyes said so much more. He hadn't shaved, the gold scruff on his face was longer than she'd ever seen it, and he looked tired, dark circles showing under his eyes, but he was smiling despite it all.

"Hi."

"I told Pop you were coming." He gestured for her to enter and shut the door behind them. "He's in the living room."

Libby walked in to find Pop sitting in the recliner, an afghan over his legs, the cast on his foot poking out the end. "Libby!" he said with a smile that warmed her heart. "I'd get up..."

"I know. I heard," she said, leaning over and kissing his cheek. "How are you feeling?"

"Fine, really. I can still walk; I just have to use that boot," he pointed to a thick, black wedge with large straps sitting next to the chair. "Pete, my boy, can you get me some supper, please? I'm starving, and you'll have plenty of time with Libby after I fall asleep," he winked at her. She wanted to smile at that comment, but it sent a pinch through her chest. She'd come strictly for Pop. She couldn't dwell on the sadness of her situation with Pete because she had to be strong for Pop.

After Pete had gone into the kitchen, he called out, "You hungry, Libby?"

"I'm fine, thanks," she said. She didn't care if she was hungry, and, truthfully, she hadn't noticed. She just wanted to see Pop and try not to think about anything else. She sat down on the floor next to him and rested her chin on her hands as she leaned on his footrest.

"So!" she said. "How are you *really*? How do you feel?"

"Honestly? This whole mess with my head isn't what's been bothering me. It's Anne. I want to be with Anne, if you really want to know."

Libby nodded, unable to say anything. The lump in her throat wouldn't let her.

"We had a good life here. We were happy. But now she's moved on to another life, and I'm left here to drive everyone crazy. I want to be with her."

He was talkative today, which was good, because Libby could hardly swallow, she was so upset. If she tried to get the words out, she'd start weeping uncontrollably. She missed Nana too, and while she wished for Pop to get what he wanted, she knew what that meant. She'd lose him.

Pop shifted in the chair and tilted his head back against it as if the weight were too much. He turned and looked at Libby, a smile on his face. "I'm fine. My leg's been bothering me a little, but otherwise I feel okay. This disease is tough emotionally, that's all." He pulled his head back up. "How about you? How are you?"

Libby was having a hard time emotionally too, but she didn't want to bother Pop with all of it. "I'm doing okay," she said.

"I'm glad you came back. I think Pete needs you." He paused, and Libby had nothing to fill the silence. She wasn't sure what to say because she knew it wasn't true. Pete didn't need her. He'd made it clear. He was doing just fine without her.

"Can I tell you a story?" Pop asked.

This should be interesting, she thought, and nodded.

"Anne had a choice once. A man, who'd lived here and who'd grown up with us, tried to seduce Anne after we were married."

Libby couldn't move. She was frozen, hanging on his every word. She knew exactly who that man was. She still had his letter. What surprised her most was that Pop already knew about him.

"His name was Mitchell Dawson. He was very career focused, so worried about moving up he left town at the first opportunity. After high school, he went off to some big college and landed a job in Chicago, I believe. He worked for a large newspaper up there. He'd always had his eye on Anne. I knew him well." Pop pulled the afghan up around his middle, tucking it down the sides of his legs.

"When he got to Chicago," Pop continued, "he was miserable. He missed Anne in particular, I suppose."

He shifted awkwardly in his seat, and Libby sat up, ready to help if he needed it. It was so good to see him the way she knew him and not in the state Pete had described. It was as if she were meant to come back at that very moment to help Pete and to hear his story, almost as if Anne had a hand in it in some way. "So, what happened?"

"He gave her a letter, telling her that he'd buy her a train ticket and she could run away with him. He was a good man, Libby, apart from his proposal. She could easily have gone."

Pete popped his head in the door. "Iced tea, Pop? Or water?"

"Water, please. I'd like to be able to sleep tonight, and the caffeine keeps me up."

"Libby? Need anything?"

"No, thanks," she said, wanting to get back to Pop's story about Mitchell. "Did she tell him 'no'—or just ignore the letter?"

"She sent him a letter with a heartfelt 'Thanks but no thanks,' and then she told me all about it. Years later, I asked her if she had contemplated his offer." A smile broke out on Pop's face. "Anne let out the most splendid laugh and said, 'If I had married Mitchell, I'd have lost out on the greatest love of my life.' That was all I needed to hear. I've still got the letter around here somewhere, God knows where. It was a reminder that Anne loved me enough to be completely open with me. Plus, I couldn't quit thinking, *my wife's still got it!*" He winked at her.

Libby giggled. It was so good to have Pop back. And she'd never heard a love story sweeter than that one. Life can throw a lot at a relationship, but right there, right then, she had proof that there really could be a perfect happily ever after.

Pete came in with a tray of food, and Pop patted Libby's arm. "Go on over to the sofa and get comfortable."

"Thank you for telling me the story," she said, sitting down, some of the anxiety she'd felt finally melting away. She knew that Pop wasn't like that all the time, and things would get hard again. She wanted to stay there in that moment where nothing was wrong; Anne's letter wasn't hanging over her head, Pop was lucid, and Pete was pleasant.

Chapter Thirty

It was July fourth. Independence Day. Libby could feel the excitement in the air as she arrived at the winery for tonight's fireworks. She hoped to see Pop. If he was himself, he would probably be there. He'd always gone. She remembered how he'd sit on the quilt or towel—whatever they had that year—and smoke his cigars while chatting to everyone who walked by. To this day, whenever she smelled a cigar, she thought of him. Libby said a silent prayer that he'd be well enough tonight. She couldn't wait to celebrate with everyone—her mom, Pop, Jeanie, Helen… Pete would surely be there.

She was apprehensive to see Pete because this day had always been a day they'd spent together. As the evening breeze wrapped around them, he'd shield her with his arms, sitting behind her, his chin on her shoulder. They'd watch together, the smell of sulfur from the fireworks mixing with his scent, his fingers entangled with hers, the feel of his breathing at her neck. She'd never get to feel that again. Seeing him tonight, and knowing that, would add a layer of tension to the night that she didn't welcome.

Libby stood next to the bar consisting of a slab of ultra glossy wood resting on top of a line of oak barrels while the man in front of her explained the type of wine that was in her glass. A grid of bottles, cork sides out, blanketed the wall behind the bar. She took a sip of her wine and set it down. Holding a linen table napkin against the bottle, the barman poured her next taste into a fresh glass. She took another sip, glad that the wine was taking the edge off her worry.

Pete came up beside her. "How are they?" He eyed the wine glasses on the bar.

There was something different about him tonight. As she looked at him, she didn't see the kid she'd dated so many years ago. She saw the grown man who had told her that day in the woods that he didn't want her. She also realized right then that she didn't still love the kid she'd known. She had fallen for the man who was standing in front of her now. The man she could never have. She chewed on her bottom lip to keep it from trembling.

She looked out at the lawn to steady herself. The sun was floating just above the horizon. Its light was coming in through the wall of glass doors leading out onto a veranda. "They're all very good. I like this one," she said, pointing to a bottle of dessert wine she'd tasted.

"Do you have a place to sit yet?" he asked.

"Mom's here somewhere. She's probably found a spot. I'll walk out with you."

"Would you grab us a couple of bottles of her favorite, please, Phil?" Pete said to the man behind the bar. The man smiled warmly at them and then disappeared below the bar top. It was barely sunset and people were starting to take their spots on the acres of mani- cured lawn outside. Beyond the grass, endless rows of grapevines stretched along the hills of the grounds.

Phil slid two slender bottles across the bar to Pete then set down fresh glasses and a corkscrew with the name Sandy Grove Vineyards etched in script along the handle. Pete dropped one of the bottles into a straw bag containing large towels. He grabbed the other bottle and led Libby toward the glass doors, their wine glasses dangling between his fingers at her back. She followed him down onto the lawn.

It only took a minute for her eyes to settle on a sight that gave her pause: in front of her, on patchwork quilts and towels, were so many familiar faces. Jeanie was pulling food out of a wicker picnic basket and handing it to Helen. Pop was in a camping chair, his feet propped on a beach bag. Her mother was next to Jeanie, fluffing her sundress over her knees, her sandals kicked onto the grass beside her, a glass of wine in her hand. Emily was scattering toys over one of the towels while Ryan had Charlotte on his shoulders, running around them all, making airplane noises. Mabel had stopped to chat with Pop, her hand above her eyes to shield the sun as she looked for her own family, presumably. Jeanie, wearing a white visor and American-flag dangle earrings, was the first to notice Libby and Pete, raising her hand and waving wildly at them. It made Libby smile so wide that it was almost a laugh.

Pete handed her the bottle and glasses and set down the straw bag once they reached their family. He pulled out the two beach towels. With a snap, he laid one of the giant towels next to Jeanie's quilt. "Pop, you doing all right?" he asked over the heads of the others.

"Great, thanks. Enjoying the warmth out here. You keep the air so cold inside…"

"Yep. Clearly fine," he smiled, giving Libby a conspiratorial glance. The old Pop would have stopped at 'Great, thanks,' and she knew his slight irritability was due to his dementia. For some reason, after seeing Pete's response, she wasn't worried. When Pop was having a good moment, like he was right then, Pete seemed to just enjoy him. The more she thought about it, the more she realized that way of thinking was probably the right way of thinking.

Pete spread the second towel onto the ground. As Libby sat down closest to Jeanie, she handed Pete the wine bottle and set the two glasses on a small camping table beside Jeanie's basket.

"Missed ya, honey," Jeanie said, leaning over to kiss her cheek. "You doin' okay?"

"Yep," she said. Pete handed her a glass of wine.

Libby took it and thanked him before leaning over to her mother. "Hey, Mom. Glad you're here," she said, scooting closer to her.

Celia tipped her head so their temples were touching, the setting sun on their faces. "Me too."

Charlotte, who had started running around the group of them, giving her daddy a break, stopped next to Libby. "Hi, Miss Libby," she said, waving a tiny hand with bright pink fingernails.

"Hi, Charlotte! Did your mommy help you paint those pretty fingernails?"

"Yes. I wanted to look fancy," she said with a grin that produced a dimple on each cheek. She wiggled her fingers in the air and then plopped down next to Libby, her little legs crisscrossed under her dress. "You have pretty hair," she said, fiddling with Libby's tresses.

"Thank you." Even though she looked like her mother, Charlotte's resemblance to Ryan and Pete was clear, and for an instant—only an instant because she pushed the thought away as quickly as possible—she wondered what Pete's little girl would look like, *their* little girl. She wouldn't allow that thought for very long because it was too painful. It would never happen.

She couldn't help but think again how badly she'd ruined things between them. For her entire adult life, she'd thought about only herself—what *she* wanted—and when she'd finally realized what she'd done, it was too late. She tried to clear her mind and focused on Charlotte's sweet face instead. The little girl was still playing with Libby's hair, her tiny fingers twirling the strands. She noticed Charlotte's long eyelashes, her little, pink pout, her milky skin.

"She's pretty, isn't she?" Pete said. It wasn't until Libby looked up to agree that she realized he wasn't speaking to her but to Charlotte. Charlotte nodded, still playing with Libby's hair. Libby looked down at her wine quickly and took a sip, not wanting to meet Pete's gaze. She couldn't think about what she felt for Pete tonight, or it would consume her, and she just wanted to enjoy the moment. It had been a very nice comment from Pete, and she could tell that he was trying to lighten the mood between them, but for Libby, it was a reminder of the relationship they couldn't have. She could feel the muscles in her shoulders tighten and she wanted to rub the knots out of them.

This was supposed to be a night of celebration, but instead she felt like she could cry at any moment. She was on edge, upset. Having him there beside her was too hard, and she didn't know if she could get through the rest of the night. Being just friends was complicated. She couldn't do it. But she had to, because that was all Pete was offering.

"Y'all hungry?" Jeanie thrust a bowl of potato salad between them. "Eat up. That's what it's here for."

"I'll take a few of those ham biscuits, Jeanie," Pop called from his chair.

"I knew you would!" Jeanie reached into the basket and pulled out a stack of paper plates, handing one to each person. "I've got chocolate-chip cookies for dessert, y'all!"

As they started passing the food around—chips, rolls, cucumber slices and potato salad—it was Helen who quieted the chatter by raising her glass of wine. "I'd like to make a toast," she said on her knees to be above everyone. Charlotte raised her sippy cup. "I am so thankful to have everyone here tonight. May we always be as content as we are in this moment." Then Helen turned to Libby, her glass still raised. "I'm glad you came home, baby girl. Cheers."

Libby touched her glass to Helen's and sipped her wine. She took in all the faces around her smiling and holding their drinks. She hadn't thought they'd be together again. A band started to play on the lawn under an enormous tent with more tables of wine. Pete refilled Libby's glass. She could barely look at him or the tears would come; she could feel them rising up. This—all her loved ones, Pete, everyone—this was what she wanted. This was what made her happy. How could she ever be happy in New York when all the people she loved were in White Stone? She took a sip of her wine and tried her best to be in the moment.

"Did you know," Pop said loudly enough for everyone to hear, "that I've been coming to this since 1963. Even back when we had it at the town fire station, before this," he waved his hand out at the vineyards. "I remember when Helen was Charlotte's age. We gave her ice cream on the hottest Independence Day in history, and it melted down her dress." He smiled, his eyes dancing in the setting sunlight. Libby felt tears in her eyes. She was sentimental. Not because everyone she loved was around her this time, but because Pop could remember. For that one fantastic night, Pop remembered.

Charlotte had pulled out a bottle of bubbles and, as the sun slipped below the horizon, the bubbles floated up into the sapphire sky. Large tiki torches burned at the edges of the vineyards and along the sides of the tents with the band and wine tables. One by one, the stars began to appear in the sky, and the blue faded to black. Then, all became quiet, and, like magic, a large *Crack*, and an explosion of color filled the sky. Red and blue and gold fanned out in the black of night and fizzled its way toward them until it disappeared. With another *Crack*, more fireworks shot up. Libby watched Charlotte. The little girl's eyebrows were raised, her mouth open in an enormous grin, her hands covering her ears.

As the last few fireworks went up, Libby sat, her arms around her knees, the nearly empty glass of wine in her hand. With all the excitement, she had only just noticed that Pete was sitting behind her. His warmth shielded her only a little from the breeze, and she wished he would put his arms around her. Jeanie had leaned back on her elbows, her head tilted toward the sky. Helen had Charlotte in her lap, bouncing her little legs in time with the music. Pop was dozing—how, with all that was going on, she didn't know—in his chair. Celia was talking to Ryan and Emily. So much of her life Libby had spent trying to achieve perfection, or close to it. She'd left everything behind in search of it, when, as she looked around, she knew now, without a doubt, it had been right there all along.

When the last of the fireworks had finished, Helen helped Jeanie pack up the dishes and blankets. Ryan picked up Charlotte, who had curled up on her side with a small blanket, her eyes blinking heavily as she tried to fight sleep. Charlotte put her head on her daddy's shoulder. Emily piled the toys into her bag and then started helping the others. Pop was still sleeping in his chair. Libby helped Jeanie with the dishes, but she kept her eye on Pete.

The night was ending, and she didn't want it to. Panic shot through her as she watched him picking up his things. She didn't want to be away from him. Ever. She had to try one more time to explain herself or the what-ifs would drive her crazy. She'd done it all wrong last time. If she could just convey to him what she was feeling, maybe he'd change his mind. She grabbed his arm and whispered in his ear, "Can we stay back after everyone leaves? I need to talk to you."

"I'll take Dad home tonight, Pete," Helen said, her eyes darting between the two of them, a smile playing at her lips. "Glad to see ya, Libby."

"It's good to see you too," she said, still glancing at Pete and waiting for an answer. His face showed no emotion, but he made eye contact and nodded.

She felt so nervous that she could hardly hand Jeanie her things without dropping them. She could feel the fire under her skin from fear. She worried that she'd make a fool of herself, pour out her feelings to Pete only to have him turn around and walk away. Again. She was unsure, scared, nervous. But what was the alternative? Just leave and never let him know all the things she'd been thinking, how she'd changed? Her pulse was racing, her mind going a hundred miles an hour, rehearsing what she might say. She hadn't planned this; she hadn't thought it all out. She'd been impulsive in asking him to stay back, but she knew in her heart that no time was better than right now to tell him what she was feeling.

The crowds departed, and Libby and Pete said goodbye to Jeanie, Celia, and the Bennett family, leaving them alone on the vast lawn of the vineyard amidst the litter and flickering torches. Pete sat down on the towel and stretched his legs out, crossing them at the ankle. He looked out ahead, his face showing nothing. She lowered herself down beside him. Above them, through the last bit of dissipating smoke from the fireworks, was a black sky so big it almost took her breath away. Millions of stars peppered the darkness. Neither of them said anything. She didn't want to, worried about how to begin what she wanted to say. She took a deep breath and looked up at the stars.

Chapter Thirty-one

L ibby fixed her gaze on one particular star, and she thought about how, by the time she saw its light, it could have already burned out. She hoped that it wasn't the same for her and Pete. He'd already told her he was moving on without her, but could she change his mind? As terrified as she was, she had to give it a shot.

"Are you cold?" he asked, a puzzled look on his face. It was July in Virginia, and the air was warm and humid, but Libby was sitting with her fingers hidden beneath the bends in her crossed arms, as she tried to warm her fingertips. They were icy from nervousness. It was as if all the heat from her body had gone straight to her face. Her stomach ached with unease.

"No," she said, uncrossing her arms. She looked into his eyes and wondered if she had the nerve to do this. "Being back here has changed me," she said before she could lose her courage. She was out of her comfort zone. This was a leap of faith. She had to take a risk and make herself vulnerable, and she still may fail. It went against everything she'd ever done in her life, but it felt more right than all of the other things she'd accomplished. She needed to do this. So she just started talking and let it all out.

"It doesn't matter how far away I am, all I can think about is you. I had it wrong, Pete. For so many years, I've had it wrong. I can't be happy in New York because you aren't with me, and I miss you so much that I don't even care about anything else anymore—not a job or an apartment. It all seems so silly now in comparison. So, by chance, do you feel anything like what I feel? Because if you do, I'm not going back to New York." Just like that old tire swing, when she'd jumped as a girl, her heart racing at the complete excitement of knowing her fate just before she hit the water. She was ready to jump.

Pete broke eye contact and took in a breath. He let it out slowly and looked back at her. "Look, you left. *You* left. You needed something else to keep you busy, and you couldn't find that something else here. Now that you've spent over a decade in New York, chasing God knows what, you've come back. It feels to me like you're bored." He looked at her, thoughts clearly moving behind his eyes. "I don't doubt that you're looking for something else, but I don't think it's necessarily something real. I feel like it's just another goal for you to reach."

Indignation swam through her. Didn't he know her better than that? How could he think that she was anything but completely serious? She'd never risk this much unless she was certain. "I'm not *bored*," she said. "This isn't about any kind of goal." She blinked to keep the tears at bay. She knew why the tears were coming. Because what he'd described was exactly what it looked like. She'd always been so focused on achievement that she hadn't looked around and noticed the people who meant the most to her. Instead, she'd left them all behind, and the fact that she couldn't change it made the guilt almost intolerable. She dragged her fingers under her eyes to catch the tears before they fell. "It's about how I feel about you."

"So it's about how *you* feel." He stood up and walked toward the vineyards, stopping on a grassy hill, his back to her.

She stood and walked up behind him, her head pounding with the stress of the situation. She had to make him see…

He turned around. "It's always been about you. About where *you* can get the best education, where *you* can move forward in life, what makes *you* happy. I'd like to be able to get on with my life without having you coming in and out of it any time that it pleases you."

Libby was shaking her head, willing the words to come out, but they wouldn't. Tears were coming instead. As they slid down her cheeks, she wiped them with the back of her hand. "You're wrong."

Until now, all her life her choices had been made for her. She didn't get to choose as she watched her daddy drive away and leave her. Her mother had trained her to hate White Stone—she didn't get to see it with her own eyes growing up. She'd been pushed to compete, to work hard, to please her mother. She'd thought her life had been her choosing, but it hadn't. Not until now.

"It isn't about me. It's about the man I see in you. It's about Pop. It's about never missing another birthday or Sunday dinner or boat ride. It's about being with the people I love."

"What about everything you've said about needing achievement to make you happy? What's going to happen when you start to miss that? I don't plan to be around when you decide to walk out again."

She could see it in his face: the disappointment she'd seen that day when she'd left at eighteen. Was he disappointed in the person she'd become? Maybe she wasn't even the type of person he wanted to have in his life. As this revelation dawned on her, a hopeless feeling took over, and she scrambled for what to do next. She wanted to be the one person whom he wanted to talk to at night, the one he wanted to spend all his time with, the one he couldn't live without. She wanted to care for him, help him with Pop, be there for him, love him. "I won't walk out," she said, her words uneven and broken from her tears.

"I don't believe you," he said quietly, looking out at the trees.

She'd never felt pain like this before. Not when Wade had left or when she'd lost her job. The misery of what she felt right now was something she could barely manage. How would she ever be able to convince him that she wasn't going to change her mind because there wasn't anything else in life that she wanted more?

"In your mind, you want this, but you just want it because you can't have it," he said, his face becoming rigid. "I don't think you even really know what you want, Libby, because only a short time ago, all you wanted was to be in New York. Now you want to be here." He shook his head, his lips pressed into a straight line.

"Don't tell me what's in my own mind," she said, putting her hands on her hips. He didn't have a clue—clearly—what was in her head. How dare he assume he did! She could feel her knees begin to shake from anger. He looked at her, a ragged, tired expression on his face.

"I have real responsibilities, Libby. Pop depends on me. I need to be with someone I can trust. Someone who pays attention to what I want and need sometimes," he said. "Life is about compromise, and you've never demonstrated even once that you know how to do that."

He was right. She hadn't given him any reason to believe that she was capable of that. She'd left. Twice.

"I can't stop thinking about you and Pop when I'm away from you," she said, grabbing his arm gently and turning him toward her. "I worry so much about Pop, but I worry about you too. I want to show you that you can depend on me. I know I haven't given you any indication that you can, but if you'll just let me show you…" She couldn't imagine how she had any tears left, but they still came—one after another.

A crew began walking the grounds, picking up the trash left by the townspeople and putting it in bags. A white floodlight illuminated the lawn, and the tiki torches were being extinguished one at a time. She saw it all, but she didn't care. She stood there next to Pete, their towels still on the grass behind them, praying for some miracle to make him change his mind.

Pretty soon they'd have to leave and she may not have another chance like this—just the two of them—where she could tell him how she felt.

"I love you so much," she said. "I always have. I've made stupid choices to make everyone else happy. And you're right; I didn't even really know myself what made me happy. Until I came back and saw you and Pop and your mom—everyone. I realized that being with you makes me happier than a job or an opportunity… anything in the world. I don't want any of that if I can't be with you. I don't care where we live or what job I have because it's meaningless when you aren't a part of it. I *know* I can make you happy because all I want to do is to be there for you and Pop and your family." She took in a breath and waited. She hung on his every movement—his blinking eyes, the twitch of his fingers—anything to give her a clue as to whether she'd convinced him of her feelings.

"I don't know, Libby," he shook his head. "We need to go." He pulled away from her and began to pack up the last few things that were left from the fireworks. He folded the towels and placed them into his bag and slid the empty wine glasses into the side pockets. He didn't say anything else. She waited.

"Tell me, what don't you know?" she pressed.

He slid the bag onto his shoulder and moved toward her. His mouth was turned down, the skin between his eyes creased, his face showing fatigue. "I don't know if I need this right now. I'm tired. I have a lot going on. I…" He pinched the bridge of his nose as if relieving an ache there. "I just need to go home." He turned away and started walking toward the car. Libby followed in silence.

When they got to the Bronco, Libby slid in on her side and didn't say a word. She was too busy thinking about his response. He'd been given one night—one night—without the burden of watching over Pop, of worrying about the realities of life, and she'd dropped a bomb on him like that. She felt awful. How selfish could someone be? Even though she hadn't meant to, she'd still thought about herself first instead of considering what a conversation like this might mean to Pete. She'd given him one more worry, one more thing to contemplate. It was no wonder he was tired.

The rush of air from the open windows of the truck drowned out the chirping of the crickets in the woods as they drove home in silence. She wanted to put her hands on his face, kiss his lips and tell him she was there for him—she'd always be there for him—and the thought that she may never get the chance to do that was nearly crushing.

She didn't know where to go from here. She was so confused. Her time in White Stone had made her realize that she wasn't happy in New York, and, if she couldn't be with Pete—if she had to see him day in and day out—it would tear her heart out, so she couldn't be happy in White Stone either. It was overwhelming. Pete pulled into Celia's drive, turned off the engine and twisted toward her just like he'd always done when they were kids. But this time, she didn't see that kid anymore. She saw the man she was in love with, and it terrified her because she didn't know what more to do about it. The ball was in his court.

"Call me if you need me, if Pop needs me," she said, feeling the sting of tears in her eyes again. She sniffled a little. She didn't want to get out the car.

"I will. Do you need me to walk you up or are you okay? It's dark…"

"I'm okay." She opened the door, got out, and shut it. As she leaned on the open window, she said, "I'm here for you regardless of our issues, whether we're together or not. If you need me, call."

Pete nodded and started the engine. "I'll wait for you to get in the door," he said, tipping his head toward Celia's front porch.

❊ ❊ ❊

Libby looked at her phone. Nothing. She didn't expect anything, but the silence was absolute torture. She couldn't control this, and it was terrifying. She'd just fled New York on a moment's notice, leaving her brand new job with barely an explanation to her boss, and now she was sitting in her mother's house in White Stone with not the first clue as to what she was to do next. Always, she'd had a reasonably attainable goal to meet and, as long as she'd done what was expected, she'd met that goal. But this wasn't a goal; it was her whole life, and she didn't know how to behave. Her stomach ached for relief, the acid settling like fire in her gut.

She'd been up for hours. Her head was pounding and her eyes still stung from lack of sleep. She'd woken throughout the night, thoughts flooding her mind. Each time, it had taken quite a while to fall back asleep. She rubbed her eyes, trying to relieve their dryness.

"Do you want lunch, honey?" Celia asked from down the hall. As restless as she was, and as terrifying as her life was at this moment, she was glad to be with her mother again. She was glad that Pop was just a drive away, and she'd get to see all the lovely faces she'd left by going to New York.

She hadn't even told Mr. Wiesner when she'd be back, because she had no idea. It all reminded her of the first time she'd ever jumped off Catherine's swing. She'd said she wouldn't do it. It didn't look fun to her; it looked startlingly scary. So many things could go wrong: the tree branch could break, the swing could come undone, she could hit the water too hard—so many things... Pete had asked if she wanted to do it, and she'd told him no. She could still see the way he looked at her—that protective gaze—and he said, "You don't have to do anything you don't want. If you decide to, I'll help you, but I think you can do it by yourself."

She'd watched as the other kids got on one at a time, each one sailing through the air and splashing into the water. She'd watched their laughter, the sun glistening off the beads of water at their shoulders, and the way it brought them all together. She'd never been taught how to live like that, but she wanted it. She'd grabbed Pete's arm and asked him to help her get on. Then, all by herself, she pushed off the tree and felt the motion of it in her stomach. She remembered holding on to that rope, her eyes on Pete as he reassured her, nodding subtly, telling her with his eyes that she'd be okay. Without thinking it through any more, she'd jumped. It was exhilarating and fun and frightening all at the same time. When she'd climbed onto the sand, dripping wet and laughing just like her friends, her heart hammering, she knew that Pete had been right. She could do it. And she drew on the freedom of that one moment for the rest of the summer.

It occurred to her that choosing the unknown and staying in White Stone wasn't much different. She worried for the things that may go wrong, but in the end, she welcomed the freedom of not having a goal to reach, not having her choices mapped out. In a way, she could just *be*.

"You don't have to make me lunch, but thanks for offering," she called back to her mother. Then she picked up her keys and threw her handbag onto her shoulder. "I'm heading into town. Do you need anything?"

"No," her mother surfaced in the hallway. "Thanks, though."

"I think I'll grab a sandwich and read in the park if you need me."

"Sounds lovely. Have fun," Celia smiled.

Libby went into town and picked up her lunch. As she walked into the park, she saw an empty bench. That insignificant little bench wasn't so insignificant anymore: it was a place to start, a place to just be. She decided to sit down on that particular bench to read her book. The sun was bright with not a cloud in the sky. Two birds were flying so high up above that they looked like the little black m's she used to draw as a kid. She unwrapped her sandwich and opened her book.

As she sat there, she realized that she wasn't reading. Her eyes were in the book, scanning the words, but the words weren't going in. She was too busy thinking about Pete and wishing she could have said or done something more. Trying not to think about it, she forced herself to read the words one at a time, but they still weren't making sense. She kept her eyes on the page anyway, the sun reflecting off the white paper, making spots in her vision.

Her issues with Pete couldn't be fixed with an email or interview. They couldn't be fixed with paint or new cabinetry. They just couldn't be fixed. Period. She didn't know what to do, how to proceed. She wanted to be around the people she loved, but she didn't feel complete unless the most important person to her was with her. She couldn't imagine being near Pete and not seeing that affectionate look in his eyes, feeling his hand in hers, having his arm around her in that protective way of his. How would she ever manage?

"Hey."

She looked up, her pulse racing, and blinked to clear the spots in her eyes. Pete was standing over her, his sunglasses on, a bag from the sandwich shop in his hand. "Mom is looking after Pop today," he said. "I had a little free time, and I was on my way to your mom's when I saw you leaving the shop." He held up his sandwich.

He sat down beside her and looked out at the grass that stretched to the tree line. Libby kept her book open in her lap to busy her hands so she wouldn't show how nervous she had become. There was so much she wanted to say, but she knew she'd already said what she had to, so she stayed quiet. He'd come to find her. She'd rather hear what he had to say anyway.

They sat in silence for a while before he finally spoke. "I've been thinking since our talk, and I wanted to find you today so I could tell you what's on my mind." He looked right into her eyes. She watched intently for some small glimmer as to what he thought, but she had to wait for his words because his face wasn't showing it. "Libby, you make me crazy," he said, turning his body toward her. "You make me so mad I can't see straight. You're stubborn, you're always in your head when you just need to be in the moment… But I've watched you with Pop. You're thoughtful and kind with him.

You flew all the way home for him. I know that you'll be there for *him*," he said. He tipped his head back for bit as if searching for something, but she knew he was just overloaded and tired, and she felt awful for putting him in this situation when he was already dealing with so much.

"I'm sorry," she said.

He pulled his head up and looked at her.

She closed her book and set it beside her on the bench. "I know how much you have on your plate with Pop, and it was so selfish of me to even mention what I want right now. I shouldn't have even brought it up. I care about you. I just want you to know that."

"I still don't know how it will all work out, but I'm glad you're home," he said.

Libby nodded, unable to control the tears in her eyes. Pete leaned back on the bench and propped his arm up behind her. She scooted a little closer and put her head on his shoulder. He moved his hand to her shoulder, and she could feel the movement of his fingers on the top of her arm. As she sat there, feeling the warmth of his shoulder against her face, she couldn't help but wish for more days just like that.

❀ ❀ ❀

Libby had spent the last two weeks helping with Pop. She'd given her two weeks' notice at Riddick Wiesner, and she planned to try and get Marty to give her the old job back, but other than that she had no plan for what was to come next. She didn't know where she'd live or what was going to happen with Pete. She just enjoyed each day as it came.

Pete walked onto the sand with two glasses of lemonade and handed one to Libby. He'd been gone quite a while. She took an icy, cold sip as she looked out over the calm waters of the Chesapeake Bay, the sun on her face. Pete sat down in the chair beside her.

There's nothing better than this, she decided. Being beside him was more like living than anything she'd done in her working career. *This is how life should be*, she thought. There was nowhere in the world she'd rather be than by his side.

"This is perfect," she said aloud, looking back out over the bay. "What's Pop doing inside?"

"Mom took him into town for a while."

They sat quietly until they'd had their lemonade. Then Pete stood up. "Can I show you something?" he asked. "Inside."

Libby got out of her chair and followed Pete across the beach. He led her inside, down the hallway, and they stopped outside his bedroom. He opened the door and allowed her to enter. There, in the center of the room, was a gorgeous wooden chest. It was huge, the wood new and shiny with lacquer. She'd never seen anything so beautiful.

"Go take a look," Pete said.

Libby fingered the latch of the enormous chest in front of her. It was nearly as big as the trunk of a car, the kind her mother used to keep all her baby clothes in. The scent of cedar came rushing toward her as she bent down to have a closer look at the smooth, oily looking surface. The natural grains—both dark and light—stretched along the top in beautiful, random streaks.

"Did you make this?" she asked Pete in nearly a whisper.

He nodded. "Do you know what it is?" he asked.

"Is it a hope chest?"

"For most people it's a hope chest," he smiled. "It's a new memory box." His gesture filled her with happiness. Standing there with him, she felt whole for the first time in her life. She'd always been chasing success, the next thing. In that moment, she realized that there was so much she could chase with him. Her mind went to their family and to the feeling of being with him. She wouldn't ever have to say goodbye to anyone again.

"So much has changed since we were together as kids," he said. "Back then, we didn't know how to appreciate what the other had to offer. With Pop, over the last few months, I've seen how generous you can be, and I've watched you give so much to everyone around you. I'm willing to try to make *us* work if you are."

They'd come so far, had so many obstacles in their way, but in the end, she had exactly what she needed and the person she loved. She put her arms around him as she thought about all the days she would spend doing her best to make him happy, the blank canvas of a life they had in front of them, the hope of growing old with him and being as content as Pop and Nana had been. She was ready to do her very best to make it work. With her face only inches from his, she said, "I'm so ready."

He wrapped his arms around her waist and looked down at her. Then he kissed her. It was like no kiss she'd ever had before. With that kiss, she could finally feel what *he* felt—he didn't hold back. His spicy scent, his strong arms around her, his unstill hands at her back, the feel of his lips moving on hers, all making her dizzy. She reached around his neck, intertwining her fingers there, pushing herself as close to him as she could get. *He didn't kiss like this back in high school*, she thought. Then she thought about how she'd get to have kisses like that over and over and over.

Epilogue

"What is this, Mommy?" Ava asks, leaning down into Pete's hope chest. She emerges with Libby's wedding veil. The little girl, with blush pink cheeks, wildly curly brown hair and green eyes like her daddy, puts it on top of her head and spins around. "It's so pretty!" she says, patting the tulle with her thin fingers.

"Are you in my memory box?" Libby giggles. "That's my veil. I wore that when I married your daddy." As all the objects in her memory box do, this one brings back many memories. So long ago, at the bonfire and then at the winery that Fourth of July, Libby didn't know if she'd ever again see everyone together. As it turned out, she didn't have to leave that family; she became a part of it instead. And not only had they come together for her wedding to Pete in the church that Anne had helped to restore; everyone had come together when Ava was born and every holiday after that. Nearly everyone. Pop and Nana had probably been watching together from up above. She hoped. She swore that she could feel their presence.

The family is here today. It's Ava's fourth birthday and Libby is getting ready, putting on her last earring while Ava plays in her memory box. "Are you ready to have your party?" she asks, unable to conceal her smile as she looks at her daughter, the spitting image of Pete.

"*Are* you ready?" Pete's voice comes from the doorway. He's on his knees, his arms spread wide.

"Daddy!" Ava runs to him and wraps her arms around his neck just like her mommy does. Pete hoists her up near his shoulders, his forearm supporting her weight. "Look what I found!" she says, holding out a photo, her mommy's veil still on her head. Pete takes the photograph as Libby walks over to them.

"That's your great-grandpa," Pete explains. "And that's your mommy, and that's me." Ava looks closer at the photo. Libby had put it in her memory box because it was the last photo she'd taken with Pop. Helen had taken it at her birthday party, on the shore, when Libby had first come back home. It was a reminder to Libby of the family she'd found.

"That was the day I jumped into the sea for your mommy," Pete laughs, but Ava doesn't seem interested. She wriggles down and pulls the veil off her head. Libby, still thinking about that day, tucks the photo neatly between two other memories in her memory box.

She asks Ava, "What do you want most for your birthday?"

To her surprise, Ava answers, "A sister!"

Pete huffs out a chuckle and pats Libby's tummy. "Maybe you'll get your wish!" he says. "But not yet. I think Grandma Celia's here. She's getting things ready for us out back. Want to go and see?"

Ava runs out of the room and they both watch through the window as she bounds toward her grandmother, with Bailey, their chocolate Labrador, following behind in wild, playful strides, a toy ball in his mouth. Pete turns to Libby. She grabs his pockets and pulls him to her. He puts his arms around her and kisses her.

"I love you," he says. "Should we go out to see everyone?"

Libby shrugs, pulling him closer, a devious look in her eye. "*Maybe.*"

A note from Jenny

Thank you so much for reading *A Barefoot Summer*! I hope that you enjoyed reading Libby and Pete's story as much as I enjoyed writing it.

You can sign up to be notified by e-mail when my next book is out. Just visit my website at www.itsjennyhale.com and click the 'Email sign up' tab. I won't share your e-mail with anyone else, and I'll only e-mail you when a new book is released.

If you did enjoy *A Barefoot Summer*, I'd *love* it if you'd write a review. Getting feedback from readers is amazing, and it also helps to persuade other readers to pick up one of my books for the first time!

Jenny

PS. Read on for an extract of my debut –
Coming Home for Christmas.

Coming Home for Christmas

Chapter One

With an aggressive nudge, I moved a box down the hallway with my foot. The mortification that I had worked so hard to keep at bay was bubbling up, despite my attempt to squelch it. As a kid, I can honestly say that I never pictured this in my vision of Allie's life. Where, along the line, did I lose the busy job, the supportive husband, and two kids? I didn't even have a dog. Don't all single people have a dog?

"You here?" I heard my mother say when I dumped an armful of hanging clothes onto my purple and white checked high school bedspread. It had slightly yellowed with age.

"Yeah." The front door swung shut, rattling the adjacent wall. It had always rattled that wall. No one knew why; perhaps it was because the whole house was the size of a deck of cards, and if we blew just the right way, we could knock it down. It had been a good house, though—full of happy memories.

I looked up from my unpacking to find my mother and Megan, my sister, filling up my doorway as if they were sealing me inside. I took in a deep breath and let it out slowly just to make sure that I could still breathe.

Megan pushed past Mom and plopped down onto my bed, sending clothes to the floor. "Wanna get a cup of coffee?"

I piled my hair up on top of my head with my fingers. Truthfully, a cup of coffee did sound nice, but I'd rather pout just a bit longer. It had been eleven years since I had even contemplated moving back home, and now it was actually happening. I let my hair loose and scratched my scalp.

Something about moving home as an adult made the space feel even smaller than it had while growing up. I hoped that I wasn't imposing on Mom too much. She'd never tell me, though, if it were too much for her. She'd just straighten the mass of shoes at the front door or stay up a little later to finish the extra laundry so that I could have a free washing machine when I needed it. That's how she is. She'd endure anything for family because having us home, she always said, meant more to her than all of the inconveniences. I love her for that.

Moving back was only temporary, until I could find a job—I had three applications out there, just waiting to hear back. Even still, it took some getting used to. Thankful as I was that she'd offered to have me, I didn't feel like an adult living back with my mother. I felt as if I'd have to start handing her the keys to my car every night before bed.

"Coffee? Yes or no?"

"It sounds good, but I have some unpacking to do."

"Oh, please. You have tons of time for that. What the heck else are you going to do around here besides unpack? Mom still doesn't even have cable, you know."

"I do so!" Mom piped up from the doorway. She slugged Megan's arm affectionately.

From the that angle, Mom was standing just as she had so many times when I was young, and a pang of nostalgia pinched my chest. *Have you finished your homework? There's a boy at the door. Do you want dinner? Don't be too late tonight; I need to know where you are before I go to sleep.* All of these moments flashed before me like photos in a flipbook. My mother's face was so much older now, so weathered; her familiar smile making new creases where her smooth skin used to be. In a way, it was good to be home. I was glad to see her. I rolled my head around on my shoulders to release the tension.

"Hey, Debbie Downer, let's go." Megan yanked me out the door, past my mother, and into the hallway where we both stumbled over yet another dozen or so boxes.

We squeezed ourselves into my sister's newest triumph, her prized BMW—an indication of the success she'd had in real estate over the years. I had told Megan many times how proud of her I was for her accomplishments, and I was, truly, but it didn't squelch the inadequacy that I felt when I saw the tangible evidence of her achievements.

"Careful," she warned as I tugged on the door handle to shut myself in. I couldn't help an eye-roll—don't think she caught it, though.

❄ ❄ ❄

Two patrons entered through the shop door next to where we sat. Cold air blew around my torso and a chill crawled up to my shoulders. I regretted taking off my coat and hanging it on the back of my chair when we came in. The door swung closed, although no circulating warmth seemed to return.

"I have another idea for employment," Megan said from behind her coffee cup. She hesitated, because I had already told her I didn't want any handouts. I had accepted one of her handouts when I'd taken the nanny job. Okay, her last offer had given me a wonderful job for eleven years, and a chance to use what I'd learned in college, but I wanted to get my own work this time; we'd already talked about it. Whatever she had to say, it didn't matter, because I was back out there. I had things in the works.

"You're quiet," she said, breaking me from my thoughts. "And you're *never* quiet."

Even though I wanted nothing to do with the idea of my sister finding me another job, the suspense of not knowing was killing me. I could at least hear her out. "Tell me whatcha got," I offered.

"Look at this," she pulled a rolled magazine excitedly from her bag and slid it across the table. The main feature was a glossy picture of the Ashford estate, an early twentieth century manor. "They're one of my clients, and they need a house manager until it sells." Megan tapped the photo.

"Intriguing." I took a drink of my coffee, and it sent a shiver through my limbs. It was really cold outside. "Why would I be good at that?"

"You are personable and organized; you'd be a shoe-in!" Megan swung her legs from under the table and scooted her chair adjacent to mine, like she'd done when we were kids when she wanted to tell me a secret. She'd always lean in as if the proximity would make our conversation more significant. Tufts of auburn curls bounced softly around her face, and I suppressed the urge to scoop them up into a ponytail. "I think they're willing to pay... *well*," she whispered dramatically.

"And why should I consider this job over the others?"

"Because you could still apply for the other jobs, but you'd make a ton of money while you're waiting. And I know how you love history. This house is *ancient*."

"So, what happened to their old house manager?"

"He left. Lots of family drama, I hear, since *he* is the one who owns the house." She uncapped her cinnamon lip-balm and dragged it across her lips. "Robert Marley, the heir to the house—irritatingly unfriendly—wants to sell the mansion. His family's all up in arms about it."

I peered at the magnificent structure on the page. The Ashford estate was the stuff of storybooks with its sprawling brick façade and a staircase that looked like an enormous smile. It seemed way out of my league.

"I don't know, Megan. I don't want you to give me another job." Even though I said the words, the idea was eating away at me.

Megan exhaled in that motherly way that always made me feel very small. Her limbs were still, other than her finger nails drumming the table. Then, she stopped tapping abruptly and said, "What if I had nothing to do with it?"

"What do you mean?"

"You could flip for it. Tails, you send in an application. No harm done."

That was how Megan and I had decided everything growing up. It started when my grandmother made up her mind that we should collect coins. Every holiday, from the time I was four, Gram would thrust new coins into our hands; some in velvet boxes, others in cellophane. She would've been horrified if she'd found out that each coin had been mercilessly torn from its package and fingered by both Megan and me as we determined who got the next flipping coin.

It's how my sister had gotten the biggest bedroom when I was nine and she was twelve, and how I had gotten to keep our fish, Oscar, in my room in the sixth grade. Now, it seems that it's how I would be deciding between normal, everyday employment opportunities or living in the clouds and applying to run a multimillion-dollar mansion.

But I didn't want Megan's help this time, or her ideas. She was the firstborn. She was the successful one. She was on her own and living nicely. I was... a glorified babysitter, living with my mother. It sounded even worse spelled out in my head. It was time that I proved myself, made something of my life.

"I won't get involved," she pressed. "I'm just the messenger," she said. When I shot a frosty glare toward her for even putting me in this position, she shrugged in the "why not" gesture and nodded toward my purse. "I know you still carry it around for luck," she said with a smirk.

As if I hadn't been humiliated enough by my recent move home, the fact that I did, indeed, have Gram's coin in my purse—only because I had no way of packing it, and it was easier just to zip it in my wallet for the time being—made my cheeks sting.

I blew air through my lips and pulled out my wallet, retrieving the coin.

Gram had given it to me in 1983, four years after it was originally minted. She'd actually given it to Megan, but I had taken a liking to it and swore that I won every time I flipped it. Megan let me have it because she didn't like the way Ms. Anthony glared at the edge of the coin. It creeped her out, she'd said. But I always wondered if she just knew how much I wanted it, and that's why she really gave it to me.

Megan pulled in a sharp breath, her eyes as big as saucers. I don't think she really believed that I had it, and I was too aggravated to explain myself.

The thought of being able to work in such an historic and fantastic home kept rolling around in my head. Even if it wasn't permanent, it would be amazing.

"Management is great on a resume."

I rested the silver Susan B. Anthony dollar coin on the top of my thumb. Its surface felt as cold as the weather outside. The late November air was just enough above freezing to cause the snow to fall in wet droplets that clung to the window, sliding down it like thin, transparent ribbons. Getting an interview for this would be like winning the lottery.

With my free hand, I pushed a loose strand of hair behind my ear, and suddenly, a fizzle of excitement swam through me. "Tails I apply for the job." I sent the coin into the air. It flipped over and over before bouncing onto the paisley-patterned carpet. A depiction of an eagle over the surface of the moon shined up at me. Tails.

❆ ❆ ❆

Coming Home for Christmas
is available now in both paperback and eBook.

CPSIA information can be obtained
at www.ICGtesting.com
Printed in the USA
BVHW070542160323
660515BV00004B/469

9 781909 490369